## ALSO BY DAN GEMEINHART

# Coyote
## LOST AND FOUND

DAN GEMEINHART

HENRY HOLT AND COMPANY
NEW YORK

Henry Holt and Company, *Publishers since 1866*
Henry Holt® is a registered trademark of Macmillan Publishing Group, LLC
120 Broadway, New York, NY 10271 • mackids.com

Our books may be purchased in bulk for promotional, educational, or business use. Please
contact your local bookseller or the Macmillan Corporate and Premium Sales Department at
(800) 221-7945 ext. 5442 or by email at MacmillanSpecialMarkets@macmillan.com.

Library of Congress Cataloging-in-Publication Data

Names: Gemeinhart, Dan, author.
Title: Coyote lost and found / Dan Gemeinhart.
Description: First edition. | New York : Henry Holt Books for Young Readers,
    2024. | Audience: Ages 9-12. | Audience: Grades 4-6. | Summary: Almost a year
    after settling down in Oregon, Coyote embarks on a cross-country road trip with
    her dad to scatter her mom's ashes, but the journey takes an unexpected turn
    when she realizes the secret to the chosen resting place lies in a lost book.
Identifiers: LCCN 2023030007 | ISBN 9781250292773 (hardback)
Subjects: CYAC: Grief—Fiction. | Lost and found possessions—Fiction. |
    Automobile travel—Fiction. | Fathers and daughters—Fiction. | LCGFT:
    Novels.
Classification: LCC PZ7.1.G46 Co 2024 | DDC [Fic]—dc23
LC record available at https://lccn.loc.gov/2023030007

First edition, 2024
Book design by Abby Granata
Printed in the United States by Lakeside Book Company, Harrisonburg, Virginia

ISBN 978-1-250-29277-3
1  3  5  7  9  10  8  6  4  2

TO ALL THE READERS, YOUNG AND OLD,
WHO HAVE ASKED ME AT SCHOOL VISITS
AND BOOK SIGNINGS AND IN EMAILS OVER
THE PAST THREE YEARS, "WILL YOU PLEASE
WRITE ANOTHER COYOTE STORY?"
HERE YOU GO. THIS ONE'S FOR YOU.
I HOPE YOU LIKE IT.

# Coyote

## LOST AND FOUND

# CHAPTER

## ONE

Sometimes stories start with a bang, and sometimes stories start with a whisper, and sometimes stories start with a robbery or a car chase or a fistfight or someone being born or someone dying. Sometimes stories start with a kitten. I mean, the funny thing about stories is that they don't really start or stop at all . . . It's just the telling that starts or stops.

And this story, it could start when me and my dad finally settled down for a bit and got off the road and into a house; or it could begin when I started real school for the first time in five years; or, heck, it could start six years before that, when something terrible happened that tore a hole in the universe (or at least felt like it did). But, nah. I think this story starts with me on a bus, finding a box.

Now, the bus wasn't moving at the time. And, no, the box wasn't a buried memory box. That's a whole different story. In this particular case, the bus was parked next to a house in Oregon that I happened to be living in. And the box held something almost as precious as memories.

So, there you go. Once upon a time, I was hanging out alone on an old bus and I was bored.

The bus was named Yager. It could be some folks don't see

the need to name a bus. Then again some folks haven't had the chance to get to know a bus as well as I have.

Heck, me and my dad (who I'll mostly just call Rodeo since that's what he likes to be called) had *lived* on that old bus for five years after that hole got torn in the universe. We'd taken out all the seats except for the first couple of rows and bolted in a couch and some shelves and a big chair we called the Throne, and I even had a room in the back with a bed and a curtain for a door and everything. Yager was weird and Yager was funky and Yager got looks everywhere we went, but Yager was home.

Even though I was the one who'd really wanted to settle down and stop living on Yager in the first place, once we finally stopped rambling and had an actual house that didn't have wheels, it turns out I still wanted to hang out on that bus a lot of the time. So I'd run an extension cord out to it and strung pretty white Christmas lights all up inside it, and it was kind of my home away from home (except it was parked right next to my home, so it wasn't really all that *away*).

On the particular March Sunday when this story started, I was laying there on the couch in the bus, half reading a book. My cat, Ivan, was laying warm on my chest, purring when I scratched behind his ears.

I shook my head and let the book drop to the ground beside me and *tsk*ed my tongue.

"It's no good, bud," I said. Ivan opened his eyes and looked into mine. Ivan is perfect in nearly every way, but one of his best perfections is how good of a listener he is. "This book is perfectly fine. But there are way too many flat-out *amazing* books in the world to waste time reading a *perfectly fine* one. Right?"

Ivan yawned in agreement.

I sighed and looked around. It woulda been a great day to have a friend over. If, you know, I *had* any friends. Not counting cats. But I didn't. Not counting cats.

I saw Rodeo's bookshelf a little ways away. So I scooted Ivan down off me and ambled over to take a look.

I knelt down, squinting at the titles, hoping something would grab me. *The Little Prince* was pretty great, but I'd read that plenty already. Same with *The Old Man and the Sea* and *I Know Why the Caged Bird Sings*. Ivan sidled up beside me, rubbing on my hip, tail held high. I eyed a tattered paperback book of poetry by Kahlil Gibran. I'd read some of it and dug it enough, but I wasn't sure I was in the mood for poetry just right then.

I went to grab it anyway, but as I did, Ivan rubbed hard on my elbow with his chin and my hand went crooked, and instead of grabbing the book, I knocked it back. It fell with a muffled thump into the darkness between the shelf and the wall of the bus.

"Crud," I said, leaning forward and turning sideways to reach blindly with one hand behind the shelf. Ivan came in close to my face, purring. "Stay out of this, cat," I said, grunting.

My fingers brushed against what I was pretty sure was the spine of the book, and I stuck my tongue out and stretched farther and grabbed.

But my fingers didn't close around a book; it was something else. It had corners and edges, but it was bigger and heavier than a paperback book. I gripped it harder and pulled it up just before it slipped from my fingers with a solid *thud*. I sat back on my knees and slid the thing toward me, into the light.

It was a box that looked like a briefcase without a handle. Made of dark wood, with tarnished metal at the corners. Just small enough to fit in that hidden space behind the shelf, but big enough that Ivan could've curled up inside it if it was open. Which, I'm sure, is one hundred percent what he would've tried to do.

I sat there for a second, looking at that box. It had a . . . a *feeling* to it. It felt secret. It felt hidden. It felt important. It felt, to be honest, like a *once upon a time*.

And there was this fact: Yager was not that big. And it had been my home for five years. I'd lived and breathed and slept and woke and eaten and laughed and cried in the cozy space between those four walls. And I'd never seen that box before. So, it *was* secret. It *was* hidden.

And it sure as heck wasn't my secret. Which meant it had to be Rodeo's. And Rodeo is a lot of things, but secret-keeper ain't really one of 'em. He was the type to brag about how productive a trip to the bathroom had been. What kind of secret would a fella like that keep, from a girl like me?

Ivan rubbed his chin against the corner of the box, the way cats do.

"Shoo," I said, but my heart wasn't in it.

I spun that box around and found two latches, snapped shut.

I swallowed. Opening up those latches was surely a step

there'd be no coming back from. Funny, how life does that sometimes. Gives you a little warning. Whispers a little promise.

"What do you think, Ivan?" I asked in a hushed voice.

"Mrawr," Ivan said. He's not a big talker.

"Okay," I said. I bit my lip. "If you say so."

I snapped open one of the latches. Ivan's ears perked at the *click*. Holding my breath, I undid the second one.

The box sat there, one big unanswered question.

All that was left was to lift the lid.

I took hold of the dusty wood with both hands.

And I raised it up.

The soft yellow glow of the Christmas lights filtered down into the box.

The box was mostly full.

And what it was mostly full of was gritty gray dust.

I frowned, for just a second. It took me a second, to realize.

It wasn't dust in the secret box.

It was ash.

"*What in—*" I started to whisper. But then it hit me. And I knew. I just *knew*.

Goose bumps sprang up on my arms.

A lump grew, dull and sharp at the same time, in my throat.

I blinked, then again, against the sudden heat in my eyes.

"Oh," I whispered. "Hi, Mom."

# CHAPTER

## TWO

I sat at our dingy little kitchen table and I stared at that box.

Closed and latched again, of course.

Because looking at what was in that box made me feel all sorts of weird and sad and confused and, quite frankly, nauseous. Not nauseous because of what it was, but because of how it made me feel. An emotional nausea, I guess.

Finding that box made me look at *everything* a whole new kind of different.

Even the table it was sitting on.

It was a flimsy, beat-up, wobbly thing with spindly metal legs and a chipped plastic top. Rodeo and me had picked it up at a thrift store, which was where we generally bought just about everything except underwear. Now, though, it was holding a box that was holding ashes that I was ninety-nine and three quarters percent sure had previously been my mother. And it made me remember another table. From another house. In another town, and another state. Another life, really.

A table that I'd shared with Rodeo, sure, but also my mom. Before she was ashes. A table that I'd shared with my big sister. A table I'd shared with my little sister. All back in that big Before.

It was wooden, and soft golden brown. Big sturdy legs. Room enough for us all, and some friends. It was scratched and scuffed, stained with paint and crayons and markers and clumsy kid hands, the center of family meals and holiday crafts and game nights. It was perfect.

And then there'd been a car accident. Six catastrophic seconds that ripped a hole in the universe and changed everything.

And then instead of it being me and Dad and Mom and my sisters at the table, it was just me and Dad and three ghosts. And it was just too sad. Too sad for me, but definitely too sad for my dad.

And so we sold the table and the house that it sat in, and we bought a bus and we left all of that behind. We even took new names when we left that life behind. So instead of being devastated Ella and heartbroken Dad, we'd been just Coyote and Rodeo, carefree travelers. Grins as wide as the world we wandered through. Nothing but the open road in front of us. And we couldn't see the sadness in the rearview mirror because we didn't let ourselves look back.

The funny thing about sadness, though, is that you can't really run away from it. Not forever.

And another funny thing about sadness is that once you stop running from it, it gets a lot less scary.

But, anyway. That box and what was in it brought up a lot for me. Clearly.

So I sat there at the crummy table as the world started to get dark out the window, waiting for my dad to get home. Because, boy, we sure had some talking to do.

Rodeo was out on one of his walkabouts. A walkabout, for anyone who's wondering, is really just a walk. I don't get why he calls them "walkabouts" and not just "walks," but there's plenty I don't get about my dear father and what he happens to call a stroll is the least of 'em.

I heard his voice, outside, finally. Talking and laughing. I looked out and saw him in the street, chatting away with our across-the-street neighbor Candace.

I frowned. She was holding what she called a dog on a bright pink leash. Its name was Fig and it was a long-haired Chihuahua and I'd been informed by Candace herself that Fig was an angel but I personally thought that Fig was, well, something other than that.

I don't dig small dogs. I don't dig Candace all that much, truth be told.

I mean, she's kinda cool, technically. She's some sort of super-smart tech coder or something and she's got this sides-shaved-and-the-rest-dyed-purple haircut that's kinda awesome (or, possibly, just trying too hard) and she's like, *nice* or whatever. But she sure spent a lot of time with Rodeo.

Judging by the leash and by how far Fig's tongue was hanging out of her mouth, it seemed that Candace and Fig had gone along with Rodeo on his walkabout. My frown deepened.

Finally Rodeo made some last laughing joke and gave Candace a fist bump, and then he wandered whistling up our front walk and into the house. Honestly. What kind of grown man gives a grown woman a fist bump?

Our life had changed dramatically in the past year, but Rodeo had not. Which was mostly for the best. He still had his long, unkempt beard. Still had his straggly long hair, sometimes tied back, sometimes not. Still had his worn and shabby clothes hanging loose on his lanky body. Still had his easy smile, and his loud laugh, and his magic eyes that just somehow invited you in and told you to sit for a while.

"Where you at, honeycakes?" he called out cheerfully as the door closed behind him.

"Kitchen," I answered, suddenly nervous. I had a sudden urge to slide the box into my lap before Rodeo saw it, sneak it back out to Yager, and return it to its secret hiding spot. I hate ruining a good mood.

But me—and the box—stayed put.

"You know that kid around the block who's been trying to learn to ride his bike? AJ?" Rodeo asked from the hallway, his voice coming closer. "Well, you won't believe what I just saw." He rounded the corner, eyes shining with delight. "We're walking past his house, not paying attention at all, when out of—"

Rodeo stopped. In every sense of the word. He stopped talking. Stopped walking. Stopped smiling, slowly. Stopped breathing, I think. 'Cause he saw me, sitting there, and more importantly, he saw what was sitting on the table in front of me.

The moment that he saw it, I knew I'd been right about what was inside.

I didn't know what to say. So I didn't say anything.

Rodeo breathed in through his nose, breath whiffling through his mustache hairs. Then out. He didn't look at me. His eyes were locked on that box.

"Ah," he said. Chewed on his lips for a second. Then, "Ah," he said again.

I swallowed, loud.

He nodded. To himself, I think.

Then he stepped forward, slow, like he was wading through water. And he pulled out the other chair with a little scrape. And he sat down, like a balloon losing all its air. His eyes never left the box.

He slid one hand across the table, toward the box. But then stopped and pulled it back.

Finally, his eyes came up to mine. They were already getting a little red, and a little extra-wet. I thought maybe mine were, too.

"You found it," he said, his voice scratchy.

"Yeah."

His eyes dropped back to the box.

"I'm sorry," he said.

I pursed my lips. "Sorry you hid it from me, or sorry I found it?"

"Well, shoot," he said. "Both, I guess."

"You . . . you had it all along?"

He nodded.

"But . . . why? I mean . . . why didn't you . . . why was she . . ."

Rodeo closed his eyes and scratched at his beard. He still had a hard time when he thought about what had happened to us. What had happened to *them*. Talking about it. Saying their names.

He was better than he had been. Way better. He'd been seeing a counselor and everything, and she was great, and he'd
come a long way. But he still had a hard time.

"It's . . . it's what she wanted. We, uh . . ." He sighed, heavy,
shook his head. "We'd talked about it, and she wanted—she
wanted to be, uh . . ." He gestured at the box with the back of
his hand. "That."

"But . . . there was a funeral," I said.

I didn't hardly remember a thing about those weeks after the
accident. I was only seven, after all. And the universe had just
had a hole torn in itself, after all. I remember lots of crying. Me
crying, and everyone else crying. Dad being a mess, just a disaster, just crying and even screaming sometimes, all a mess. Lots
of people hugging me and rubbing my back and trying to get
me to eat. And I remembered a funeral, or something. A stuffy
room. More crying. Some talking that I didn't listen to. I threw
up, I think.

"Sure," Rodeo said. "There was a service."

"With coffins," I said, and my voice broke. "I saw them." An
image, blurry, sickening. One of the coffins was small. Small
enough for my little sister.

"Yeah," Rodeo said. "Two coffins, little bird."

"Just two?"

My dad nodded. And he rubbed at his eyes with a knuckle.

"Just two."

"My sisters," I whispered.

"Mm-hmm." He cleared his throat, then again. "I, uh, didn't

know. What to do, I mean. With, uh. Didn't know what they woulda wanted, so they were . . . uh . . . well, they were, you know, buried. But I knew what, uh." He breathed. "I knew what your mom wanted. So."

I think I mentioned that my dad had a hard time talking about it.

"It's weird," I said. "That . . . that you had this all along. Hiding it. That you . . . brought it with us, all that way, all that time we were on the road, but that you never told me?" I don't know why I asked it like a question. I guess it was one, kind of.

"Yeah." Rodeo exhaled the word, like a surrender. "I s'pose. But, lord, Coyote, I . . . I just couldn't let her go, you know? But, also, I couldn't . . ." He trailed off. Looked away, lost. "I couldn't. So"—he gestured again at the box—"yeah."

We sat there in silence for a while, us two. Well, us *three*, kind of. Which was weird.

"So," I said. "Are we supposed to, like, bury her, or something? Or put her in one of those vase things?"

Rodeo sighed. "Nah. She didn't want to be locked up like that."

Feeling surprisingly generous, I didn't bother pointing out that for six years he'd kept her locked in a box, hidden behind a bookshelf.

"She wanted to be scattered. You know, set free."

"Where?"

"She had a special place in mind."

"Did she tell you where she wanted to be . . . scattered?"

Rodeo nodded. "Yeah. Yeah, she did."

"Where?"

"I don't know."

I blew a breath out through my nose, feeling rapidly less charitable. "Not exactly in the mood for games over here, old man."

Rodeo laughed a little, a raspy half chuckle. "No. I guess not. But I wasn't joking, darling. She didn't *tell* tell me." He shrugged and looked at me. "You want the whole story?"

"Of course."

"All right." Rodeo took a steadying breath, his eyes down on the table. "Well, one day we had a conversation. This was—"

"That ain't how you start a story," I interrupted.

Rodeo's eyebrows went up.

"Oh. Right. Sorry." He cleared his throat. Almost maybe hid a little smile inside that bird's-nest beard of his.

"Once upon a time," Rodeo began, "me and your mom had a talk. This was a while back, a couple of years before . . . well, *before*. We just had one of those talks, you know, about what we wanted, you know, if we died. And your mom said she wanted to be cremated, and her ashes scattered. I said the same, by the way. But your mom, she didn't like morbid conversations. Thought they were bad luck. So she had an idea. Instead of telling each other where we wanted our ashes scattered, we should write it down. Keep it secret. Then, if the time came, well, we could look and see. So we did that."

"You both wrote down where you wanted to be scattered?"

"Yep."

"Well? Where?"

"In one of her favorite books. Each on a different page. And that was that."

"And you . . . have that book?"

Rodeo nodded.

"I do. Out there in Yager right now."

I looked toward Yager. Well, I looked at the wall. But on the other side of that wall, I knew, was Yager. And in Yager, apparently, was a book. And in that book, apparently, my mom had written down her own final resting place.

"Did you . . . ever look? At what she wrote?"

Rodeo shook his head.

"Not even . . . after?"

Rodeo sighed and shook his head again.

"Especially not after," he murmured.

"Right," I said, nodding and chewing my lip. "It's funny. That for all these years, I've always felt so far away from Mom. And it turns out she was right there in that bus with me the whole time."

We both looked at that box, sitting there between us.

"Yeah," Rodeo said. He blew out a big breath. He shifted back, like he was gonna stand up, which I knew was almost certainly what he really wanted to do. The man had spent years running away from feelings and sadness and hard conversations.

But, lately, he'd been trying.

And so he leaned back forward, and reached past that box, and took one of my hands in his.

"How you feeling about all this, Coyote? Like, really?"

"Emotionally nauseous," I answered, matter-of-fact.

"Oh. You sure had that one ready."

"Yeah, well, I had some time to think."

"Okay." He gave my hand a squeeze. "Listen. I spent years putting this off. I wasn't just hiding that box from you. I was hiding it from me, too. But I'm getting better. Thanks to you. And my counselor. I'm finally putting my pieces back together. And I'm ready. Ready to give it a shot. So if you want, we can go out to that book right now, and fire up Yager, and take your mama to—"

"No," I cut in. I shook my head, and when I looked up at my dad, I was surprised by how blurry my eyes were. "I just got her back, Dad. I'm not ready to let her go just yet." I reached out with my free hand and put it on the box. I sniffed. "Is that okay?"

Rodeo squeezed my hand even harder. "Oh, darling. 'Course it is. Lord knows I know all about that. And, whenever you're ready, we'll do it. We'll do it together."

We looked into each other's eyes. We were having a moment there, me and my dad and that box of ashes.

The moment was interrupted by a thump. Ivan appeared up on the kitchen table and shot our moment a dubious, one-ear-back look. Then he ambled over to the box, gave it a sniff, climbed on top, turned in a circle, and then laid down facing us, paws tucked into his shameless chest. He gave us a slow, satisfied blink.

I shook my head and *tsk*ed my tongue at him. No respect for the dead.

"But when we go," Rodeo said, "we're not taking that damn cat."

I snorted.

"Of course we are, old man," I said, letting go of his hand to give Ivan a scratch. "Now, what's for dinner?"

# CHAPTER
## THREE

No big surprise, but that box stuck in my mind like a splinter. All that night through dinner—green chile mac 'n' cheese, by the way, a Rodeo specialty—and in and out of my dreams and as I was brushing my teeth the next morning and while I was riding the bus to school.

It's funny, riding a bus to school; the first time I got on, I looked around and thought, *Where the heck do you sleep?*

But I got to school safe and on time, which I guess is a bus's main job in most situations. I wasn't particularly thrilled to get there, though. I'd spent years dreaming about actually going to an actual school with actual classrooms and actual kids. It had seemed sure to be a social upgrade from the decidedly chill, spectacularly solo, hippie-dippy "homeschooling" Rodeo had been giving me on the road. But, in this case, there turned out to be a significant gap between dreams and reality. Truth be told, I don't really fit in all that well.

It started on my first day, back in the fall. First period. First thing, really.

I'd found my way to my first class and sat down, and a boy looked me up and down and gave me kind of a sour look and asked, "Is your last name Chesterfield?"

It wasn't as random as it seems; I was wearing a "Chesterfield Family Reunion, 1997" T-shirt I'd gotten at a thrift store.

"Nope!" I answered, naively excited to be having my first real conversation with a future classmate and, inevitably, a *friend*.

"Then why are you wearing that weird shirt?"

"It's got a cartoon hot dog on it and it was only a buck! How could I go wrong?"

Well, it turns out, I could go wrong. My grin was not returned. There were some snickers, but they weren't the friendly kind.

Then, there was attendance.

"Ella?" the teacher called out, which is my legal name.

"That's me," I said, "but I go by Coyote."

More snickers.

"Coyote? Like the animal?"

"Yes, ma'am."

The teacher smiled, but it was a tight-lipped smile. "And why do you want to be called *Coyote*?"

I blinked. "Does it matter?"

A murmur had gone through the class, and I realized that I'd maybe sounded kind of, you know, attitude-y. But truly it had been an honest question.

The teacher had sniffed. And she'd tightened her smile up a bit. "This is your first day joining our class, Ella. Welcome. And where did you live before you moved here?"

I thought about the previous years of my life, living on Yager, waking up in a new place every morning, the gas stations and truck stops and campgrounds and national parks and highways and big cities and small towns.

"Gosh," I said. "The whole world, really."

It was, apparently, another wrong answer. Which, apparently, was the only kind of answer I knew how to give. If my dad had heard that answer, he probably would have smiled and nodded and given me a fist bump and said something like, "Good answer, little chickadee."

But my dad wasn't in Mrs. Clark's first period seventh grade Life Science class. Which was probably for the best. No one gave me a fist bump. There were some smiles. But, again, not the friendly kind.

That's about as well as my first day of real school had gone, and about as well as every day since had gone. When I'd told Rodeo about it that afternoon, he'd pulled me into a tight hug.

"Aw, shoot," he'd murmured into my hair. "Sorry, bud. I guess you're the lone lobster in the crab pot. But I've always preferred lobster, if that makes you feel any better."

"Not really," I'd said, frowning at the idea that either way I had to get boiled alive and eaten.

So my dream-come-true of going to school turned out to be more of a rude awakening. But, hey, I was used to not having friends. I'd had five years of practice.

True, it felt somewhat lonelier to be friendless when you were surrounded every day by literally hundreds of possible friends, but what are you gonna do?

And there were bright spots. One in particular. Which was right where I headed on this particular morning, and was in fact right where I always headed on every particular morning.

I walked through the library doors and felt my whole body take a relaxing breath.

There's a limit to how bad a school can be if it's got a library. That's just a fact.

"Good morning, Coyote," Ms. Jordan, the librarian, greeted me. Ms. Jordan is probably the oldest teacher at the school, based on hair grayness and wrinkle count. But based on eye twinkle and laugh volume, she's the youngest. She's got a full-lunged belly laugh that is about as far from a *shush* as a sound can be.

"Good morning," I answered, and headed toward my regular spot at a table over by the window.

"You have a nice weekend?" she asked.

I thought about the box of human remains that was currently sitting on my kitchen table.

"It was interesting," I said, dropping into a chair.

At that moment, the library doors swung open and Ostrich walked in.

To be clear, she was not an actual ostrich. And nor was her name Ostrich.

Ostrich is what everyone called her because, allegedly, she resembles an ostrich.

To be fair, they had a point.

She was very tall. With a long neck. And big kind of bulging eyes that were regrettably exaggerated by her thick glasses. Oh, and she kept her hair cut close to her scalp, shorter even than most of the boys. She kept her hair cut so short because, as she told me the first time we met, she'd gotten head lice in the third grade and it had been a particularly bad case of the head lice and eventually her parents had given up on the special combs and toxic shampoos and just buzzed her hair with dog-grooming clippers and she'd gotten kind of used to the cool air on her scalp and really didn't want to risk another episode of head lice and so she'd kept that style ever since.

And, again, that was the first time we met.

Plus, her actual name is Audrey.

So, there you go. Audrey the Ostrich.

I mean, it's mean, and it's not okay, and I certainly never called her that, but there was no denying the overall point. I'm not saying that she looked like an ostrich, but if you *had* to pick an animal that she most looked like, I think nine people out of ten would say "ostrich" without being given any hints. The tenth person would say "giraffe."

It didn't seem to bother her, though.

She was . . . *unique*. A real one of a kind.

That same first time I met her, I'd been sitting right there in that same spot. I'd started coming to the library every day before school and at lunch, sitting there by the window. She came every day, too, and sat at a table on the other side. But then one day at lunch, she'd marched right up to me.

"You've been coming here every day," she'd said.

"Yep," I'd answered.

"You don't have any friends," she'd said. I think it's important to note at this point that Audrey is never mean on purpose. Those last two words are key.

"I'm the lone lobster," I answered with a shrug, and instantly realized that Rodeo was, in fact, rubbing off on me, and that might not, in fact, be the best thing for my social life. The girl, though, was unfazed.

"Okey dokey," she said. "Can I sit here?"

"Okey dokey," I said, and that was that.

We'd sat together every day since. We weren't exactly *friends*, really, but we were at least both lobsters. When I explained the whole "lobster" thing to her I laughed and said, "Look at us, a Coyote and an Ostrich, who are both lobsters. We could be a petting zoo," and she'd furrowed her brow and said, "I don't think petting zoos have lobsters. Or coyotes," and I'd said, "Good point," although I'm not entirely sure it was.

But, anyway.

This day-after-the-ashes morning, she walked in and sat down across the table from me and pulled a pencil and her sketchbook out of her backpack and jumped right into shading whatever dragon she was currently working on. Audrey has quite a thing for dragons. Some folks would call it an "obsession," but I don't think that word goes quite far enough.

"Good morning," I said.

"We'll see," she answered without looking up. She wasn't being grumpy. She was just being realistic.

Ms. Jordan joined us, like she did every morning, carefully setting down three steaming mugs on the table between us, like she did every morning. She called us the Coffee Crew but she was the only one who drank coffee.

"Thanks," I said, and took a sip of my cocoa. Audrey blew on her mint tea, eyes still on her drawing. Audrey is good company, but she's not always great company.

"So," Ms. Jordan said, settling in, "weekends?"

Audrey sighed and set down her pencil. The rule is that if Ms. Jordan supplies us with beverages, we have to provide her with conversation.

"My stepdad brought home a kite for me," she said. "It was a dragon."

"That was nice of him."

Audrey shrugged. "It got stuck in a tree. In like three minutes. Which a real dragon would never do."

I didn't bother pointing out the ridiculousness of the term "real dragon." I'd made that mistake before.

Ms. Jordan turned to me.

"I found my mom's ashes yesterday."

Ms. Jordan's eyebrows went up.

But Audrey just blinked behind her glasses. She's a big blinker. "Did you lose them?" she asked.

"No. My dad was hiding them."

"Where did he hide them?"

"Behind a bookshelf."

"Oh." She blinked again. "If I were hiding someone's ashes, I'd hide them in the fireplace."

"Why?"

"Because they'd blend right in."

Ms. Jordan and I looked at each other.

Then she threw her head back and whooped out a few of her trademark guffaws.

Audrey just blinked at her. She hadn't been making a joke.

"What are you going to do with them?" Audrey asked me. For a dragon person, she was surprisingly no-nonsense.

"I don't know yet."

"I think you're supposed to bury them."

I shook my head. "Apparently not. She wanted to be scattered. In a certain place."

"Then why don't you do that?"

I opened my mouth. And then I closed it. It was tricky to swallow, for just a second.

"These things can be complicated," Ms. Jordan said gently. Audrey and Ms. Jordan know all about my tragic backstory, by the way. That kind of thing tends to come up.

"I don't see the complicated part," Audrey said. "She wanted to be scattered. So scatter her."

See that right there? Not on purpose.

"*Emotionally* complicated," Ms. Jordan said, looking rather intensely into Audrey's rather intense eyes.

"Oh," Audrey said. "I guess I could see that. Sorry." She picked her pencil back up and returned to her shading. "My dad didn't die. He just moved to an apartment in Salem. With a pool. So I don't have to worry about burying him yet. Or not burying him."

"You're lucky," Ms. Jordan said kindly.

"Well, it's an outdoor pool," Audrey said. "So it's only open in the summer."

Ms. Jordan didn't have anything to say to that.

She did reach across the desk, though, and put her hand on

mine. "It can be helpful to have someone to talk to about these kinds of things, honey," she said. "Do you have an adult in your life that you trust?"

I thought about Rodeo. When I'd left that morning, he'd been drinking coffee straight from the pot and stomping his foot because it was too hot.

"I have a cat," I offered.

My Coffee Crew conversation didn't really help me get a lot of clarity on the whole Mom's ashes thing. Ms. Jordan did give me an extra warm hug before I left, though, which was nice. And she made me an appointment with the school counselor.

But when I got off the bus at the end of the day (with a few kids coyote-howling at me out the windows as it drove away, which they do every day, which is apparently hilarious), I was still feeling as emotionally complicated and emotionally nauseous as ever.

"Aloha, sweet thing!" Rodeo called from his office. His office, by the way, is actually a hall closet just big enough to hold him, a folding chair, and a laptop. He claims to be writing a book, which I find both fascinating and alarming.

"Hey," I said, not able to muster much enthusiasm.

Ivan was sleeping in the sunny spot on the back of the couch. He gave me a wide-mouthed yawn, but he was far too exhausted from a long day of napping to walk over to greet me.

I let my backpack fall to the ground and walked into the kitchen to grab a banana, and then I saw that box sitting there on the table. Funny, I'd spent all day thinking about it, and the sight of it still kinda took my breath away. It wasn't a bad feeling, but it was a *big* feeling.

"Hi, Mom," I whispered.

The banana forgotten, I walked over and picked up the box. Gently, like it was holy. Which it was, really.

And I walked back to my room.

And I sat down on my bed, cross-legged, and slid my back against the wall, with the box on my lap. And then I took a deep breath and unsnapped the latches and lifted the lid and looked inside, at all those ashes.

My hand, shaking just a little, reached out. Gently, gently, gently, I touched a fingertip to the ash. I closed my eyes and tried my best to remember how she looked. Her hair. Her smile. The way she moved. The way she smelled. The way she laughed. The way she'd press her lips to the top of my head and kiss me. All that. All that, just ashes now.

I heard my dad, whistling his way down the hall.

His whistling stopped when he stuck his head in the door and saw me, sitting there holding my mom in my lap.

Me and that box had been interrupting a lot of his good moods lately.

"When's the last time you looked?" I asked him, my voice gentle to keep him close. "Inside, I mean? At . . . what's in here."

Rodeo dropped his head and looked down at the shag carpet. But then, with his head still down, he raised his eyes to mine.

"The last time?" he said. "Honeybear, there wasn't a first time. I've never looked in that box."

I nodded. I got it.

"Do you want to?"

Rodeo swallowed. "No," he rasped out. "I do not. I'm sorry."

"Nothing to be sorry about," I said, because there wasn't. Folks get to choose.

A few moments slid by. I looked down at my mom.

My dad stepped forward, quiet, like he was walking into church. Sat down on the bed. Put a hand on my leg. Breathed in, breathed out.

"Little bird," he said. "I talked to my counselor today. About this, about you finding this box. It was good. Real good. And, whew." He rubbed his chin and then nodded and turned his eyes on me. "It's time."

"Time for what?"

"To do what I shoulda done a long time ago. To scatter her ashes. To set your mom free, like she wanted."

My breath caught, and my fingers tightened around the box.

"What? Why? What's the rush?"

"Rush?" he said gently. "It's been six years, darling."

I don't know why, exactly, but I freaked out. On the inside. I'd been feeling kinda lost, I guess, with school and not fitting in and everything. Like a little boat, tossed around in a storm. And then I found that box, and it was kinda like a lighthouse, or something. Holding it in my hands, I felt, I don't know, *rooted* somehow.

When I held that box, when I sat there with my mom, I knew who I was. It was a feeling I didn't know I needed until I had it and someone tried to take it away.

I guess maybe sometimes you don't know you lost something until you find it again.

"We can't do that," I said quick.

Rodeo's brow furrowed. "Why not? I'm ready. And it's what your mom wanted."

*But* I'm *not ready!* my heart wanted to shout. But I didn't. Me holding on to my mom felt too personal, too private, too . . . little kiddie, honestly, to just say out loud. Not to mention more than a little selfish.

"We . . . can't, yet, though," I said, mind racing. "Because, you know . . ." I was floundering, but then my mind flashed and I saw it. "School! You can't just pull me out of school! There's laws and stuff about that."

"There are?"

I shrugged. "Pretty sure."

"Huh. Yeah," Rodeo said thoughtfully. "I mean, I wouldn't want to pull you out of school anyway, laws or not. Huh." He blew out a big breath and nodded. "Okay. So we wait a bit. 'Til spring break or summer or something."

My shoulders slumped and my stomach eased and I let out a tight breath. Summer was basically forever away. I didn't have to lose what I'd found just yet.

"In the meantime, though, there *is* something we can do," my dad said.

"What?"

He licked his lips. "We can go look in that book," he said. "We can see what she wrote. We can find out where we're going."

# CHAPTER

## FOUR

$S$o, a few minutes later, we were standing outside Yager's folding door. I was feeling pretty emotionally nauseous again. I was gonna see a message from my mom. And I wasn't gonna be able to write back.

"You know which book?" I asked, buying time.

"'Course. Little black book. Red and white lettering. In my desk drawer. It's called *Red Bird*. Poems by a lady named Mary Oliver. She was our favorite."

"Okay. And you know what page it's on?"

"Yeah. We taped 'em shut, to keep the secret."

We stood there for a second.

"You ready?" I asked.

"Mmm" was all he said.

Another few seconds went by.

"You know what?" he said. "Why don't you look? Why don't just you go in and then tell me what it says?"

His voice was getting all shaky. He sounded like how I felt.

"I thought you wanted to do this," I said.

"Yeah. Yeah. Me, too. And I do. In theory. But, boy." He rubbed his jaw. "Seeing her handwriting? Whew. I don't know, little bird. Feels kinda like looking in that box. I don't know."

He swallowed, and his eyes were all glisten-y. "I mean, I saw that book a hundred times these past few years. It was always there, in my desk drawer or on my bedside table. I even read it, every year, on our anniversary. Did that just last summer."

I was kinda floored. I thought he'd pretty much spent the last six years trying to forget about what had happened to our family. I'd had no idea.

He shook his head, scratched at his chin. "Could you do it for me, darling?"

I reached up and gave his shoulder a squeeze. "Sure," I said. "'Course I can."

I looked at the waiting door to Yager, suddenly feeling pretty nervous myself.

I took one more *here we go* breath, then I pushed open the door.

And I walked up the stairs.

And I walked back past the bus seats, to Rodeo's desk. Now, Rodeo's "desk" was really nothing of the sort, just like his "office" in the house was really just a closet. His desk was basically a long double shelf that he'd built and bolted to the wall that mostly held junk and snacks and, usually, some potted tomato plants. But built into the bottom of that shelf was a drawer I never poked around in because as far as I knew it was just where he kept the bus registration, insurance paperwork, all that stuff. I certainly hadn't known it also held a book my mom had written her in-case-I-ever-die wish in.

I grabbed the drawer knob.

*"Come on, Coyote,"* I whispered. And then, out of nowhere,

my anxiety died down. And some weird version of *excited* took its place. After all these years of missing my mom, I was about to get another piece of her back.

This was a hard thing, for sure, but it was a *good* thing. Maybe an *awesome* thing, even.

I pulled open the drawer. Saw the messy pile of paper. Started pulling it out, a sheet or two at a time. There wasn't that much. I arched an eyebrow at an unpaid parking ticket from Mississippi from two years before. Rolled my eyes at a flyer for a hot-dog-eating contest in North Dakota that Rodeo had thought was hilarious and had apparently kept for three years, right there with our vehicle title and my birth certificate.

And then I was standing there, a bunch of papers in one hand, looking down at the dark wood bottom of the drawer.

"Huh," I said. I scrabbled my hand around to the back corners. Nothing. I tossed the papers on the shelf and pulled the drawer all the way out. Definitely empty. Crouched down to look into the hole. Even more nothing.

"*Dang it, Rodeo,*" I said. It was so like him to be all flaky and misplace something irreplaceable. Well, I knew it had to be on Yager somewhere. There's no way he'd take it off the bus and forget that he had.

And that's when I saw his bedside table. Which, for the record, was just an old flimsy wooden crate that he had sitting next to his blanket nest.

The book was always in his drawer, he said. Or on his bedside table.

The table I was looking at was empty.

But a vague little memory began prickling like an itch. Got a little less vague. Got even more prickly.

It was dim, and it was blurry, but the memory rose up like a catfish in my mind. I could see the book, sitting there on that crate. A little black book, paperback. A while back, but not forever back. Rodeo had said that he'd read it just last summer on their anniversary, and that felt about right.

In the memory, I was rushing around. In the memory, I was feeling kind of impatient. In the memory, I picked up the book.

"*Oh crap,*" I whispered. Not in my memory. In real life.

In the memory, I added the little book to a stack of books I held in my other arm.

"*Oh crap oh crap oh crap oh crap,*" I whispered. My stomach lurched with both emotional and actual physical nausea. I stopped breathing. Then breathed really fast for a second. Then stopped breathing again.

Here's an important historical fact about me and Rodeo's five years on the road: Living a life without school or TV or phones or computers, we burned through a whole heckuva lot of books awfully quick. And since we never spent more than a day or two in one place, libraries weren't really an option. So we had to buy a lot of books. More books than we could store in a house on wheels. So, our home library was in constant rotation. We'd pick up books wherever we found them: new bookstores, used bookstores, garage sales, thrift stores. Then we'd have them for a while, read them, pass them back and forth. Then, whenever we decided we had a batch we were done with, we'd drop them off somewhere. The same kind of places we picked them up in: thrift stores, used bookstores, flea markets.

Just a few hundred miles from wherever we got them.

It was a fine system. Unless, of course, the wrong book accidentally ended up in the drop-off stack.

And guess whose job it was to gather up a stack of books to drop off?

We'd pull into a parking lot somewhere and Rodeo would say something ridiculous like, "Whip us up a quick batch of books, darling!" and I'd gather old books off the floor, the couch, wherever. And I'd march them inside and drop them off, and we'd get ourselves a bunch of new-to-us ones. I'd never take books off me or Rodeo's actual shelves, of course. Those were keepers. But off an old wooden crate? Maybe. Probably.

Aw, shoot. Definitely.

I was supposed to ask first. Make sure he was done with it. Because once when I was like ten, I accidentally dropped off some spy novel that he was in the middle of reading and then we had to spend a month hitting every bookstore we could until we found another copy because he just had to find out how it ended. It was a whole thing.

And I did ask. *Almost* every time. Unless, you know, I was feeling rushed or impatient or fed up with Rodeo's sleep-in-a-pile-of-blankets-and-leave-junk-all-around-the-bus ways and just muttered "oh, screw it" under my breath and grabbed any book I could find.

I knelt there, sick to my stomach.

"*I lost it*," I whispered.

My mom's favorite book. The book with her handwriting in it. The handwriting where she told us how she wanted to, finally, be laid to rest. The book that my dad was standing out there waiting for, right at that very minute.

I blinked and blinked and blinked and then rubbed at my eyes. Took a couple jaggedy breaths.

What would I tell him? *How* could I tell him? How could I look him in his eyes and tell him what I'd done, tell him that we'd never know what Mom had written, never know how to let her rest in peace?

Seconds ticked by. Minutes, maybe? I couldn't tell.

But, then, I knew. It couldn't be put off forever. Nothing can, really.

I wiped my eyes one more time. Tried to steady my breathing and gulp down my nausea. Then pulled myself to my feet and took that long walk toward my waiting dad to face the music.

Rodeo was standing right where I left him, outside that bus door.

I slumped down the bus stairs, shaky and sweaty. Closed the door behind me, just to buy a couple seconds.

"How was it?" he asked.

I couldn't meet his eyes. I sniffled. Swallowed a big ball of broken glass. Shrugged. And then I opened my mouth to say it.

"I lost the book, Dad. It's gone."

I mean, that's what I *planned* on saying. I swear. But all that came out was a little squeaky wheeze.

My dad stepped forward and wrapped me in a tight hug. He pressed his mouth to the top of my head.

"Shhh," he said, quiet. "It's okay. You don't have to tell me right now." And for a second I was confused, thinking, *How does he know I lost the book?* But then I realized, of course, that the *telling* he was talking about was telling him what Mom had written. "Whenever you're ready, okay, darling?"

I froze. There was a choice to be made.

So I made one.

I nodded. Right there into my dad's shoulder.

Now, I didn't *lie.* I just nodded. I'd planned on facing the music, but then my dad had changed the song, and I'd just kind of, you know, hummed along. Nothing wrong with that, right?

Rodeo gave me a squeeze.

"I'm sorry," he said, "about all this," and I said *me, too,* but only in my mind, because my actual mouth actually said, "I'm going inside." Rodeo gave me a couple more pats and then let me go, and I slid out of his arms and brushed past him through the back door.

Not because I needed to be alone, though I did.

But because I needed to talk to my friend.

# CHAPTER

## FIVE

*f*unny thing: Me and cell phones turned out to be a lot like me and school. Man oh man I wanted one, but man oh man it just wasn't a love connection.

Once we settled down, I'd begged and begged Rodeo for my own phone, and finally he'd given in, and I'd just been over-the-moon excited, and then . . . I don't know. Everyone else couldn't get enough of those things. But I quickly figured out that the longer I sat looking at one, the emptier and flatter I'd feel when I was done. Which didn't happen if I was reading a book. Or playing with Ivan. Or looking out the window, even. So mostly my phone just sat by my bed, plugged in. It was a handy alarm clock, and that's about it.

There was, though, one highly awesome thing about my overrated phone: Salvador. I could push some buttons on that dumb smartphone and then hear the voice of my best-and-let's-face-it-only friend in the whole world. And when you only have one friend in the whole world and they live four hours away in a whole other state, it is in fact highly awesome to be able to push some buttons and hear their voice.

So that day, after I kinda sorta lied to my dad about an irreplaceable and apparently lost book, I closed my bedroom door and grabbed my phone like it was oxygen. There were a million little notifications, but I ignored them and went straight to the actual phone app and dialed the person that was just about my only contact.

Salvador picked up on the fourth ring.

If you don't know who Salvador is, well, my condolences. All you need to know, really, is that he's pretty freaking awesome and he's my best friend, and that may seem like a silly label given my actual friend count of one (not counting lobsters), but the title of best friend has got nothing to do with quantity and everything to do with quality, and Salvador is one hundred percent quality. We'd only just met the year before; he and his mom had been on the road, kinda like me and Rodeo. They'd needed a ride, we'd given 'em one, a whole bunch of stuff happened, and *bada bada bing!* We'd been best friends ever since.

"Hey, Coyote."

"Salvador!" I said, my voice already starting to break a little.

"Did you get my texts?" he asked.

"What? Oh. Probably."

"Probably? Did you read them?"

"No."

Salvador huffed.

"You are so weird. You are the only kid I know who would rather, like, actually *call* than just *text*, which is like a thousand times easier."

"Yeah," I said. "Right. 'Cause I really wanna look at words on a screen instead of hearing my best friend's voice. Especially right now."

"Well, you could still—" Salvador started to say, but then I guess what I'd said registered with him. "Wait. Why especially now?"

I heaved out a ragged sigh. Then, suddenly worried that Rodeo would accidentally overhear, I crawled under the blanket on my bed.

"You're not gonna believe this," I whispered. "I lost the book that was gonna tell me where to scatter my mom."

There was a fairly significant pause.

"I think you're gonna need to back up a little, Coyote."

I heaved out yet another sigh. "Fair. So, I found my mom's ashes."

"You found her *ashes?*"

"Yes. In a box. On Yager. Dad had been hiding them."

"Your dad was hiding your mom's ashes?"

"Oh my god, Salvador, this will go so much faster if you don't make me repeat everything. Just assume if I say something, it's true."

"Okay. But I just wanna say for the record that a lot of times you say stuff that's totally wild, but you say it like it's totally normal, and it takes the rest of us a second to catch up."

"Okay. I guess I can see that. Anyway. She wrote down where she wanted her ashes scattered in this old poetry book, but at some point *I got rid of the book by accident and now it's gone and I don't know where to put her!*" By this point I was talking about as loudly and emphatically as someone who's whispering under a blanket can.

"Oh," Salvador said softly. "Okay. Wow. Yeah."

—— 38 ——

"I know. Right? What can I do, Salvador? This is, like, an epic disaster!"

Salvador thought a second. "Is it, though?"

"Yes!!" I shouted, then remembered the top secret nature of the conversation and brought it down a couple hundred notches. "*Yes!*"

"Okay. Okay. I mean, I get why you're upset, but . . . do you think your mom would be? Like, don't you think she'd be okay if you just, um, *scattered* her wherever *you* wanted?"

I opened my mouth. Closed it. "You're missing the point," I said at last. "*I* want to do it in the right place. *I* want to do it how *she* wanted. Doesn't it matter that *I* want to do it right?"

"Sure, sure. Sorry." I heard him click his tongue, like he was thinking. "Well, what did your dad say? Was he upset?"

"Um," I answered. "No?"

Another pause.

"Coyote?"

"Hmm?"

"You didn't tell your dad you lost the book, did you?"

"It's complicated."

"Why would that be complicated? You should really just tell him you threw the book away."

"It's . . . emotionally complicated," I said. "And I didn't throw it away. I'm not a monster. I dropped it off at a thrift store or used bookstore somewhere."

There was another pause. When Salvador spoke again, his voice was different. Hopeful. "Well. It's not *gone*, then, is it? It's still out there. It's just . . . lost."

My breath caught. I saw where he was going with this. And I liked it.

"And if it's lost," I said, throwing off the blanket and sitting up, "I could find it."

"Exactly." He paused. "Well, maybe exactly. How long ago was this?"

"I don't know."

"Okay. *Where* was it?"

"I don't know."

"Um."

"But. You're right. It *is* out there. Somewhere."

"Yeah . . ." Salvador's voice had gone from hopeful to cautious, but my heart had gone from tragic to hopeful, so it didn't bother me.

I stood up from the bed. Cleared my throat. "How are you doing, Salvador?"

He blew out a breath. "You're getting ready to hang up on me, aren't you?"

"Yeah. But it'd be rude to just make it all about me. So how are you?"

Salvador sigh-laughed. "Fine. Pretty great, actually."

"Sweet. Your mom good?"

"Yeah! She's taking night classes to be a nurse."

"Wow. She'd rock as a nurse. Tell her I said 'hi.'"

"Will do. Say 'hi' to Rodeo for me. And Ivan."

"Salvador says 'hi,'" I said to Ivan, who was lying at the foot of my bed. Ivan was unimpressed. "Thanks, Salvador." I took a breath. "I miss you, man. Like, a *lot*."

"Yeah. I miss you, too, Coyote."

"Obviously. Well, I gotta go."

"I know. Good luck. Let me know what you find out."

"You'll be the first call I make, amigo."

"Or you could text me . . ."

"Hm. Bye, Salvador."

I stood there in my room, mind and heart racing. I'd been on a bit of a roller coaster, emotionally speaking. But it ended in a hopeful spot. And hopeful spots are generally the best kind of spots.

My hope was barely a spark, though. I'd built enough campfires to know that a spark is all you need, sometimes, but if a spark is all you got, it's gonna take a lot of work.

"Buckle your seat belt, Ivan," I said to my cat. He put his ears back and gave me some significant feline side-eye. "We got some work to do."

# CHAPTER

## SIX

*A* few minutes later I was back in my room. But now I had our big ol' atlas opened up to the map of the whole United States, spread out on my bed. And I had a pen in my hand, and a notebook open to a fresh page.

"Okay," I mumbled to myself, "I should be able to figure this out."

My dad said he read the book every year on his and Mom's anniversary. I knew for a fact that they were married on the Fourth of July, because my dad had always said they picked that date because fireworks went off when he looked at my mom, but my mom had always said they'd picked it just so my dad could remember it. And I knew for another fact that I'd gotten a very important phone call from my grandma when I was in Naples, Florida, last summer. I remembered that phone call because it was kind of a big deal and started off an entire dramatic race-across-the-country journey that had ended, more or less, with me living here.

Anyway, I was one hundred percent sure that we hadn't done any book drops after that phone call, which I knew was toward the end of summer. The memory felt kind of August-y to me. So all I had to do was remember where we'd traveled in July and August last year, and then remember where we'd stopped and done book drops. The book had to be in one of those places. No biggie.

I wrote *Naples, Florida* at the bottom of the page. That was the end point. Now I just needed a starting line.

I squinted my eyes, thinking hard. We'd gotten Ivan last summer, too, in Oregon, but that had been at the beginning of the summer. June-ish. So the catastrophic book drop was after Oregon. That was a start. I sucked my lips, trying to scour back through my memories.

"Let's see, let's see, let's see," I mumbled. The Fourth of July. Rodeo is a big fan of fireworks, so we usually tried to catch a show every year. What about last year? My eyes flashed open as the memory sparked into my brain like, well, a firework.

We'd watched a fireworks show a couple days after we left a lake in Colorado. I remembered that lake in Colorado because I'd met a girl there. *"Fiona,"* I whispered, nodding. She'd been cool. And then we'd left without saying goodbye, which sucks, and drove to . . . I tapped my pencil on my lips, thinking . . . Cheyenne, Wyoming! I was sure of it. They'd had some sort of "Frontier Days" festival going on. We'd gone to the fireworks show and then stuck around the next day and walked around town and, I was one hundred percent certain, had hit a second-hand store. I still had the Willie Nelson T-shirt I'd bought there. I wrote *Cheyenne, Wyoming* at the top of the page. Boom.

I spent the next hour or so scraping through my mind, poring over the map, and jotting down notes. I had to try to remember where we'd gone, but more importantly, where we'd stopped and done a book drop. And then I had to get on my phone and try to see if I could find the *exact* secondhand store we'd stopped at in, say, Pittsburgh. It was, to be honest, kind of a nightmare.

But not as impossible as it seemed at first. Looking through my memories, I figured out that when you're moving all the time and living on the road, all the places *do* kind of blend together in your mind, sure; but the *events* don't, because they're all happening in different places. Living like we did now, with the same house and street and school and scenery every day, it was kinda hard to tell the days apart. It was way less hard when I was remembering a fireworks show in Wyoming (fantastic), and then an escape room in Pennsylvania (we lost), and then a picnic on the coast in Maine (lobster rolls: delicious).

So, pretty soon, I had what I thought was a pretty accurate timeline of where we'd traveled between Cheyenne, Wyoming, and Naples, Florida, the summer before. And I had what I thought was a fairly *possible* list of places that I *might* have left that priceless copy of *Red Bird* in. I wasn't a big fan of the words "possible" and "might" in that sentence, but at least it was a start.

I looked at my paper, at the seven places I'd written down:

*Cheyenne, Wyoming*
*Emporia, Kansas*
*Chillicothe, Missouri*
*West Lafayette, Indiana*
*Pittsburgh, Pennsylvania*
*Freeport, Maine*
*Bel Air, Maryland*

Yikes. Seven spots, in seven cities, in seven states, spread across, like, two thousand miles. I was tempted to think it was like looking for a needle in a haystack, but honestly, finding a needle in a haystack seemed like a better bet than what I was doing.

And then another even more alarming idea flashed into my mind. Something that hadn't occurred to me. And it was that Willie Nelson T-shirt that started it.

The super-obvious-but-nevertheless-blood-chilling aha that I had was this: People buy things at secondhand stores. Things like Willie Nelson T-shirts. But also things like old books of poetry.

I'd foolishly been thinking of this whole thing as just me having to figure out which store it was in, then going and getting it. But . . . what if someone else did first? What if tomorrow, someone strolled in and bought the book? It'd be gone forever, and I'd never know where. What if someone had done that yesterday, or really *any* day since July the year before?

My stomach dropped out of my body and through the bed and onto the floor.

I had to find that book. And I had to find it before it was too late. I had to find it *now.*

I was sitting there staring at my fairly hopeless notes when my door swung open.

"Hey, monkeyface, do you—"

"Dad! Knock!"

"Sorry!" he said quick, stopping in his tracks and covering his face and turning away. But then he seemed to notice two things at once: I wasn't naked, and I had a map spread out on the bed. I covered my notes quickly with my arm, but it was way too late for me to hide the rest of what I was doing.

His eyebrows went up.

"What are you doing?" he asked, voice quiet.

I opened my mouth, but nothing came out.

"I think I know, birdie," he said. "I know exactly what you're doing."

My heart sank. My desperate plan had become a failed plan before I'd even got started.

"You're planning it out, aren't you? Mapping out where we got to go. Because of that book that your mom wrote in."

I swallowed. And then, once again, I nodded. In my experience, nodding is the best kind of lying because you don't have to trust your shaky voice and you feel a little less guilty after, since you didn't actually *speak* a lie. A nod is not a speak.

He lowered his eyebrows, eyeing the map and the couple of sticky notes I'd stuck on it.

"We have to . . . go pretty far, huh?"

I nodded, deciding to stick with what worked.

"Sweet." He drew in a big ol' breath and then let it out, shaking his head. And then he smiled. "You know, darling, this is gonna be something. I just . . . I just know your mom would love this, us doing this together. Us setting her free, just like she asked. It's gonna be special. And it's gonna be . . . *right*, you know? Doing what *she* wanted."

I saw the tears rising in his eyes just before he went blurry from the tears rising in my own.

He stepped toward me, fist held out, and I gave him the fist bump he was asking for.

Rodeo's eyes started to drift toward the map, and I slammed it closed as quick as I casually could without looking like I was trying to hide a terrible secret.

He took a big, bracing-himself breath. "So . . . where we going?"

My mouth went dry. I realized, too late, I really should have had a plan for this moment. Of course he would ask. It wasn't, like, a small detail.

"We're going," I said, brain racing, "to the place," I continued, swallowing dryly, "that Mom wrote in that book."

It wasn't amazing.

My dad's brow furrowed a little. "Right," he said. "And . . . what did she write?"

I took a shaky breath. "She wrote," I said, "um, where she wanted her ashes scattered."

I wasn't exactly *killing it* at this whole think-quick-and-say-something-to-save-your-butt thing.

His forehead furrow deepened. "Yeah," he said encouragingly. Gave me a confused little smile. "And can you . . . tell me where that is?"

All I had to do was make something up. Pick some faraway place to buy myself some time and give myself a chance to find that book and make it right. "Boston, Massachusetts!" I could say, or "Myrtle Beach, South Carolina!" and then I'd be good and my secret would be safe for a while and for a few thousand miles.

I opened my mouth.

But I couldn't do it. Couldn't lie out loud to my dad, standing there all patient and gentle. Lie about something so big and important. But I couldn't quite talk, either. Earlier, I'd lied with a nod, kinda. This time I told the truth by shaking my head.

I shook my head. And that was it. The truth was out. My dad knew I'd lost the book and now he was gonna be sad or devastated or mad and it was gonna be awful.

"You . . . can't?" Rodeo frowned, just a little.

I managed to find my voice, or some of it. "Nope," I croaked.

He blinked at me. Then his forehead smoothed out. And he kinda stepped back so he could lean against the wall. His shoulders sagged.

"Oh," he said, quiet. I knew he'd put the pieces together. "I get it," he murmured. His head dropped down.

My eyes filled with tears. What was he gonna do? Punch a hole in the wall? Nah. Collapse to the ground, sobbing? Possibly. Look back up at me, eyes filled with disappointment and betrayal? For sure. What I was pretty sure he wasn't gonna do, though, was forgive me for what I'd done. Even if he tried to. Even if he said he did. How could he?

But then he looked back up to me. And his eyes were all teary, like I'd been afraid. But . . . he was also smiling. Which was confusing.

"I get it," he said again. "That's part of it, ain't it? It's not just a place. It's a . . . a *quest*, right?" He wiped his eyes and shook his head. "She didn't just write down a spot, did she? Your mom gave us . . . a *journey*. I *get* it."

I realized my mouth was hanging open. He didn't get it. He

*definitely* didn't get it. And I saw my solution. I didn't have to lie to my dad. I just had to agree with him. You can't get mad at someone for just agreeing with you, right?

So I nodded. My head had been doing an awful lot of lying lately.

"Of course she did," my dad said, his voice hoarse.

I cleared my throat. I needed to say something. But I didn't want to lie. So I chose my words carefully.

"I've got a direction we're gonna go," I said, patting the closed atlas. Which was true. "But I can't tell you what she wrote in that book yet." Also incredibly true. "And then, at some point on our journey, I'll tell you the truth." True, true, true. Not a single lie in there. I'm not gonna say that made me feel all that much better, but it was a fact.

My dad was full-on grinning now. "Oh, man," he said. "It's *perfect.*" He sucked in a big, lung-clearing breath and then blew it out. "I can't wait for this summer."

"About that," I said, stomach churning. "I was thinking. Why wait? We've got this awesome, super-important quest to go on. Let's do it! Like, tomorrow!" I tried to keep my voice all positive and casual, but I was picturing that Willie Nelson T-shirt, imagining that clueless stranger walking out of a thrift store with my mom's book in their hands.

"But . . . you'd miss school."

"I can live with that," I said, with one hundred percent sincerity.

Rodeo *tsk*ed and shook his head. "Nah, little rabbit. You were right the first time. You oughta be in school. We'll go first chance we get. But no rush. We got this, darling." Then he gave me a little farewell wink and backed out of the room and closed the door. I looked back to my notes.

I swallowed. I had to find that book. I *had* to. It meant too much. To my mom. To my dad. To me. And now I had lies stacked on lies piled on secrets. I had to find that book.

"It's not gone," I said, echoing Salvador. "It's just lost."

I looked at my notes, scanned those seven distant, far-flung towns. Any one of which might have my book in it at that very moment; any one of which might have somebody *looking* at that book at that very moment, thinking of buying it. I swear I could *hear* a big clock of doom ticking in the background, counting down to the moment I lost that book forever. I had to wait to visit the stores, apparently. But I didn't have to wait to start looking. I *couldn't* wait, actually. So I grabbed my phone.

"Ready or not, haystack," I muttered to myself, "here I come."

# CHAPTER

## SEVEN

I'm gonna go ahead and fast-forward the story a bit here. Because, basically, some boring stuff happened and then some very exciting stuff happened, and I think it's best to just skip the crust and go straight to the peanut butter and jelly, if you know what I mean.

The boring crust stuff: I made a whole bunch of phone calls, trying desperately to find that book or at least narrow down that list of seven haystacks. And that's when the real frustration kicked in. A couple places didn't answer and never called back. A couple places were just *very* unhelpful.

Like, "What? No, I don't know if we have that book, and *no*, I ain't gonna go check! Come and look yourself if it's so important!"

That, but with a few other choice words thrown in.

So I did a little less crossing off than I'd hoped. But not zero.

A couple places checked their shelves and let me know that they didn't have my book; then I just had to hope that they'd *never* had it. One place was super nice, and they searched their computers and let me know that, nope, not only was *Red Bird* by Mary Oliver not in their current selection, they hadn't sold a copy of it in the last year. Gold. I gave 'em a big "thank you" and crossed them off my list.

I never got that great, "Yeah, we've got it right here, we'll send it to you!" conversation, but I also never had a "Shoot, we had your book, but we already sold it and it's gone forever" conversation, either. My long shot was still long, but it was still a shot.

In the end, I'd narrowed my list to four places. Four places that *might* maybe possibly have the book I needed. Four places that, at any moment, some rando stranger might wander into and buy my mom's book and, basically, ruin my life.

Now, to the peanut butter and jelly.

So, there I was—ashes found, book lost, clock ticking, list narrowed, pressure mounting. Dying to get on the road to get to those stores to get that book, but with no way to make it happen as fast as I desperately needed it to. I was actually literally considering buying a bus ticket and running away to find the book myself, which even *I* knew was a horrible idea. But that's how desperate I was.

But then something happened. Something terrible. But a terrible something that did change my frustrating timeline for the better.

It went like this:

Friday afternoon. The last ten minutes of the school week, which are by far my favorite ten minutes of the school week (not counting the Coffee Crew).

The little electronic chime went off, which meant that an announcement was coming over the PA system, which meant that Mr. Swenson told everyone to shut up. Literally. He probably needs to retire.

Anyway, the principal came on the intercom, and we could all tell right away from her voice that this was actually big news and not just like "the volleyball game got rescheduled" kind of news. So we all actually shut up.

And then she said it. Her third sentence started with her saying, "Due to the ongoing and escalating COVID-19 coronavirus situation," and ended with her saying, "school will be canceled until the end of spring break, beginning this afternoon."

She probably said more, but none of us heard it.

There were cheers in the room. And fireworks in my heart.

That long, long wait I'd been seething at had just evaporated. Spring break was two weeks away. And we were getting out *now*.

School was out for three weeks. *Three* weeks.

Amid an uproar of high fives and cheers, I sat at my desk and felt a smile stretch across my face.

Three weeks was enough time. Enough time to visit those four possibilities. And the three weeks started *now*.

Against all the odds, the boulder that had been in my way had just evaporated.

Don't get me wrong. I hadn't read all that much about the pandemic thing, but I knew it was no joke. I mean, folks were *dying*. So I wasn't cheering and pumping my fist like almost everyone else.

But, hey. I had a quest to go on. And now I could. That was a good thing, even if it came from a whole steaming pile of bad.

One more quick fast-forward. Just about a half an hour or so.

I walked in our front door. I was bouncing and crackling, inside and out.

I closed the door behind me and leaned back against it, eyes closed and grinning, just for a second.

When I opened my eyes, I saw Ivan ambling toward me, tail high in greeting.

"Pack your litter box, bud," I said.

"That you, darling?" Rodeo called from his closet.

"Get out of that closet and into the bus, Daddio!" I hollered. "It's time to fire up Yager and hit the road again!"

# CHAPTER

## EIGHT

When I told Dad about school being canceled, he surprised me by *not* shooting both fists up into the air and giving a big ol' "Yeehaw!"—which is kinda what I'd assumed he'd do. Instead, his eyebrows shot up and his shoulders sagged down.

"Seriously? Canceled?"

"Seriously!" I said, waiting for the high fives to start. They didn't.

"Geez," he said, rubbing his chin. "This is all getting pretty darn serious, ain't it?"

"Well, at least...," I started to say, hoping to get the conversation back into seeing-the-bright-side territory. But my dad wasn't ready for that quite yet.

"Huh. School canceled. Man. I mean, the news has been grim for a while now. Hospitals full and nursing homes closed and all that. But, heck. This is kinda scary, little bird."

"Uh, yeah," I said. I heard what he was saying, and he wasn't wrong. But I'd been stressing all week about losing that book forever, and now out of nowhere I had a chance to maybe get it back, and I knew that if I couldn't talk Rodeo into grabbing that chance, it might be gone for good. So I took a breath and got to work. "This is a crappy situation," I said. "No doubt. But ... like, even used toilet paper's got a bright side, right?" My dad frowned. I forged on. "If you . . . like, turn it over, I mean. So you can't see, you know . . ."

"What?" Rodeo asked, eyebrows crinkled. Fair.

"Okay, forget that," I said, shaking my head. "We're gonna leave that metaphor behind. So to speak." I blew out a breath. I wasn't really hitting it out of the park here. I reached up and grabbed both my dad's shoulders until he was looking right at me.

"Dad," I said, looking deep into those magic eyes of his and trying to put a bit of that magic in my own. "Sure, this whole world is pretty darn cloudy at the moment. But, listen. We've got a quest to go on. An epic one. An *important* one. And now we can do it. That's a heckuva silver lining, old man." I put a smile on my face. "Coyote and Rodeo. On the road again. Come on, Dad. It's time. Let's do it."

A matching smile slowly spread across Rodeo's face as I spoke. By the end of my little speech, he was even nodding along a little.

"Heck to the yeah," he said. "Coyote and Rodeo, on the road again."

I gave his shoulders a squeeze and stepped back, mission accomplished. "I bet we can get on the road by dinnertime," I said, rubbing my hands together.

"Easy, tiger!" My dad chuckled. "I gotta get some stuff together first. I'm like a real-life grown-up now. Make sure rent is paid ahead, mow the lawn, that kind of garbage."

I frowned. This whole my-dad-as-a-responsible-parent thing was definitely a new look for him. I didn't care for it.

"Fine. On the road by dark?"

He pursed his lips and shook his head.

"First thing tomorrow?" I tried.

He cocked an eyebrow.

"Ugh. Right after lunch tomorrow?"

He waggled his head, then nodded. "I could probably swing that. Twenty-four hours, and we're off."

"I don't eat lunch at 3:30," I said. "You got twenty-one hours, real-life grown-up. Get to work."

Then I went straight back to my room and grabbed my phone. One notification: a missed call from Salvador.

This time, he picked up on the first ring.

"Hey, Coyote, guess what?"

"Holy heck, is your schoo—"

"Our school is canceled!" he interrupted.

"Mine, too! For how long?"

"*Indefinitely!*" he shouted. I've never heard a more boring word said with more enthusiasm in my life.

"We're off for *three* weeks! Can you imagine?"

"I know. This is so wild."

"Me and Rodeo are hitting the road tomorrow. I've got it narrowed down to four places. I'm gonna find that book, Salvador."

"That's amazing! Where you going?"

"Uh, Pittsburgh, Maine, Wyoming, and, uh . . . Kansas. Yeah. Not in that order, though."

"Man. That's cool. I'm just gonna be sitting around."

I chewed a lip thoughtfully. No one was there to see it, but I did.

"Hey, Salvador."

"Yeah?"

"Do you think, if you asked real nice, that your mom would let—"

"Yeah! Heck, yeah! Well, I mean, I can ask! Do you think that Rodeo wou—"

"Of course he would!"

The cool thing about having a best friend is that a lot of times you're just on the same page without even really trying.

Best fast-forward ever: Five minutes later he was calling me back.

"She said yes! I can come, Coyote!"

"Are you serious?"

"Yeah! She still has to work, and she's still doing her nursing stuff. Apparently they're going to do the classes, like, virtually? On a laptop?"

"How could you possibly go to school on a laptop?"

"Who cares?" he asked. "So I'd really be on my own at home anyway. This way she figures that at least there will be an adult supervising me."

I blinked. "Who?"

"Your dad."

"Oh! Right. Well, if that's good enough for her . . ."

I hung up with Salvador just about more excited than I could stand. I walked out into the living room in time to see Rodeo walking over from across the street. Which was confusing. Because, as far as I knew, he didn't need any help from Candace to mow the lawn or pay the bills. He was smiling and doing the dorky little bouncy dance walk he does when he's excited. So at least our moods matched.

He swooped in the front door and I hit him with it.

"Guess what? Salvador is coming on the trip with us!"

Rodeo's eyes went wide. "Are you serious?" he asked, his voice going high. He high-fived me. "Right freaking on!"

One of the cool things that makes Rodeo different from most parents is that with a lot of stuff I don't have to *ask* his permission, I can just kind of *tell* him, and he's totally good with that.

"We'll have to go a little bit out of our way to pick him up," I said.

"Worth it!" Rodeo, who has pretty good taste in people, is a big Salvador fan.

"This is really coming together great," I said.

"Right?" Rodeo agreed. He rocked back and forth on his heels a bit. Smacked his lips. Itched his nose. He was acting suspiciously like someone who was getting his nerve up to say something.

"You know what'd be fun?" he finally said. "If Fig came along!"

I frowned. "Fig? Like, the little rat dog that lives across the street? That Fig?"

"Yeah!"

"Why in the world would we bring Fig along?"

Rodeo scratched at his beard, and his eyes darted off to the side. "Well. Fig can't really be left all alone. And if Candace comes along, then, you know, that'd be an issue, so . . ." His voice trailed off.

My jaw dropped open. "Wait. Is this your way of telling me

you want to bring your"—I almost said "girlfriend" and stopped myself just in time, since gagging would have really tripped up my momentum—"your friend along on our special trip? This is *actually* what you thought the best way to bring it up was?"

Rodeo shrugged hopelessly. "I mean. I guess? You're bringing your friend, right?"

I opened my mouth. Closed it again. Gave it another shot. "Are you seriously comparing Candace to Salvador?"

"She can do her job remotely, from her laptop," Rodeo said, actually braving eye contact to make his case. "And she said she can hook Yager up with a wireless hotspot."

"What makes you think Yager *wants* a wireless hotspot?"

Rodeo squinted. "Uh. Well. What?" Then he shook his head and charged on. "We'll be able to get farther, faster. Because she can split the driving with me. Like Lester!" His eyes were all shiny with hope, since he knew that I was a big fan of Lester, a top-notch fella who'd helped us out on our last long journey. I narrowed my own eyes against the hope in my dad's.

"She's nothing like Lester. I don't even think she plays an instrument."

"I . . . well . . . that's not what I meant, really."

I held my glare steady.

"Look," Rodeo said, calming down all his nervous tics and scooting in a little closer. "It really will be helpful to have another driver. Plus, this way Ivan will have a friend along!"

"Ivan will already have a friend along," I said. "Salvador." Salvador is Ivan's second-favorite person. He's a distant second, but still.

"It'll be fun. She's great. You'll see." I realized, to my horror, that he wasn't *asking*. He was *telling*. Which, I suppose, was fair, given I'd done the same thing with Salvador. But still.

But also still: I had a heckuva big secret to keep. I needed to weave across basically the whole country and search four random stores without my dad getting suspicious. Candace might actually be a good distraction.

"Fine," I said, in the way folks often say that word, which is almost exactly the opposite of how they say "Great!" I saw Rodeo's eyes and they looked all worried, and then I felt bad because I remembered how happy he'd looked before he walked in. And he wasn't wrong: *I* was getting to bring a friend. Fair's fair. I guess. I made myself smile. "Okay. Yeah. It'll be fun."

The worried look in his eyes gave way to relief. "Aw, you're the best, sugar beans," Rodeo said, and grabbed me in a hug.

I squeezed him back, but in my mind I was going through how in the world I was gonna pull this thing off.

But then something caught my attention. Or, rather, my nose's attention.

I sniffed. Put my head closer to Rodeo. Sniffed again.

"Did you . . . *wash your hair?*"

Rodeo's eyes got all shifty. "Maybe. So?"

I felt my lip curl. Rodeo never washed his hair. At least not with, like, *soap*.

"You smell like a goddamn popsicle."

"It's supposed to be . . . kiwi lime flavored. The shampoo, I mean."

"Flavored? You mean *scented?*"

"Oh. Sure, kiwi lime *scented*, I guess. It has . . . vitamin E? Do you like it?"

I shook my head at him. "I don't even know you anymore." I pursed my lips. "Wait. *Did* you taste it?"

Rodeo's eyes got twice as shifty.

"Good lord," I said.

Rodeo scowled. "Well, geez. I mean, you'd *have* to, wouldn't you, just to see? With that much food in it?"

"Aaaand . . . you're back," I said. "Thought I lost you for a second there." I squinted at him. "What did it taste like?"

He grimaced. "Not like kiwis, I'll tell you that. Or limes."

"Well, at least it wasn't watermelon flavored," I said. I *loathe* supposedly watermelon-flavored foods. And, I can only assume, watermelon-flavored toiletries.

I shook my head and clapped my hands. "Okay. You. Take care of . . . whatever it is you need to take care of. Pack your most delicious shampoo or whatever. I'm gonna get my room on Yager ready."

Rodeo nodded and bounced off, and I headed through the kitchen toward the back door. And that's when I saw the box. *The* box. I'd set it off to the side, on a little cabinet in the corner.

I took a breath and walked over to it. Traced my fingers along its edges. In all the excitement about the trip, I'd almost forgotten the real reason. It was a good reason. But it wasn't really, like, a grin-and-high-five sort of reason.

"Well, Mom," I whispered. "You ready?"

I looked up. Caught my own reflection in the kitchen window.

A better question came to mind, and I asked it.

"Well, Coyote?" I asked my reflection. "Are *you* ready?"

"I don't know," my reflection answered. It was an honest answer. But I had a couple thousand miles to get ready.

I set my jaw. And I smiled, an I-don't-know-about-this-but-it's-apparently-happening-so-I-better-put-on-a-brave-face kind of smile.

"Ready or not," I told myself. "Here I go."

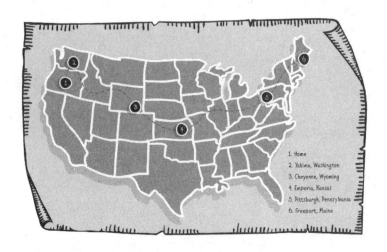

1. Home
2. Yakima, Washington
3. Cheyenne, Wyoming
4. Emporia, Kansas
5. Pittsburgh, Pennsylvania
6. Freeport, Maine

# CHAPTER

## NINE

*I* was the first one on the bus the next day. Perched on the first seat, right behind the captain's chair. My cat beside me. My mom on my lap. Most folks would have probably had the opposite arrangement, but there I was.

Ivan's litter box was in my room. Rodeo's mattress was on the floor, for Candace. He was gonna sleep in his usual blanket pile. Salvador could have the couch.

I heard Rodeo and Candace coming, chatting and laughing. I tried to recapture some of the charitable—some would say "saint-like"—attitude toward her I'd managed the day before.

"It'll be fun," I whispered to myself, forcing a little smile.

Rodeo bounded on first.

"Ready to hit the road, darling?!" he asked, eyes sparkling, body all twitching electric. My smile grew, both in size and sincerity. Rodeo, whatever else folks might say about him, is a great traveling buddy. He plopped into the driver's seat and drummed on the dashboard. "What about you, Yager?"

Candace climbed up the bus steps, Fig cradled in her arms. Her eyes were kind of sparkly, too. Candace's, I mean. Fig looked terrified.

She was sidling past Rodeo when I held up a hand. "Whoa!" I said, and she stopped, eyes wide.

"What?" she asked.

"Aren't you even going to ask her the questions?" I said, locking eyes with Rodeo in the rearview mirror. "Are we just rolling with no rules at all now?"

Rodeo turned in his seat. "Oh. Right. Okay." He leveled his eyes on Candace. "Everyone has to answer three questions to get on the bus. One: What is your favorite book?"

Candace bit her bottom lip. "Um . . . does a magazine count? I love *Popular Science*."

Rodeo looked to me.

I was speechless. Her favorite book was a *magazine*?

"Next question," Rodeo said quick. "What is your favorite place in the world?"

"Hmmm," Candace said, thinking. "There is this bar in Portland that has killer live music and, like, the most *amazing* Thai food. Best pad kee mao you've had in your life."

My jaw actually dropped open. A bar? Her favorite place was a *bar*?

"And, uh, lastly," Rodeo stammered, eyes darting anxiously between me and Candace, "what is your favorite sandwich?"

Candace laughed. Which I didn't appreciate. To be fair, *most* people laughed at the last question, but still.

"Oh, fun," she said. "Uh, I guess I'd have to say . . . sloppy joes. That's a sandwich, right?"

A sandwich? I wasn't even sure sloppy joes counted as a *food*, let alone a sandwich, let alone someone's *favorite* sandwich.

It's probably for the best that I was so stunned that I couldn't muster a response.

A magazine, a bar, and *sloppy joes?* They were, without a doubt, the worst three answers I'd ever heard to our questions. By a mile. Rodeo, though, didn't seem to notice.

"Welcome aboard!" he said, then murmured to Candace while looking nervously at me, *"Quick, get on."* So maybe he did notice.

"Can I join you here?" Candace asked, looking at the space beside me.

"Sorry," I said, offering a tight smile. "Three per seat is the limit." She looked at Ivan, then at the box on my lap.

"Okay," she said brightly after a moment, and slid into the seat across from me. "Gosh, this is fun. Thanks for letting me tag along." She smiled at me and cocked an eyebrow. "Me and Fig are super stoked."

Here's the deal. I wasn't wild about Candace coming along, for reasons I wasn't quite ready to deal with, on a personal level.

But, also, she really was—if I was forced to admit it, while hooked up to a lie detector, and with my life on the line—kinda cool. She was super smart and nice and generally pretty fun. And I'm a big-enough person to acknowledge that. And while saying Rodeo "raised me" is probably giving him an awful lot of credit, if he *did* raise me, he raised me to be kind. He was always saying stuff like *There's way too much meanness out there, Coyote; you gotta put as much kindness into the universe as you can* and that kind of garbage. Which, I'm also big enough to acknowledge, is not actually garbage.

It was possible that Candace didn't deserve a seat on our bus; given her answers to the questions, "probable" might be a better word. But it was also relatively certain that she didn't deserve a whole bunch of meanness from me that had basically nothing to do with her actual behavior or personality.

So I smiled at her, and I tried awful hard to make it look genuine.

"It'll be fun," I said, for the second time that day, and tried to ignore the fact that the more often someone repeats something like that, the less likely it's true.

Rodeo was fidgeting around in the driver's seat in front of me, putting his sunglasses on, adjusting the mirror, getting his bottle of Squirt in the cupholder just right.

Fig let out a whiny little whimper from Candace's lap. Beside me, Ivan went stiff. Slowly, he leaned out and cocked his head so he could look across me to see what other unwelcome trespasser had been invited into his home.

Fig's oversized ears perked up when she saw Ivan. They'd met once before, in a carefully chaperoned meet-and-greet in our living room. Fig had been very excited to meet Ivan. The feeling had not been mutual.

Now, on the bus, she yipped in recognition. It was, I think, a friendly hey-it's-you!-remember-me? kind of yip.

Ivan saw it for what it was: obnoxiously clueless and desperate.

Some cats puff up and get all dramatic when they see a dog, but Ivan has far more dignity than most cats, and Fig was *barely* a dog. So Ivan just glared.

His ears went back. He looked up at me.

*Her?* he said with his flat ears and his tail whipping. *Seriously?*

*Tell me about it,* I said with tightened lips and raised eyebrows.

Yager chugged loudly to life, and my heart skipped a little beat. The deep rumble of that engine—a rumble you could feel through your feet, and into your heart—sounded like adventure, like journeys, like horizons coming closer. And, to me, it felt like home.

"Pick some music to start off this here adventure, little bird!" Rodeo crowed.

Rodeo was holding his phone in his hand, and a cord snaked from it into the dashboard. I had dragged him kicking and screaming into modern life—it had taken me an incredible amount of arguing to get him to get his own phone—but one thing he head-over-heels loved about it was having, like, a *billion* songs at his fingertips. I'm pretty sure it's the only thing he ever actually uses his phone for.

But mine is basically just the world's most expensive alarm clock, so who am I to judge?

I decided to throw another olive branch Candace's way.

"What are you in the mood for?" I asked. "Rock, country, blues?"

"Rock," she said without hesitation.

I thought for a second. "Black Keys," I said to Rodeo.

"Heck freaking yeah," he said with an appreciative nod. A little thumb work later, and a wailing guitar and shuffling drumbeat were pouring out the speakers.

He dropped Yager into gear. "Give me a hitting-the-road howl!" he cried.

I threw my head back and howled. I looked over to Candace, who was staring at me and Rodeo, eyebrows high, but a down-for-anything smile on her face. I gave her an all-the-way genuine smile back.

"Go on," I said. "You heard the man."

She laughed. And then she opened wide and let it out.

It wasn't the best howl I'd ever heard. But it wasn't bad for a first try. And lord knows it was better than her answers to the questions.

Yager lurched into motion.

I leaned my head back and closed my eyes, still smiling, fingers holding tight to my mom.

We were off.

A few hours later Rodeo pulled Yager up to Salvador's house, honking the horn, music blaring and me leaning most of the way out of one of the windows. It wasn't a super low-key arrival.

My heart did a happy skip when Salvador came squinting out onto his porch, hands stuck in his jean pockets, a possibly-slightly-but-understandably-embarrassed smile on his face. He was taller than the last time I'd seen him, but he was still the skinny-necked, sweet-faced, quiet-smiled boy who'd been (and still was!) the best possible friend I could have had, just when I'd needed one the most.

"Salvador!" I hollered, and all the embarrassment stretched out of his smile, and I hopped down off the bus and ran up the little sidewalk and just grabbed that boy in a hug. It could be he was expecting more of a handshake or even one of those chin-lifting "what's up" things, but I didn't care. There's nothing like having no friends to make you appreciate how awesome having a friend is.

"Hey there, Coyote." He laughed into my shoulder.

"You grew out your hair!" I said, stepping back. "And got muscles, kind of!"

He blushed and looked down. "Yeah!" he said, then shook his head. "I mean to the hair part. Not the muscles."

"No, definitely the muscles! Your arms were spaghetti noodles before and now they're like, I don't know, ziti?"

"Okay?" he said, laughing.

We hadn't seen each other in person since Thanksgiving, and I guess a lot can change in four months. There was even the hint of a little shadow on his upper lip. Which was too surprising and awkward for me to bring up.

Growing up is funny because you're just going along, being a kid and feeling like a kid and acting like a kid and then one day you've got a friend with a mustache.

"Coyote!" Salvador's mom said, coming out the door behind him.

And then there was this whole big reunion thing with me and Salvador and Ms. Vega and Rodeo, with lots of hugging and smiles. Everyone in that group is a pretty big fan of everyone else. Since we'd all settled down in our current, stuck-to-the-ground homes, we'd visited a couple times in both directions and we were always pretty darn happy to see each other.

At some point I realized that Candace had come out, too, and was standing a few feet back up the front walk kind of awkwardly, with Fig on a leash.

"Oh!" Ms. Vega said. "And who is this?" Her English was really coming along.

"Uh. That's Candace," I said. "She's . . . our other driver."

"And our neighbor!" Rodeo said, laughing, beckoning Candace closer. "And friend!"

"Yeah," I said, and then there was this whole thing where everyone made a big deal about how precious Fig allegedly is and then it turned out that Candace speaks, like, fluent Spanish, and I guess technically that's cool but also kind of annoying because does everything have to be about her *all* the time?

And, of course, once we wrapped up the "hellos" it was pretty much time to slide right into the "goodbyes," so then all that happened. Salvador got lots of hugs and kisses from his mom, which seemed to mortify him but which I thought was pretty adorable. And he was given lots of warnings about eating right and sleeping and several firmly delivered rules, which I'm pretty sure were mostly about not being on his phone too much because I heard *telefono* in there like twelve times.

"Don't worry, Ms. Vega," I assured her. "I definitely will *not* let him stare at his phone all day. Plus, I brought, like, thirty books, so we're good."

Ms. Vega grabbed both my shoulders with her hands and she looked right into my eyes. "Good luck," she said, very seriously. "With your mama."

I breathed deep. "Gracias," I said. "Good luck with your laptop."

And then she gave us a whole bag full of warm tamales, which completely made Rodeo's day.

And then, once again, we were on board the bus.

But this time, I had Salvador with me. Which is one heck of an upgrade.

As soon as the bus door closed, though, Candace tried to ruin everything.

"So," she said brightly, kneeling on her bus seat to look back at where Salvador and I were sitting on ours. "Where we headed, Coyote?"

"Um," I said, kicking myself for not having quick answers to annoying questions ready. "East."

Candace arched an eyebrow. "East? That's a little"—she waggled her head—"vague."

Which was, of course, a little . . . annoying.

I propped a not terribly sincere smile onto my face. "Oh. Rodeo didn't"—I waggled my head—"tell you?"

Candace blinked and her own smile faded a bit. It's possible my hostility was coming on a little strong.

I did a five-second through-the-nostrils calming inhale and tried again. "This trip," I said, forcing cheerfulness into my voice, "is not really about a destination. It's about the *journey*. My mom didn't want us to just have a finish line. She wanted us to have an adventure along the way."

I was veering dangerously close to lying there, which I'd been trying to avoid. Since I'd lost the book, I had no idea what my mom actually wanted. For all I knew, she'd written *whatever you do, don't have an adventure along the way* in that book. But the chances of that were pretty slim. And in the meantime, if I had to maybe sorta possibly lie to keep my secret, then so be it. Especially if the lie was just to Candace.

"Oh!" Candace said, brightening. "Like a scavenger hunt?"

Boy. She was really putting my patience to the test. A scavenger hunt? Did she think my mom was a ten-year-old at summer camp?

"No. Not like a scavenger hunt. More like . . . one of those old-time spiritual journey walk things they do? A pilgriming."

"*Pilgrimage*," Salvador whispered in my ear.

"A pilgrimage," I said. "So we're gonna do it right. I don't want y'all to think about the destination. I'll take care of the navigating. I want you to embrace the *journey*. Look out the window. Listen to the road. Forget about the maps. *Go with the flow.* And when we get there, you'll know."

That flimsy, paper-thin eyeroll of a sales pitch would probably only work on, like, two people in the whole world.

Candace, apparently, was not one of those two people. It was pretty obvious. Her lips kinda tightened and her brow furrowed. She wasn't buying it.

But, luckily, my dad definitely *was* one of them. Which wasn't, of course, actually *lucky*, because I knew that weirdo inside and out, and I'd tailor-made that sales pitch specifically for him.

His eyes got all misty. And when he talked, his voice was all scratchy.

"*Heck yeah, huckleberry*," he said. "*Heck freaking yeah.*"

"In the meantime," I said. "Head southeast. Tonight we crash in Twin Falls, Idaho!"

"Yeehaw!" Rodeo cheered. He fired up the bus. "And what, pray tell, is our kickoff song?" he asked at a full holler.

Candace kind of snort-chuckled.

"What?" I asked. Possibly rudely.

"Do you guys do the whole 'starting song' thing every time?" she asked.

I looked at her. "No, we're just gonna start a road trip in utter silence like a bunch of sociopaths," I said, then felt immediately bad about my arguably toxic tone, and so I added, "You choose this time."

Candace considered and then called out a band I'd never heard of which turned out to be some kind of punk group which, frankly, wasn't really to my liking. If I wanna sit around and listen to someone shouting I can just flush the toilet while Rodeo's in the shower.

"Couch time," I said to Salvador, and we headed on back. I needed a little space from at least one of the people at the front of the bus. And their rodent-on-a-leash.

"It's cool to be on the road again," Salvador said, leaning back and clasping his hands behind his head. "Like old times!"

"Totally," I said. "This is going to be epic."

"Candace seems cool."

I chewed on my tongue. I was finally getting a face-to-face convo with my bestie and I didn't feel like ruining it by talking about Candace. "How's school going?" I asked.

"Great!" he said with a grin.

"I mean before it got canceled."

"Oh. Still pretty good, actually." And then he told me a bunch about his classes and playing basketball and lots of stuff about his friends. His friends and him did *this* and his friends and him did *that* and honestly it was starting to make me feel kinda weird and jealous and finally when there was a break I just blurted out, "Are you popular, Salvador?"

"What?"

"Are you popular?"

"Uh. I don't know. I guess, maybe?"

"Do you have a lot of friends?"

"I guess. Enough."

"Who do you sit with at lunch?"

"Friends, I guess?"

"Do you ever eat alone in the library?"

"No."

"Huh."

Salvador got a little wrinkle between his eyebrows. And his voice got all gentle and careful, which I thought was unnecessary. "Are *you* popular, Coyote?"

"Not remotely."

"Oh."

"There's more important things than being popular," I said.

"Yeah. Definitely."

I looked away and cleared my throat. I was realizing that I may have steered this conversation down a road I wasn't all that thrilled about. It was better than talking about Candace, but just barely.

"Is everything . . . cool?" Salvador asked.

"Peachy," I said, but I didn't really sell it.

Salvador got a troubled look on his face and leaned in. "Is anyone, like . . . *mean* to you?"

In my head I heard coyote howls, and snickers, and taunts, and hallway comments. Some secret bathroom tears.

I half laughed and rolled my eyes and said, "Pfft, *no,*" but I couldn't look him in the eye and I have always been a fairly terrible liar.

And then something kind of hilarious happened. I saw it.

Salvador's body tensed up. His eyes narrowed and his nostrils widened. And his hands balled into fists. "Who?" he said. "Who's being mean to you?"

Salvador got *mad.* Which was pretty silly. But also pretty, like, *sweet.*

That noodle-armed boy's anger made me feel like a million bucks. Which, I know, is weird. It wasn't some stupid boy-girl damsel-in-distress thing. There's no *girl* that needs to be *saved* by any *boy.* But friends—any kind of friends—do need to look out for each other. If you've been feeling all alone, knowing that someone's got your back is a great feeling. I may even have teared up a little.

"Oh, just a few crabs," I said, waving my hand.

"What?"

I blew out a breath and looked him in the eye. "It's no biggie. I'm a weirdo. And not everyone knows that's a good thing, yet, is all."

"You're not a weirdo, Coyote."

"I am definitely a weirdo," I said. "And I'm good with that. Weirdos are the bestos."

"Bestos?"

"See?" I said, holding up my hands. "Weirdo."

"Listen, Coyote—" Salvador started to say, all serious and heartfelt, which was super nice, but I honestly was just kind of done with that portion of the conversation.

"It's fine, Salvador," I cut in. "Really. It's fine, I'm fine, you're fine, it's all fine. Moving on."

"Okay," Salvador said, but he was still frowning and looking at me kind of intensely. Another good thing friends do is give each other space when they need it, though, and Salvador was a good friend.

"What's this?" he asked, picking up the box with my mom's ashes in it. He shook it by his ear and arched a playful eyebrow. "Candy stash?"

"That's my mom."

Salvador's eyes went wide. "Gah!" He tossed the box like it was a live rattlesnake and jerked his hands back, and it landed with a thudding scrape on the bus floor. "Crap! Sorry! I didn't mean to throw . . . her? It? I didn't mean to . . ."

"It's okay," I said. "I probably shouldn't just leave her lying around like that."

I looked at Salvador. His eyes were still wide. His face was kinda pale, and I swear he was actually *panting* a little.

I couldn't help it. I laughed. A little at first, then a lot.

He scowled. "It's not that funny," he said, but he was trying not to smile. He failed. And pretty soon we were both laughing, heads back on the couch.

"Okay," he said between laughs. "You're right. You're a weirdo."

"Oh, abso*lute*ly," I said. "But you're the one throwing moms around."

I reached down and picked up the box and held it on my lap and our snickering settled down.

Ivan, drawn by the ruckus, wandered over and hopped up on the couch and walked right across me and into Salvador's lap.

"Do you . . . wanna see?" I asked, looking down at the box.

And then Salvador did something that was super cool. He didn't just shrug and say "sure, why not?" and he didn't shudder and say, "ugh, no thanks." Like, maybe, most folks would've done.

He thought for a second. And then he looked to me. Into my eyes. "Do you want me to?" he asked.

It was my turn to think for a second. I'd found those ashes, and it had changed everything, and I hadn't shared them with anyone yet. Rodeo hadn't wanted to look at them. Candace was, well, not really a prime candidate. And I didn't have any other friends. But, I realized, I *did* want to share them. And who better with than Salvador?

"Yeah," I said. "I do."

"Okay."

So I unclicked the latches. And I swallowed. And I lifted the lid. And there she was. My mom.

"Oh," Salvador said, soft.

"Yeah," I said.

And then, to my surprise, I got sad.

I got really, really sad. I don't know why. My mom had been dead for years, and I'd looked at those ashes all week. But, sitting there on that bus, next to my best friend who always had my back, I got really sad, looking at those ashes. Really, really sad.

And my breath got all shaky. And I sniffled, then again, then again.

Salvador didn't say anything.

But he put a hand on my arm. And he held it there.

And I rested my head on his shoulder.

And we sat like that, for a long time, me and my friend and my cat and my mom, as the sun set outside the bus windows.

# CHAPTER

## TEN

The first two days of the trip were pretty uneventful, other than me routinely kicking Salvador's butt in cards. He may remember it differently, but whatever. We listened to some music. Had some convos. Ate a surprising amount of to-go meals, because a lot of restaurants were starting to go takeout only because of the whole pandemic thing, which felt super weird. Fig made a million pathetic attempts to befriend Ivan, but Ivan had too much taste and dignity to go there.

And then, we were there. The first stop on my secret treasure hunt. A secondhand store in Cheyenne, Wyoming. I started to get all nervous and fidgety and excited as we pulled into town. Cheyenne, Wyoming, is a great place if you're the kind of person that likes a place like Cheyenne, Wyoming. And I was. But the task at hand was a little too emotionally high stakes for me to just kick back and enjoy that Cheyenne vibe.

Working out how to get us to the store was pretty easy: I'd already managed to guide us to within driving distance of the joint, then I had Salvador mention that he needed another book to read, and then I just happened to remember a store that we'd stopped at the summer before. A few songs later, we were pulling into the parking lot.

My heart jumped into third gear.

"*Yep,*" I whispered to myself, looking at the building. "*This is the place.*"

I remembered, dimly, walking through those doors. Remembered, maybe, having a stack of books in my hands.

It had been less than a year since I'd been there, but man, I'd been through a lot since then. I was an entirely different person, almost. Rodeo definitely was.

"Man," he said, one hand on his stomach. "I hope they got a bathroom that locks." Okay. Not *entirely* different.

"Masks!" Candace reminded us, and we all took one from the stack in her hand and hooked 'em over our ears to cover our mouths and nose. It was, apparently, what everyone was doing now to hopefully help stop the spread of the virus. Candace had brought a whole box and we'd been putting 'em on anytime we went inside anywhere.

Together, our whole crew minus Ivan and Fig walked in through the double doors of the Second Chances Secondhand Store. The little bell above the door jingled as we entered.

"Howdy," said the woman slouched behind the counter, and I said "Howdy!" right back and then asked, "Books?" and the lady pointed with a thumb over her shoulder and around a corner.

Rodeo headed toward the bathroom in the back and Candace started browsing through the clothes and Salvador and me walked toward where the front desk lady had pointed.

This had been one of those places that had answered my phone call, but said they couldn't look for the book for me. At the time I'd thought they were just being unhelpful, but when I walked around the shelf full of old VHS tapes and vinyl records and saw the book section, I totally got it.

"Oh," I said, and Salvador said, "Uh," and then I said a word I won't repeat.

It was a *wall* of books. Wall to wall. Floor to ceiling, almost. Plus some books piled on top of the books on the shelves. Plus a bunch of piles on the ground. *Thousands* of books. No sections. No visible organization of any kind.

My jaw dropped. My heart dropped.

For a moment, we both just stood there, looking.

"How are we ever gonna find it?" I whispered.

"Not by standing here," Salvador said. "Let's start looking." Good partner, that guy.

"Whatcha looking for?" a voice asked. Me and Salvador both jumped. We turned to see a kid standing there, staring up at us, chewing gum like a llama. He was maybe eight years old, with brown hair sticking up in all directions, a shotgun blast of freckles across his face, and a pair of buck teeth like I'd never seen before. He was wearing blue jeans and no shirt whatsoever and he was skinny as heck so I got an eyeful of ribs and elbows and collarbones.

Me and Salvador exchanged a glance. The kid had truly come out of nowhere.

"Who are you?" I asked.

"Rawley," he said. He pointed a thumb over his bony shoulder. "My mama works here. I ain't got no school 'cause of the Covid. So here I am."

Then he sniffed and spit. Right there on the floor.

He was the most Cheyenne, Wyoming, kid I'd ever met.

"Whatcha looking for?" he asked again.

"Who said we're looking for anything?" I asked, peeking around to make sure Candace or Rodeo wasn't within earshot.

"You did," he said. He pointed at me with his chin. "*You* said, 'How are we ever gonna find it,' and then *you*"—he chin-pointed at Salvador—"said, 'Let's start looking.' 'Member?"

"Okay, okay, *sshhh*," I said. I could tell this was the kind of kid who could accidentally blow a secret in no time flat, so I knew I needed to get him on our side quick. "Yeah. We're looking for something. A book. But it's a secret. You can't tell my dad or Candace."

The kid frowned. "Is your dad the weirdo that went into the bathroom?"

"Yes."

"And is Candace that punk-rock lady over there?" he asked, pointing.

"Yes."

He shrugged. "Okay. Why is it a secret?"

I licked my lips. "Because it's a surprise. A surprise *present*. For Candace. It's her birthday."

Rawley crinkled his eyebrows. "You're getting her a used book for her birthday?"

"Yes."

"Some present."

"Hey," I hissed. "It happens to be a very *special* book that means a lot to me. I mean, to *her*."

He shrugged again. "All right. I'll help. What book is it?"

I hesitated, but just for a second. I kinda wanted to tell him to buzz off, but I also knew that an extra pair of eyes could be helpful for that wall chock-full of books staring us down.

"It's called *Red Bird*. By Mary Oliver."

"What's it look like?"

"Oh. Uh. I don't know?" I snapped my fingers. "My dad said it was black! With red letters, maybe?"

Rawley held out his hand. "Phone," he said.

Me and Salvador just looked at him. "C'mon, phone!" he said, shaking his hand at us.

I pulled out my phone and unlocked it and handed it over. Rawley did some rapid thumb typing and in seconds had a picture of the book on the screen.

"Here it is," he said.

That internet thing, man. When it's handy, it's handy.

The book was indeed black, with the title and Mary Oliver's name in red letters, and a black-and-white picture of a leaf in the center. It was kind of plain. Kind of simple. Kind of perfect. It looked, honestly, exactly like the kind of book you'd find the secret to your mom's final resting place in. Or, at least that *I* would.

I got goose bumps. And the whole crazy quest got a lot more real, and felt a lot more important.

We weren't just looking for a book. We were looking for *that* book. That simple, perfect book that once upon a time my mom had held in her hands.

I looked up at the wall of books. None of which were facing us.

"What about the spine, though?" I asked.

Rawley did some more fast typing. "Got it," he said. "Some used bookstore's got a bunch of pics of their copy."

In the picture a wrinkly hand was holding the book so the spine faced the camera. No surprise: simple. Black. Red and white letters.

I blew out a breath. "All right. Let's go."

We split up, with Salvador starting on one end and me on the other and Rawley checking all the random stacks on the floor.

The hunt was exciting at first, when each and every book you looked at *could* be the one. But it was less so every second. And, eventually, just kind of exhausting and frustrating.

Shelf by shelf, book by book, spine by spine, we scanned and squinted and searched. Stooping and stretching and squatting. Rawley chomping his gum the whole time.

And then me and Salvador and Rawley met in the middle. I had a book in my hands, sure, how could you *not*, but it wasn't *Red Bird* by Mary Oliver. We stood there, shoulder-to-shoulder, looking at the wall of books that had defeated us.

"Sorry, Coyote," Salvador said.

I shook my head. "Man. I really had a feeling I was gonna find it."

"I didn't," Rawley said honestly, his fingers hooked through his blue jean belt loops.

"What were you looking for?" a different voice asked, and for the second time since we'd walked in, Salvador and I jumped and turned to see who was talking.

And it was, unfortunately, Candace.

"Hey, Candace," Rawley said between gum smacks.

"Uh. Hey," she answered, probably trying to figure out how the topless gum-chewer knew her name. Then she just kinda stared at me and I realized I hadn't answered her question.

My mouth went dry. "Um," I said.

"They were helping me," Rawley said, fairly heroically bailing me out. "I was looking for a book."

"Oh yeah?" Candace asked. "Which one?"

Rawley chawed his gum a couple times. I realized he was thinking, and I also realized that it was highly possible that Rawley wouldn't be able to come up with the title of a single book to pretend to be looking for.

"The Bible," he said at last.

So I was wrong. I guess.

"The Bible?" Candace said doubtfully.

"Yes, ma'am," Rawley answered, then shrugged. "I've heard good things."

Candace's eyes narrowed. She looked back and forth between me and Salvador. It was dawning on me that Candace might be too smart for my own good. Fooling Rodeo was not a huge challenge. It was like pretending to throw a ball for a dog but then hiding it behind your back. Done.

Candace, though, was proving to be a tougher nut. Which sucked. Because if I wasn't careful, she could derail my probably-doomed-but-not-yet-entirely-hopeless plan. I felt my jaw clench. And my own eyes narrowed, to match hers.

"Whatcha got there?" Rawley asked, pointing at what Candace was holding.

"Oh," Candace said, looking down. She held up a black

leather jacket covered in straps and buckles. "Check this out. Pretty killer, right?"

"Yeah," I said, eyes still narrowed. "If you're going to a costume party."

"Ouch," Candace said, shooting me a little wounded look that was probably supposed to make me feel bad but which really just made me feel triumphant.

Okay, and a little bad, maybe, but just a tad.

I stuck my tongue out at her. Which, of course, she couldn't see, because I was wearing a mask. But still.

"Heck, if you're going to a costume party, I got just the thing for ya," Rawley said, grabbing Candace by the elbow. "How do you feel about furry vests?"

"Um, pretty positive, actually," Candace answered as Rawley started to lead her away. He shot us a quick look back over his shoulder and winked.

"I betcha you're a medium, right?" I heard him ask, and then they were gone.

"That kid's solid," Salvador said.

"Heck yeah, he is."

I heaved a sigh and pushed the book I was holding into Salvador's hands. *The Mad Wolf's Daughter.*

"What's this for?"

"We said you needed a book, right? You're not gonna do much better than this one. Come on."

So me and Salvador walked out of that Cheyenne secondhand store with a great book in our hands, but the wrong book.

But, the funny thing is, it wasn't a total loss. It felt like it at the time. A whole lot of looking and absolutely zero finding. But, even though I didn't realize it in that moment, something monumentally important actually happened, right there in that secondhand store in Cheyenne, Wyoming. Later, I'd realize how close we'd come. The little clue that we'd missed.

That was later, though.

In the moment, it was mostly just dejection and disappointment and trying to put on a brave face.

Me and Salvador and Ivan and Fig sat there in silence on Yager in the parking lot, waiting for Candace and Rodeo.

"Hey," Salvador said after a minute. "One down. Plenty to go. We just crossed off one whole entire place where we know for sure that book *isn't*. That's, like, *progress*, right?"

It was, to be fair, actually a pretty good point. Or, at least, not a terrible one.

I blew out a heavy sigh.

"Thanks," I said. "You're right. We had four places to look. Now we only have three. Yee-fricking-haw." It sounds more bitter than it was. I smiled when I said it. At least the last part.

"Yee-fricking-haw," Salvador said with a little smile.

Rawley's shirtless self appeared in the secondhand store door and he pushed it open and stood in the sunlight, holding the door for Candace and Rodeo. He saw us in the bus and gave us a funny little salute from his forehead. Me and Salvador waved back. Good kid, that Rawley.

"Oh, hey, Candace!" I heard him holler just before she got on the bus. "Happy birthday!"

"What?" Candace started to say, but luckily Rawley had already stepped back inside and let the door close behind him.

"Weird kid," I heard Candace say to Rodeo as they climbed aboard Yager. But I noticed that besides the black leather jacket, she was also holding a leopard-spotted furry vest. So.

"Where to next?" Rodeo asked.

I shook the disappointment out of my head. I still had a show to put on. "Head to Kansas City," I said, which was *not* where we were going, but would take us in the right direction.

"Oooh," Candace said, "barbecue!"

"That's what I was thinking!" Rodeo said. "Starting song?"

I needed to turn my vibe around. And nothing can do that better than the right song.

"'I Will Survive'!" I shouted. "The original!"

Candace laughed. "Do you even have that one?" she asked Rodeo.

Rodeo went stiff. He looked over his shoulder at her. "That," he said, "is a disco *anthem*." He shook his head at her. "Of *course* I have it."

In seconds, an opening piano riff rippled out of the speakers.

Then a voice. Singing words that I knew by heart. It was my *getting-ready-to-go-to-freaking-school-in-the-morning-when-I'd-rather-go-almost-anywhere-else-in-the-world* song.

I saw Salvador mouthing along, too. Apparently it's just one of those songs that everyone somehow kind of knows.

Even Candace started nodding to the beat, lips moving, and then she closed her eyes and started *singing* along. Technically. Really belting it out, but . . . Candace was not a great singer. Or even a minimally decent one. She was terrible. And that's not me being mean. That's objective fact. Even Salvador was curling a lip.

But, whatever. It kinda worked. And then we were all singing along. Mumbling the words we didn't know, but really putting feeling into the ones we did.

Beat by beat, head bob by head bob, my vibe did indeed turn around.

One haystack down. Three to go.

My needle was still out there.

And I was gonna find it.

# CHAPTER
## ELEVEN

We stopped for dinner in a little place in Denver that Candace found on some app.

"Usually we just kind of stop at wherever looks good when we're hungry," I said when she suggested it to the group. "We don't need, like, a whole plan."

"Okay," Candace said with a shrug. "But this place supposedly has the best tater tots in Colorado. Who doesn't like tater tots?"

"I like tater tots," Salvador said unnecessarily.

"I *love* tater tots," Rodeo added.

"Fine," I said. "Tater tots it is." I tried to look all casual and *over it*, but it was tough because my mouth was literally watering. I freaking love tater tots.

While we waited in the parking lot for our order to get done—the tot restaurant was takeout only, too—it started to rain. Like, kind of a downpour. Which I actually love, because it sounds super cool on Yager's roof.

Finally, Candace's phone *dinged* to let us know our order was ready, and Rodeo headed out and came back dripping with rain and bearing a few bulging plastic bags that instantly made the whole bus smell like absolute freaking heaven.

Besides each of us ordering our own dinner, we'd gotten three orders of tater tots to share. We all gathered around the couch, and Rodeo popped open the to-go containers of tots, and then we all sat there for a second, just looking and sniffing. They were golden brown. And steamy. And shiny. They looked *perfect*.

I was suddenly secretly grateful for Candace and her dumb app.

Our moment of respect observed, we dug in. Big time.

A perfect tater tot should be crisp, but not so crisp that it, like, cuts the roof of your mouth (which I've had happen). And it should be good and salty, but not so salty that it makes you pucker. And it should be almost *too* hot, so that you have to kind of blow and puff while you chew.

It's a real high-wire act, making a perfect tot.

This place did it. They really did.

"Well, Coyote," Candace asked between chews. "Verdict on the tots?"

I finished a wet chew and poked with my tongue at some tot chunks stuck to my front teeth. "Phenomenal," I admitted. I wasn't gonna slander perfect tots just to make a point.

As I slurped down the tots, I noticed Rodeo kept looking out the window and frowning. I followed his eyes and saw a guy sitting on a suitcase against the restaurant, huddled out of the rain, eating out of a to-go container like we were.

Finally, Rodeo stood up. "I'm gonna go invite that guy in out of the rain," he said.

Candace looked where he was looking and then gave Rodeo kind of a funny look. "You . . . don't even know him," she said.

Rodeo gave her a little smile. "I know he's sitting in the rain," he said, and then headed out.

I love my dad.

I watched the conversation through the rain-speckled bus window. Rodeo walked up to him and put on a mask and then started talking and laughing and pointing at the bus. It seemed to take a little convincing, which is fair, but after a bit the guy stood up and grabbed his suitcase and followed Rodeo our way, and then they were both climbing up the stairs onto Yager.

He was a skinny little old guy, Asian American, wearing a suit and tie almost as wrinkly as his face. He put on a mask as he climbed Yager's stairs.

"Welcome aboard," I said, then pointed at the Throne, which seemed like it was a good socially distanced space away from us. "Grab a seat."

"Thank you," he said, and his eyes smiled above his mask.

"Would you like us to mask up?" Candace asked, which was technically kind and thoughtful.

The man thought for a moment, then shook his head. "It's okay," he said. "But thanks for asking."

He saw us scarfing down the tots and then rummaged around in his own food bag and pulled out some little plastic things of sauce. He pulled off the lids and jumped up to set them next to our tots on the table.

"Their special lemon-pepper sauce," he said. He had a very clear, precise, kinda slow way of talking that I dug. "Trust me."

"Yeah?" Rodeo asked. He dipped a tot into the sauce and then popped it into his mouth. Did a couple of chews. His eyes went wide. "Oh mah gah," he said around the hot tot. "Eh oh ukkin ood!"

I turned to the old man. "He says it's really good," I said, with a little sideways glare at Rodeo. I don't mind his filthy mouth, but I don't like it when he swears in public.

He looked away guiltily, 'cause he knows it.

Rodeo washed the tot down with a swig of Squirt.

"Nice tip!" he said to the guy. "Local secret?"

"Oh, I'm not local. Just passing through."

"Us, too!" Rodeo beamed. He's always excited to meet a fellow traveler. "What brings you to Denver?"

The man waved a hand at the empty baskets on the table.

"The tater tots," he said, like it was obvious. "I read they were the best in Colorado."

Out of the corner of my eye I could see Candace trying to make some sort of grinning eye contact with me, but I wasn't in the mood for her gloating.

"Well, heck, where'd you come from?" Rodeo asked.

"Most recently? Reno, I guess."

"You came all the way from Nevada to Denver for tater tots?" Rodeo asked, his voice the kind of amazed whisper a person uses when they finally meet their soulmate. His eyes slid to me. "A D.E.A.D. Dream, darling!"

"D.E.A.D. Dream?" the man asked.

"Drop Everything and Drive," I explained. "It's a thing we do. If one of us gets a real hankering for something, no matter how far, we hit the road and go and get it."

The man threw his head back and laughed. "D.E.A.D.

Dream! Delightful!" He shook his head. "But I guess mine was more of a D.E.A.R. Dream . . . drop everything and ride. I took the train."

"Fan-freaking-tastic," my dad said. "My name's Rodeo. Pleased to meetcha."

"Rodeo like with the bull riding?"

"Eh, more like Rodeo with the barrel racing. Less cruel."

"Ha ha! My name's Wally. A pleasure."

Rodeo and Wally nodded at each other, both with smile wrinkles around their eyes. Kindred spirits from the get-go, those two.

I saw Candace start to frown a little bit.

I gave Wally a little wave. "I'm Coyote Sunrise," I said.

"Rodeo and Coyote?" Wally said, eyebrows high. "I'd be surprised if there wasn't a fun story behind those names!"

"Well, then I hope you like surprises," I said, thinking of Mom's box of ashes. But then I shook my head and put the sunshine back into my voice. "But we're having fun now."

Wally looked me in the eye for just a second. "Well, I'm glad you're having fun now," he said with a little nod.

I liked Wally. I liked Wally a lot.

"This is Salvador," I said. "He's my best friend and a violin virtuoso." Salvador and Wally exchanged nods. "And that's Candace." Candace started to smile and open her mouth but I was already moving on. "So where you headed next, Wally?"

"No idea. I took the train here. Got my tater tots. Gonna head to the station tomorrow morning and buy a ticket to somewhere else."

I looked at Rodeo. Pursed my lips questioningly. He shrug-nodded. Candace was looking back and forth between us.

"You don't have *any* idea where you're going next?" I asked.

He shrugged. "Chicago? Miami? Or Maine, maybe? I've always wanted to go to Maine. Never really seen a lighthouse before."

"Maine?" I said. "Seriously?"

I looked to Rodeo's sparkling eyes. Candace was *definitely* frowning now. She leaned over and whispered something in Rodeo's ear. His brow furrowed. He mumbled something back.

"*We're* going to Maine!" I said.

"You are?" Wally said.

"We are?" Rodeo asked.

"We are," I said with a nod. "Well, kind of."

"Huh," Rodeo said.

I tilted my head toward Wally and shot Rodeo questioning eyes. "What do you think?" I mouthed.

He started to half smile and nod, but then Candace tugged on his sleeve and they did a little more sour-faced whispering.

"*But we don't even know him!*" I was pretty sure I just barely heard Candace hiss into Rodeo's ear. "*What if he's, like, unstable?*"

If Candace doesn't like unstable people, I have no idea what she's doing hanging around with Rodeo.

And I didn't plan to just sit there and let Candace boss Rodeo around and ruin our trip.

"Hey, Wally," I said, quick. "Wanna ride along with us?"

"Ride along?" he asked, looking around the bus. I suddenly wished I was better about tidying up. I saw his gaze distinctly linger on Rodeo's blanket nest. Out of the corner of my eye, I could see Candace poking Rodeo in the ribs.

"Yeah! It'll save you a train ticket!" I said.

I could see him considering doubtfully. Honestly, I'd be suspicious of anyone who *didn't* have doubts before hopping aboard Yager.

"We're not creepy," I added. "We're actually pretty great company. For the most part." I felt like I deserved immense credit for not looking at Candace when I said that last part. "None of us are sick, as far as we know. And we can mask up the whole time if you want. Come on. It'll be fun!"

"It's okay with you?" Wally asked Rodeo.

Rodeo hesitated for only half a second. "'Course it is, brother." Rodeo *definitely* deserved immense credit for being his usual hospitable human self despite the rather intense negative vibes emanating off Candace right next to him.

"We . . . don't really have enough beds," Candace said, trying to make her voice apologetic.

"I could just throw my sleeping bag on the floor and he can have the couch," Salvador offered. "If you don't mind couches, sir."

My heart sang. The next time I have to do one of those things in school where you list your strengths or talents or whatever, I'm definitely putting down *choosing best friends*.

"I don't mind couches," Wally said thoughtfully. "It would be at least as Covid-safe as the trains, I guess. After all, it'll just be us five people, instead of a train full of strangers, right?"

"That's right!" Rodeo agreed. "We'll be, like, a little . . . quarantine squad."

"They call that a pod, I think," Wally said.

"A pod? Like killer whales? I dig it, man!" Rodeo clapped his hands.

I was already a lobster and a coyote. I didn't know how many animals one person could be. But if being a killer whale was what it took to get Wally on our bus, I was down.

Wally looked around one more time. Then he closed his eyes and nodded. "Yes," he said, then smiled at us. "Let's go to Maine together."

"Yeehaw!" I cheered, pumping my fist. "Welcome aboard, Wally!"

"What about the questions?" Salvador asked.

"Right! Okay, Wally, you gotta answer our questions to ride the bus. Ready? One: What is your favorite book?"

Wally took off his mask as he thought it over. "My mother used to read me the original *Winnie-the-Pooh* stories, when I was a boy. By A. A. Milne. With the lovely pen-and-ink drawings. I haven't read them in many years, though. Is that all right?"

I sighed. "Very all right, Wally. Very all right. Kind of a home run, actually. Next: What is your very favorite place in the world?"

"Oh. A big question. Well. There is a park, where I used to walk my dog. Lucy, was her name. And there was a bench in the park, that looked out over a pond. And sometimes, before her hips got too bad, Lucy would get up on the bench beside me and lay her head in my lap so I could pet her. That bench, in that park, is my favorite place. As long as Lucy could be there with me."

His eyes had wandered away as he talked, and when he was done, they came back to mine. And he smiled. And Wally had a *great* smile. It was gentle, and soft, but *warm*. It was a smile that put an arm around you and welcomed you in. A smile that you couldn't help but smile back at. A smile that just made you feel *good*. Like lip balm for your soul, kind of.

I always said that Rodeo had magic eyes because they made folks feel safe and peaceful; well, Wally had a magic smile.

I gave him a smile back and shook my head.

"I gotta say," I said. "You're putting in an all-time great performance on these questions. Whew. Okay, last one. What is your favorite sandwich?"

"A Reuben. With corned beef, not pastrami," Wally said. He'd really had that one ready, apparently. "Everything is better when you have a Reuben sandwich."

"Amen, brother!" Rodeo said. "*Love* me a good Reuben."

And that was that.

I avoided eye contact with Candace as we finished up our dinner and walked the garbage to the can outside and got Wally all settled in. Winning is great, but it can also be kind of awkward.

Wally sat down in one of the second-row seats, and me and Salvador sat in the one in front so we could turn around and talk to him. Rodeo was settling into his blanket pile when Candace looked over to me from the driver's seat.

"Should I just put 'Maine' into my phone?" she asked. She sounded a little grumpy.

"No!" I said, probably a little too fast and too loud. "I mean, I'll keep handling the navigation. There are some stops I wanna make."

"Oh. Okay. Where to, then?"

"Um," I said, digging out my phone and frantically opening the map app. The next bookstore stop was in Emporia, Kansas, but we weren't gonna get that far tonight. I picked another town along the way. "Just put in Hays, Kansas. That'll get us in the right direction."

"Mmmkay," she said, clicking around on her phone. "And . . . start-off song?"

She was being a surprisingly good sport. I'll give her that.

I turned to Wally. "Song request? To set the mood?"

Wally drummed his fingers on his chin. Then his eyebrows went up. "'Good Vibrations,'" he said to Candace. "By the Beach Boys."

"Christ on a cracker!" Rodeo called from his pile. "Where have you been all my life, Wally?"

Sound poured from the speakers. Yager shook and growled into life, and then into motion.

"So how long you been on this trip?" Salvador asked Wally.

"Let's see," Wally answered. "Seven months. And seventeen days."

Me and Salvador exchanged a look.

"Long trip," Salvador said.

"Yes," Wally said with a smile and a nod. "I wasted most of my life at work. Now I am making up for it."

"What did you do? For work, I mean?"

Wally sighed. "Corporate law. It's almost too boring to talk about. You've seen a person in a suit at a desk before?" I nodded. "Okay. Just picture me. Doing that. For forty years."

"You're still wearing a suit," I pointed out.

Wally looked down at his rumpled suit and shrugged. "Old habit. I worked very hard for a very long time and made a very decent amount of money. I was very good at my job."

"So why'd you quit?"

"I got tired of spending every day doing something I didn't love, surrounded by people I didn't really like."

"I know the feeling," I said.

Wally blinked at me. "You've . . . worked in corporate law?"

"Middle school," I said.

"Ah, yes." He nodded and didn't smirk even a little bit, which I appreciated. "So I quit my job and sold my house and bought an RV and decided to see more of this world than I could see from my desk."

I looked around. "Where's your RV?"

Wally chuckled. "I am a very bad mechanic. And a very anxious driver. And an RV is very big. After a month I sold the RV for enough money to buy bus and train tickets for probably the rest of my life. Now someone else drives and changes the oil and fixes the flat tires, and I just get to look out the window."

"That's . . . awesome," Salvador said.

"So now you just . . . travel around and eat tater tots?" I asked.

"Yes. I just travel around. And I say 'yes.'"

"Say yes . . . to what?"

"To almost everything. I said no for a long time. No time for vacation. No time for family. No to danger, to risk, to adventure. To fun. I was very careful, and very prudent. And very bored. Very boring, too, I'm sure. And then, when I left, I decided to start saying 'yes.' Yes to almost anything that comes along."

"Like to us," I said, remembering how when we'd asked him to hitch a ride with us, he'd closed his eyes and said yes.

"Exactly. Getting on this old bus with a group of strangers is exactly the kind of thing I would have said 'no' to my whole life. But, so far, I'm glad I said 'yes.'" He paused and fixed me with a serious look. "You're not going to murder me, are you, and then cut me into pieces with a chainsaw and put me into a suitcase and throw me off a bridge?"

"Not planning on it."

He looked to Salvador.

"No, sir. I don't even have a suitcase."

"Good," Wally said, smiling.

I narrowed my eyes at him. "*You* have a suitcase."

"Ah," he said, holding up his hands. "But no chainsaw."

I liked Wally a whole awful lot. Right from the start.

And then, of course, he asked us some questions. About us, and what we all were doing on that bus eating tater tots in Colorado. Of course. I mean, look at us.

"You want the long version or the short version?" I asked him.

"We're driving to Maine, right?"

"Correct."

"The long version, then."

And so I told him. The whole thing. Starting six years ago with a car accident and a hole in the universe. Then on through meeting Salvador last summer and a race for a memory box. And right up to finding some ashes and an out-of-the-blue pandemic shutting down school. I did *not* tell him about the lost book. That little piece of info was still on a best-friends-only level of secrecy, and even though Wally was moving quickly right up the ranks, he wasn't quite there yet. Who knew if he might accidentally spill the beans and tell Rodeo.

Wally listened quietly to the whole tale. He nodded once or twice, murmured occasionally. Closed his eyes when I mentioned the hole in the universe.

"And so, here we are," I finished. "On the road. To scatter her ashes. Where she wanted them."

Wally pursed his lips and looked out the window at the darkness, and the lights. "This is a big thing you're doing," he said at last.

"Yeah," I sighed. He didn't even know the half of it.

"A hard thing, maybe," he said.

"Yeah." He didn't even know a quarter of it.

"A *good* thing," he said.

"Mmm," I replied. He knew, like, ten percent of it. Because what I was mostly doing was lying about very important things to very good people in a very big way. Including to him, at that very moment. I'm not sure "good" was the best adjective to describe it.

"I wish you luck," he said.

"Thanks," I said, and I meant it, though I couldn't *quite* look him in the eye when I said it.

"Now," he said, yawning. "I am an old man. And it's time for the couch."

# CHAPTER

# TWELVE

My next haystack to search was a used bookstore in Emporia, Kansas. Emporia is *not* on the big interstate route that any normal person would take to get from Colorado to Maine. Luckily, I wasn't a normal person. And my dad definitely wasn't, either. My plan (which is a generous word) to get us there went like this:

"Hey, Wally! You ever seen a buffalo?" That was me, asking a question while we were on the couch chowing down on a grocery store breakfast the morning after the tater tots. There was a brief thunder as Ivan ran by, chased by Fig. They'd started doing this playful chase-game thing, which looked dangerously like friendship to me.

And I'd thought that Ivan had good taste.

"Yes," Wally said, ruining my plan. Which shows you about how good of a plan it was.

"Oh," I said, realizing I probably should have had a plan B.

"I haven't," Candace said, coming to my rescue out of the blue.

"You haven't?!" I exclaimed, leaping at the lifeline with enough enthusiasm to make Candace's jaw freeze mid-chew.

"No?" she said through a mouthful of bagel.

"Holy smokes!" I said, then hollered to Rodeo, who was reading up in the driver's seat, "Hey, Rodeo! You hear that? Candace is dying to see her first buffalo!"

"Um, I didn't—" Candace started to say, but Rodeo reacted exactly as I'd hoped and known he would.

"What?!" he said, standing up. "You've never seen a buffalo?!"

"Well—" Candace began, but I wasn't about to let her stop being useful when she'd just finally started.

"Don't worry. We're gonna fix that." I clicked around on my phone—or pretended to, anyway, since I already had the tab open and ready. Another round of thunder, as Fig darted past, this time chased by a puffy-furred, ears-back Ivan. "Look at that!" I said, really selling my phony delighted surprise. "There's a place with buffalo that's almost on our way! The Tallgrass Prairie National Preserve!"

Candace was looking at me, fairly confused.

"Uh, we don't really have to go out of our way to . . ."

"Sure we do!" I interrupted. "This is a *quest*, remember? There's no such thing as 'out of our way.' If someone in the pod really wants to go somewhere, we do it. Right, old man?" Rodeo had walked back to us.

"Ab-o-ut-ey," he said through a mouthful of half-chewed banana.

But Candace shook her head. "I never really said that I wanted to—"

"You didn't have to," I cut in. "I could see it in your eyes. And don't worry. We got your back. You want it, we do it. That's the pod code. Right, Salvador?"

Salvador, who knew exactly what I was doing, nodded. And kinda sighed. He'd let me know that he really thought I should just tell my dad about losing the book. But I had it under control. And he was an awesome-enough friend to have my back anyway.

"Uh, yeah," he said. "Pod code."

"See?" I said. "We're going."

And that was that. Candace sure seemed to think she was super smart. But she was no match for me.

And once we'd hit the Tallgrass Prairie National Preserve (which was actually pretty awesome), what do you know—Emporia, Kansas, was more or less right around the corner.

"Hey," Rodeo said when we just coincidentally walked by the used bookstore in Emporia after lunch. "I think we've been here before!"

"I think so!" I said. I knew so. "Last summer, maybe?" Last summer *absolutely*.

The store was smallish and packed to the brim with books. Organized, thank any and all gods, by topic. Which meant there were three shelves that were set aside for poetry. Only three shelves I had to scan for *Red Bird* by Mary Oliver.

There was a moment—a beautiful, soul-crushing moment—when I thought I had it. I saw a narrow book with *Mary Oliver* in plain white letters on the spine and my breath caught and I actually got a little dizzy and I snatched it off the shelf and then my heart sank like a cast-iron canoe when I saw it was just some other book by Mary Oliver.

Salvador's head snapped over when I gasped and snatched,

but he gave me a comforting elbow nudge when he saw the cover. We couldn't talk because Rodeo and Wally were both browsing in the store, too. We were lucky we got away with all the gasping, snatching, snapping, sinking, and nudging.

Rodeo bought a couple paperbacks and he and Wally wandered out and I went up to the old man at the counter, who was deep in some science fiction book.

"Excuse me. Is there any chance you have any other Mary Oliver poetry books around? In the back, maybe?"

The man looked up from his book. He may have been smiling, or frowning, but I couldn't tell because of his mask. This whole wearing-a-mask-everywhere thing was going to take some getting used to.

"Afraid not," he said. "Anything we have would be in the poetry section."

Behind him, a telephone hanging on the wall started ringing. He didn't even glance at it.

"Do you remember if you've sold any books by her? Like in the last year? The one called *Red Bird*?"

The man squinted at the ceiling. The phone jangled and jangled. "Hmmm. *Red Bird*?"

Salvador held his phone across the counter with the pictures of the book that Rawley had found. "It looks like this."

The man peered at Salvador's phone. He clicked his tongue. "I don't *think* so. Pretty sure not. I've got a pretty good memory for books."

*Ring. Ring. Ring.*

"Do you . . . wanna answer that?" I asked.

"No," the man said simply. I remembered, now. This was one of the stores that had just never answered the phone when I'd called, doing my research. "I never do."

"Why not?" I asked, and worked hard to make my voice sound curious as opposed to furious, which was closer to the truth. I'd driven hundreds of miles out of my way and had my soul crushed because this guy didn't bother answering his phone.

He looked at me. Patiently. Like I was the infuriating one.

"If I wanted to talk to somebody on the telephone," he said, "I'd call them."

It wasn't a bad answer. I mean, it was absolute nonsense, but it was absolute nonsense that did make a certain kind of sense. As someone who'd recently been scolded by their best friend for refusing to answer texts, I didn't really have a lot of ground to stand on. But, still.

*Ring. Ring. Ring.*

"Oh, for the love of tacos!" I spat, and marched around the counter and grabbed the phone off its cradle.

"Hello?"

Salvador was watching me with wide eyes. The bookshop man went back to reading his book.

"No," I said, replying to the question the person on the other end of the line had asked. "I don't think so," I said. Salvador was now giving me a has-my-best-friend-gone-off-the-deep-end? look. "Um. I'll check."

I put my hand over the phone's receiver and sighed.

"Excuse me," I said to the bookshop man. "Are you interested in possibly saving thousands of dollars by transferring your existing credit card debt to a new Sapphire Club card with a very low introductory interest rate?"

"I don't have any credit cards," the man said without looking up from his book.

"Do you want one?"

"Absolutely not."

I put the phone back up to my mouth. "You're really barking up the wrong tree here, ma'am. Good luck with the next one," I said, then hung up.

The bookshop man marked his place in his book with a finger and glanced up at me. "See?" he said.

"Have a nice day," I said with a smile that, if anyone could have seen it through my mask, was spectacularly insincere.

I tried to get my head straight as me and Salvador slumped back toward Yager. Half of me wanted to cry and half of me wanted to punch something, but all of me had to act cool and unbothered when I climbed back aboard. People who don't have something to hide rarely walk out of used bookstores seething and devastated.

"More progress," Salvador said to me under his breath. "Now there's only two places that book could be."

I didn't answer. Salvador was being nice. He was being awesome, actually. But both of us knew that the book could be in a *million* places, and I'd only identified four *possible* places out of those million, and two of those had already been ruled out.

I wasn't just down to two choices; I was down to two *chances*. And when something means the world to you, a two-in-a-million chance doesn't feel all that hopeful.

"Yeah," I said, "you're right," but neither one of us believed it.

"Done already?" Candace said from the driver's seat as we climbed the stairs into Yager. She'd been napping on the couch when we'd pulled in. "I was just about to come in and look around!"

"They don't have any magazines," I said acidly and kept walking. I was all set to walk straight back to my room and do some solo decompression when I saw Rodeo, sitting all by himself in one of the seats in the second row. Well, Fig was sitting with him, but I'm not sure what that counts for.

"Hey, little bird," he said, kinda soft, and I slowed down.

Besides choosing best friends, another thing that I'm really good at is reading my dad. Feeling his moods. Sensing where he's at and what he needs. Let's be honest; for the last six years, I'd spent far more time taking care of him than he had taking care of me. I ain't bitter. If I had to take care of someone, I couldn't do much better than ol' Rodeo. Taking care of that man was like eating the sweet, tart seeds of a pomegranate: a lot of work, but worth it once you got the hang of it.

Anyway. I could see from the slump of his shoulders and the shape of his face and the vague tone in his voice that he wasn't firing on all cylinders. He'd been his usual chipper, funky self when he'd walked into that store. I mean, he'd been walking backward and snapping his fingers. Sure signs of a good mood in the world of Rodeo. But something had happened.

"I'll be back in a sec," I said to Salvador, who gave me a look and then headed back to join Wally on the couch. I slid in next to Rodeo.

"Hey there, weirdo," I said, scooting until our shoulders hit. Fig yawned and wagged her tail and wiggled her way up into my lap and I rolled my eyes and reluctantly scratched behind her ears so she'd sit still and I could work on Rodeo. "Pretty cool bookstore, right?"

One of the many things I knew about taking care of my dad was that the best way to get him to talk about his feelings was to absolutely *not* talk to him about his feelings.

"Yeah," he said. "Good selection." He sighed and scratched at his eyebrow, and my stomach flopped a little. I was reading the signs and the signs weren't great. "I, uh. I saw a book in there."

Now, if he'd have been in a yeehaw-everything-is-just-peachy Rodeo mode, I definitely would have had a sarcastic comment for that brilliant observation. He was not, though, so I did not.

"Oh yeah?"

"Mm-hmm." He took a deep breath and looked out the window.

"Should we hit the road?" Candace asked from the driver's seat.

I shot her an irritated look. "Knock yourself out," I said, and turned back to Rodeo.

"Uh . . . where should I head?"

It was, without a doubt, a fair question. So I summoned all my patience and turned back to her. "Just put in Pittsburgh, okay? Thanks, Candace." Insincere Smile #2 for the day.

The bus's great engine coughed and growled and we eased into motion.

"So you saw a book, huh?"

"Mmm." He traced a finger along the window. "It was, uh. It was . . . one of her favorites. One of your, uh, mom's, I mean."

"Oh." I kept my voice gentle, but casual. "What book was it?"

I braced myself for the answer. If he said *"Red Bird"* and it turns out they *did* have the book but just in the wrong section, I was prepared to leap right out the window of that moving bus and run back and grab it.

*"Beloved,"* he said. "Toni Morrison."

I nodded. I hadn't read that one. But I mentally added it to my to-read list.

He took a full, deep breath. Rubbed his eyes. "I want you to know that I'm . . . that I'm having a hard time with this, darling. This whole thing."

"Okay," I said. With Rodeo it's important to not try to talk him out of his feelings. Or deeper into them.

He shook his head. "I know it's the right thing to do. It's time. It's past time, probably. But, man. All these years. The good times, and the bad times, I always knew . . . I knew that she was just . . . *right there.*" He gestured back with his head to the shelves behind us, the shelves where I'd found the box. "No matter how hard it got, I knew she was there. It's gonna be . . . oh, man. It's gonna be hard letting her go."

I leaned in closer, so that our shoulders and our arms and our legs were touching. I could feel his shaky breaths. "Of course it is," I said.

"And this Maine thing is really throwing me off, too," my dad said, frowning and scratching at his beard. "I mean, as far as I know, your mom had never even *been* to Maine."

I licked my lips. Lord. Every time I think I'm out of the woods.

"Yeah? Huh. Well. Kind of a weird deal, I guess," I said, shooting hard to make my voice sound *casual* but, to my ear, hitting more of a shooting-hard-to-make-my-voice-sound-casual tone. My mind was racing, or trying to. "But, remember, this is a *journey* thing, not a *destination* thing. We're heading *toward* Maine as part of it all, but we're not spreading her ashes there." I crossed my fingers in my lap, hoping that was the truth. I mean, it was probably true, right? Like Rodeo said, why would she want her ashes scattered in some place she'd never been before?

Rodeo sorta smiled, under his beard. His eyes got kinda misty.

"Aha." He squinted. "Hey. I bet it's, like, a four corners thing, right? Like she wants us to hit Maine, and then Florida, and then California, and then back to Washington? 'Cause she knew how much I loved road trips? Is that what she wrote?"

I licked my lips and pasted on a hopefully-not-too-wobbly smile.

"I can't tell you," I said, which was one of the truer things I've ever said.

"I love it," he said, shaking his head. "That your mom gave us this trip to do together. Man. She was something special, wasn't she?"

I couldn't quite talk. But I managed to cough out a little "Yeah."

Rodeo took in a big breath and then let it out. "I wanna do this," he said. "For you. For her. For me, even." He reached over and squeezed my leg and took in a shaky breath. "And I think I *need* to do this. I . . . I never talk about this, but I've felt . . . guilty, and responsible, and *ashamed*, for all these years. About what happened. Like I let them down. Your mom, and your . . . your . . ." His voice cracked and he coughed and then kept going. "Your sisters. Like, if I would've been the one driving, if I'd have been the one to go to the store, then maybe it all wouldn't have happened. I've felt like it was all my fault."

I started to talk, to tell him how wrong he was, but he stopped me, gently, with a shake of his head.

"I know, I know," he said. "It wasn't, really. But for years I've felt like I let your mom down. Now, though, with these ashes and that book, I feel like, kind of, in a small way, I can make it right. By doing what she asked in that book, I can, I don't know, put right that wrong. Make it up to her, a little. I feel like, if I can do this, and set your mom free how she wanted, that maybe I can really start being okay again."

By this point I was actively trying not to throw up. As if I hadn't been desperate enough to find the book. As if I hadn't been devastated enough that Emporia had come up empty. I was honestly trying not to hyperventilate and vomit at the same time. And, possibly, burst into tears.

Rodeo turned his head and tried to look into my eyes, but I just couldn't do it, so I looked down at Fig and her weird bald belly, and for once I was grateful that she was there. My dad blew out a big sigh.

"Anyway. Sorry I'm getting all heavy. I gotta shake this. You got a once-upon-a-time for me, sparrow?"

Really. I was having a hard-enough time as it was holding it all together and then he wants me to tell him a story? But I had to. I had to get that man through this patch of clouds. We had a long way to go, still. This was my ride, my quest, and he was trying to hold on for me, even if just by his fingertips. So I swallowed down my queasiness and gave it my best shot.

"Once upon a time," I said, "there was a . . ." I put on a little half smirk and leaned back to look him up and down. His scraggly beard. His whole skinny, threadbare self. "Badger," I finished, then nodded.

He smiled, a little. "Handsome fella?" he asked, his voice scratchy.

"God, no. Mangy son of a gun," I said. We both laughed, just a little. "But he was handsome on the inside. Just . . . solid gold under the fur, that guy."

"But?" Rodeo asked.

"Of course he had a butt," I said, and we both laughed some more. Small, careful chuckles. "But, he was . . . stuck. Caught. In the sharp metal teeth of a trap. Had him right here." I latched on with my fingers to his forearm. Rodeo's cautious smile faded. "Had him good. He couldn't shake free. And the more he tried, the more he hurt. Right down through that fur, and through that gold, right down to the bone." I gripped his arm tighter, and tighter. He watched my hand with his troubled eyes. "He knew he needed to get free. He had to get that trap open. But he couldn't. It wasn't his fault. He was stuck." Rodeo's brow was furrowed, his mouth tight. "But he was also lucky," I said.

"How?" Rodeo asked hoarsely.

I let a soft breath out. "Because he wasn't alone," I said, and my dad's eyebrows went up, just a little. "You see, this shaggy badger, he had a pup."

"Yeah?"

"Yeah. A girl pup."

"Ah. And was she a total pain in the butt, this pup?"

"Of course," I said. "I mean, she was like *twice* as smart as he was, so."

Rodeo's smile came back, a bit.

"The old badger couldn't get out of that trap alone. But that pup of his, who was so terribly smart, she didn't leave his side. She wouldn't. Not ever." I leaned in, a little closer, so I could look in his wounded badger eyes. "Not ever," I said again. He dipped his chin. "So, together, they got him unstuck." With my other hand, I reached and grabbed his free one, and pulled it to my fingers that were gripping his arm. I pinched one of my fingers and lifted it up, away from where it held him. He did the same to another of my fingers. And another. And another. And I pulled my thumb free. "It was hard. But they did it, together. They were strong enough, together."

I let go of his arm. He flexed and unflexed his fingers.

"He was free," I said.

"And they lived happily ever after?" he asked.

"Oh, who knows. But, whatever. You can't start the next story 'til you finish the one before. And they were ready for the next story."

Fig wiggled her way out of my lap and onto Rodeo's. She

rolled over onto her back and curled her paws and blinked her ridiculously huge eyes at him.

"Ugh," I said, and was all ready to shoo her away, but Rodeo laughed and scratched her belly and her tail wagged furiously. She was, possibly, some version of cute.

Rodeo and I both watched her for a few breaths as he scratched her chin and she closed her eyes in pleasure.

"Thanks, Coyote," he said, kinda low and gruff. "That was a good story."

I snorted. "That was barely a story, Daddio. Give me a little time to get ready next time and I'll really wow you."

Fig was now looking at Rodeo in adoration and licking his hand with her creepy little tongue.

He blew out a big breath and wiggled his shoulders and scratched Fig's neck with his fingernails. Her eyes were rolling.

"Thanks for making this happen, darling. Thanks for taking us on this quest. I need this, hard as it is. I'm a mess, I know. But you're gonna get us there, aren't you?"

Now, I'm not a great liar under the best circumstances. But lying about something like this? Something so personal, so important, so . . . *sacred*? Ugh. Way, way worse. I couldn't lie about that. But, also, I wasn't exactly ready to spill the actual, horrible truth. Especially given all of the stuff that Rodeo had just said. No way. So I, kind of, like, split the difference.

I squeezed my dad's knee. And I leaned over to plant a kiss on his scruffy cheek.

Now, in *my* mind, that squeeze-and-kiss was meant as an

actually-you're-totally-wrong-and-I-just-can't-get-up-the-nerve-to-tell-you-the-truth-and-I'm-super-sorry sort of squeeze-and-kiss. That's a thing, right?

But, my dad being my dad, he almost certainly interpreted that squeeze-and-kiss as a you're-absolutely-right-old-man-you-sure-hit-the-nail-on-the-head-I-got-this-completely-under-control-and-I'm-definitely-not-totally-lying-about-all-this sort of squeeze-and-kiss. I was counting on it. It ain't *my* fault that he chose to think that.

So, it wasn't a lie. It was just an instance of unfortunate miscommunication. That just happened to be on purpose.

My dad blinked wetly. He nodded. Lifted one hand away from petting that rat dog and patted my hand that was lying on his knee. *Lying* in both senses, by the way.

I was being rocked by such intense waves of emotional nausea that I was practically seasick. I gave my dad's knee another squeeze and then I slid away and stood up, Fig's enormous eyes watching me the whole time.

That damned dog knew I was lying, I could tell. She licked her lips and wagged her tail. So smug. I narrowed my eyes at her.

I walked back past my best friend and my new friend on the couch. Ivan was curled up on the couch between them, accepting their petting without begging for it, the way an animal with any sort of dignity or self-respect should. I closed the curtain to my room and collapsed onto my bed.

Now, more than ever, I had to get that book.

"Pittsburgh or Maine," I whispered to the ceiling. "Maine or Pittsburgh." It *had* to be in one of those places. It just had to be.

I'd dragged three people and one neighbor and a cat and some sort of canine rodent a thousand miles across the country and the emotional stability of at least one of us was kind of hinging on finding that book and, maybe most of all, everything my dad had said had been right: We were doing this with my mom and we were doing this for my mom and we had to do it right.

I looked over to my bookshelf, where I'd cleared a space for the box of ashes. I reached and picked it up and lay back down with that box on my chest, my arms hugged around it.

"We'll find it, Mom," I whispered. "I promise."

# CHAPTER
## THIRTEEN

I fell asleep like that, back on my bed, hugging my mom.

And maybe that's why I woke up remembering her. Maybe I dreamed about her, too, I don't know. Maybe she visited me while I slept, watching over me, the way some people say. I hope not, honestly. That's always struck me as creepy, some dead loved one standing there watching you sleep. And boring, too, for them. But who knows.

Anyway. I woke up and it was sometime in the afternoon and I blinked at the light coming in the windows, and it was just there, this memory.

It must have been just before. Just before . . . the hole in the universe and all that. Just before I lost her.

It was springtime, and we were walking through the apple orchards behind our house. Just going for a walk, like folks do. I don't remember for sure, but I was probably complaining about having to go for a walk, the way kids do when they don't know that the person they're with is gonna die and they're gonna miss them forever. It was one of those spring days when there are dark clouds scattered across a blue sky, so that sometimes it was cool and shady and sometimes it was bright and sunny, as the sun came and went. All the apple trees were in bloom. Covered in pretty little white flowers. It was toward the end, though, so a few of the petals were just starting to fall. There was a little breeze.

And then it happened. The rain started. A steady but soft rain. It felt almost warm. You could hear the drops tapping the leaves and the branches and the blooms and the grass, all around. And as we walked beneath those trees, the raindrops and the breeze started shaking, gently, the apple blossoms loose, and they drifted down around us, and then they were everywhere, falling down on the grass and on our shoulders and in our hair.

My mom gasped and dropped to a knee beside me. And she put her arm around me. And she whispered into my ear, hushed and breathless, like it was magic: *"Listen,"* she said. *"Look. It's raining flowers."*

I blinked around at the world. And it *was* magic. The air smelled like rain, but it also smelled like flowers, and everywhere was the sound of rain, but the rain wasn't falling on us because we were under the trees, and so it looked and sounded and smelled like it was raining apple blossoms.

For just a few moments, the world was a world in which flower petals fell from the clouds.

That's the kind of person my mom was. The kind of person who could make it rain flowers. The kind of person who noticed. The kind of person who stopped and spoke in a magical whisper so that you'd notice, too. And you'd remember.

Even after the day was gone, and even after the flowers were gone, and even after *she* was gone. You'd remember her, and that moment.

"I promise," I said again.

# CHAPTER

## FOURTEEN

It was, Candace's phone told us, fourteen hours from Emporia, Kansas, to Pittsburgh, Pennsylvania. A whole truckload (or, I guess, a busload) of momentous things happened from Pittsburgh on, but only two momentous things happened between Emporia and Pittsburgh.

Here's the first one: It was a couple hours in, and I'd finished my little nap and my big memory, and I was sitting in one of the bus seats kind of half reading and, occasionally, calling the thrift store in Maine. The Maine store was one of the ones, like Emporia, that just never answered their phone. After watching that Emporia bookstore dude sit there like a monster while the phone rang behind him, I'd started calling the Maine store again. Maybe the owner would finally break and pick up. Or maybe some intelligent, take-control customer like myself would answer it for them. There was a chance. So I'd sit there, reading, while the phone rang in my ear. It was even less fun than it sounds.

So, there I sat. An excruciating mixture of desperate and bored. Ivan was on my lap. Fig was curled up on the seat against me, which I decided to allow because she was kind of warm and it didn't feel like the worst thing in the world. Plus she did this big tongue-curling yawn thing every time I scratched behind her ear, which some folks would've found cute. Wally was sleeping in one of the other seats. Rodeo was driving. He was chatting with Candace, who was kneeling on the seat behind him.

None of that was the momentous part.

This was: I just happened to glance up, one time, between chapters. And I saw something.

Candace was scratching Rodeo's back.

With her fingernails.

In these slow, scratchy circles.

My mouth dropped open.

It was not just a *friendly* back scratch. And it was definitely not a *neighborly* back scratch, which I don't think even exists.

Now, I'm not totally clueless. Usually. I know that Rodeo is a grown man and that he'd been tragically single for years and years and that maybe, someday . . . you know. And when Rodeo had started hanging out with Candace and going for walks and laughing and talking and all that, I wasn't completely naive about what maybe, possibly, might be happening.

I'm thirteen, not three.

But, still. That's all fine as a theoretical possibility when it's just something that you try not to think about. It's a whole different banana when it's looking you in the face, scratching your dad's back.

And then, when I thought it couldn't get any worse—her hand drifted up. And she started, like, *massaging* his neck. And kind of twirling her fingers through his fruit-flavored hair. And they kept talking and laughing like nothing was happening.

I slammed my book shut and picked up Ivan and stomped back to where Salvador was lying on the couch.

I picked up his feet and slid underneath them to sit down and said, "Has your mom ever had a boyfriend?" and he rubbed his eyes and said, "I was sleeping," and I said, "Sorry but this is important," and he shook the cobwebs out of his head and said, "Okay, what was your question?" and that kind of thing is exactly why I picked that boy to be my best friend.

"Has your mom ever had a boyfriend? Like, since your dad?"

Salvador made a look of mildly confused disgust. "Why would she need a boyfriend?" he asked. "She has me."

I rolled my eyes. Boys.

"Well, buddy, I think you and I are going to have to have an awkward conversation at some point."

He scowled. "No, I mean, *gross*, but, I don't know. She's pretty busy. And . . . why?"

I glared at the front of the bus. Salvador's eyes followed mine. *She* was still up there, massaging his neck like there weren't maybe people around who were trying to read or at least not throw up.

"Oh," he said, "yeah. I was wondering when we were gonna talk about that."

"What do you mean?" I demanded.

"I mean, it's pretty obvious that they're, like, at least a *little* more than friends. And it's pretty obvious you don't like her. So, yeah."

"Well . . . well . . . I *don't* like her!" I said.

Salvador huffed out a breath. "I know, Coyote. We all know.

But did you ever think that maybe . . ." He broke off and took a deep breath and closed his eyes like he was bracing for something, and when he talked again, he said it all in one breath fast. "That maybe you don't actually don't like her? That maybe you're just against her because you're, like, jealous of her being friends with your dad, and, you know, worried about her, like, replacing your mom or something?" He swallowed and looked at me nervously through one squinting eye. "Sorry."

I sat there blinking at him. Dumbfounded. "What?" I finally managed to spit out. "Of *course*. Of *course* that's why I don't like her! Was that supposed to be, like, *perceptive* or something?"

"Oh. I thought maybe you were, like, in denial or whatever."

"No. Her personality is . . . *fine*, I guess. But I think someone elbowing into your life and trying to steal your dad is a perfectly good reason all on its own not to like them."

"I'm not sure that's . . . really what she's trying to do."

"Well, you didn't see the entire disgusting display I just had to witness," I said, jerking a thumb toward the front of the bus.

"Yeah," Salvador said, kind of doubtfully.

We sat there for a while. Me, fuming. Salvador, doubting. Ivan, purring on my lap next to Salvador's feet. Fig pitter-pattered over and hopped on Salvador and curled up on his chest and ogled me while he petted her.

Finally, Salvador broke the silence. "But, like . . . would it be that bad, really? Like, is having a girlfriend the *worst* thing in the world?"

I narrowed my eyes. I smelled a rat. And it wasn't the rat-sized dog blinking its huge eyes at me.

"Why did you say it like that?"

"Like what?" Salvador asked, looking away.

I kept looking at him. He kept looking away. A blush rose in his cheeks.

"Oh my god," I said. I tilted my head. "Salvador. Do you have a girlfriend?"

"Kind of," he mumbled, looking closely at the back of Fig's head. His feet were twitching.

"You serious? Like, a *girlfriend* girlfriend?"

He shrugged a "yes."

I pursed my lips. "What's her name?"

Salvador cleared his throat. "Um. Isabella?"

"Why'd you say it like that? Is it Isabella or not?"

"No, I mean, yes, I mean, yeah, her name's Isabella."

I arched an eyebrow. "Have you kissed?"

"What? Coyote . . ."

"Tell me."

Salvador's face was an entirely new shade I'd never seen on him before. "Well, uh, yeah, I guess? We kissed?"

"You don't sound too sure. I think you'd know it if you did."

"Fine. Yeah, we kissed. We totally kissed. Okay?"

I narrowed my eyes and shook my head. "You got a lot of nerve. I can't believe you, Salvador Vega."

"What? You . . . you can't be mad at me, Coyote. I mean, it's not like we, like we're, like . . ."

I reared back my head. "Ugh! Is that why you think I'm mad? Gross, Salvador. I have zero interest in pressing my lips against yours. I've seen you eat out of a garbage can."

"Then . . . what's the problem?"

"The problem is you didn't tell me. Until now. And we're supposed to be best friends. What kind of best friend doesn't tell you when they have their first kiss?"

Salvador frowned and scratched at the back of his neck. "I didn't think . . . uh, I didn't think . . ."

"Yeah. You got that part right."

He scratched at Fig's weird skull for a minute.

"Have you?" he asked, still looking away. "Had your first kiss, I mean?"

"No. But I'm in no rush. I'm not looking forward to it."

"You're not?"

"Nah. I'm looking forward to, like, my *seventeenth* kiss."

Salvador blinked. "Your seventeenth? Why?"

I shrugged. "I feel like kissing is probably something you get better at with practice. Like, maybe by around seventeen or so you'd start to get the hang of it. But those first few must just be super awkward and clumsy."

Salvador pursed his lips thoughtfully. "You're not wrong," he said. "Do you, like, have a boyfriend, though?"

I laughed.

He looked at me kind of sideways. "Is that a 'no'?"

My turn to look away. "I don't even have a *friend* friend," I said.

Another silence stretched between us.

"That's a bunch of bullcrap," he said.

"It's not. I don't have a single friend, Salvador."

"Even more bullcrap."

I was breathing a little harder than I wanted to. And I was still not meeting his eyes. "Salvador, you don't know. You don't—"

"Yes, I do. I *do* know that you have a friend, Coyote." He picked Fig up and set her on the ground and sat up so he could look me in the eye or at least in the face because I still wouldn't make eye contact with him. "Because you've got my number. So you'll always have at least one friend, Coyote. No matter what."

I shook my head. "I'm just . . . some weirdo who gave you a ride once. Some girl you feel sorry for because her . . ." I stopped. Couldn't quite say it. I've got a little Rodeo in me after all. A whole lot, maybe. "Some girl you feel sorry for."

Salvador smacked his lips. Rocked forward and back a little bit. Breathed through his nose. He was, I realized, mad.

"Me and Isabella," he said, "we got in a big fight. Just a little while ago. The night you called to tell me about losing the book. I was hanging out with her when you called. And I answered, and I walked outside to talk to you. And she was like, 'Why are you taking calls from other girls when we're hanging out?' Fair, right? But you know what I said?"

I swallowed. "Kiss me?"

"No. Shut up. I said, *sorry*. But when *this* girl calls, I answer. Every time. And I always will. No matter what. I don't even answer every time when my *mom* calls. But I do for you, Coyote."

I sniffed. I gave Ivan a little pet.

"And you won't even answer my texts," he said.

My head snapped to look at him. "Come on. I mean, I *hate* texting."

He shrugged. "I hate taking showers at truck stops. But here I am."

Boy. He was right. He was one hundred percent right. Leave it to a best friend to make you feel like a million bucks *and* a total piece of crap in one conversation.

"Salvador," I said, looking him in the eye, "I will text you back every single time you text me, from now on. Every. Single. Time. That's a promise."

He smiled. A kind of embarrassed smile. "You don't have to, if you don't want to."

"I want to."

"Fine."

I glanced again up at the front of the bus. Candace had both hands on Rodeo's shoulders now, and they were singing along together to whatever was playing out of the speakers.

"Ugh. I can't watch this. I'm going to my room."

I slid Ivan to Salvador's lap and stood up. And I looked down at Salvador, sitting there still looking kinda half-sleepy, with my cat on his lap. And then I stooped right back down and gave him a hug.

"Thanks, Salvador," I said. "You're the best."

"You, too, Coyote," he said.

I started to let go, then stopped. Sniffed. Sniffed again. "Wait a minute," I said. Sniffed some more. "Did you . . . change deodorants?"

"What?"

I straightened up and looked down at him with my arms crossed. "You used to smell like pine trees. Now you smell like . . . coconut?"

He blushed a little and shrugged one shoulder. "I guess."

"Why did you . . . oh, lord," I said. "It's Isabella, isn't it? Did you switch because of her?"

Salvador blushed even harder. "Um. Well. She . . . she said she didn't like the tree one. She likes coconut better."

I shook my head at him. "What is happening to everyone?" I said. "My dad smells like kiwi and you smell like coconut. I'm basically living with a fruit salad at this point."

The whole world was going bananas. At least the guy part. And at least in the smell department.

Salvador was still blushing pretty furiously. I started to feel bad.

"It smells nice," I lied. "And, hey, they're *your* armpits."

"Thanks?" Salvador said.

I started walking away.

"That eating-out-of-a-garbage-can thing was a low blow, by the way," Salvador said after me. "You're the one who threw away a perfectly good hot dog."

"It was *half* a hot dog," I said over my shoulder, "and I threw it away because I dropped it on the ground, so if anything, I was being easy on you. You ate garbage can food *off the ground*."

He had no comeback for that.

I flopped down on my bed. I had a lot to think about.

My phone buzzed under my pillow. I fished it out. There was a text from Salvador.

*Hey*, it said. I smiled.

*Hey*, I replied.

I'm a promise keeper.

# CHAPTER

# FIFTEEN

So, that was the first momentous thing that happened between Emporia, Kansas, and Pittsburgh, Pennsylvania. A horrifying neck rub followed by an important conversation.

The second thing, unfortunately, was even more horrifying than the neck rub, which I wouldn't have believed was possible. But it was. By a mile.

We stopped for gas. Somewhere in Indiana. I don't know where exactly, and frankly I don't care because I'm never going back there again.

Candace was walking Fig around on her leash so she could "do her business," as Candace put it, which I really thought was dressing it up quite a bit. Me and Salvador and Rodeo masked up and walked into the convenience store to browse the snack selection. Wally had volunteered to wash Yager's windshield while the gas was pumping.

I was standing there trying to decide if I was the kind of person who would eat dill-pickle-flavored potato chips when the little bell above the door jingled and then the big bearded guy behind the counter said, "Nope!"

Now, "nope" isn't that dramatic of a thing to say, maybe, but it was *how* he said it that made my head snap up. He said it mean and loud and ugly.

I scanned the situation.

Wally had come in the door. He was standing there, eyes wide above his mask, looking at the dude behind the counter, who was pointing a meaty finger at him.

"Out! You ain't welcome here. Get on out, *now*!"

Wally blinked. "I'm sorry?"

"Get out," the dude said again, but this time with a couple of extra words I won't repeat.

"Hey," I started to say. Maybe. I'm not sure I got any sound out.

Wally seemed paralyzed.

"You deaf?" the man asked. Then my heart dropped to the floor because that dude bent down and reached under the counter and when he stood back up he was holding a baseball bat in his hand. For real. The man was getting red-faced now and he pointed the bat at poor Wally. Skinny, sweet, wrinkly, "Good Vibrations" and *Winnie-the-Pooh* Wally. "Get out of my store. I don't want your damn Covid flu. Y'all brought it over here and you ain't coming in my store!" That's the edited version of what he said, anyway. And then he called Wally a couple of names that I will never not ever repeat not ever.

Here's what I wish I could say: That I jumped right in. That I shouted that jerk down. That I ran to Wally's side and stood up for him.

But I didn't. I stood there like my flip-flops were nailed to the floor. I stood there, shocked and terrified and breathless and useless.

"What's going on?" Rodeo asked, walking out of the bathroom and wiping his hands on his jeans. He'd only heard the last couple choice words but they were more than enough and he was marching toward that dude and his eyes were glittering but not in a happy way.

The dude shot Rodeo a dirty look. To be fair, Rodeo got that look at a lot of gas stations. But this was most definitely different.

"None of your business." He turned his furious face back to Wally. "You got like three seconds to get out or it's gonna get ugly." But it was already ugly. It was already horribly, disgustingly ugly. Then he banged the counter, hard, with his free hand, and we all jumped, or at least I know that I did, and he shouted, "Get! Out!!"

"Okay," Wally said, ducking his head. "Yes. I'm sorry." And he turned and shuffled quick out the door. Wally apologized. *Wally* apologized.

"You two," Rodeo said to me and Salvador as he walked past us, his voice quiet but intense. "Go outside, all right?"

"But—" I said, or thought of saying; honestly, I'm not sure.

"Out you go," he said. "Salvador?"

"Come on, Coyote," Salvador whispered, and he tugged on my sleeve. That finally got me moving. Not up toward the counter to tell that guy what a piece of garbage he was and to tell him to go out and apologize to Wally, like a friend would do. No. Toward the door. To walk out without saying a thing. Like a coward would do.

Which is what we did. Which was, maybe, the smart thing to

do. But which also felt worse than using tin foil as toilet paper. I'm assuming.

We walked out the doors and they whooshed closed behind us, and then we were walking toward Yager and Wally was already starting to climb inside, and he looked so small and I was *shaking*, like, *trembling*.

I looked back over my shoulder and saw Rodeo. Standing right across the counter from that guy. And he was talking. Not yelling. Talking. But talking hard. His head was nodding and he was pointing at the dude's big bearded face and he was talking. I don't know what Rodeo was saying. But he was saying it strong. And he was saying it right into that man's face. I'm guessing he was saying all the things that I should have said. I hope he was.

"We should go back in there," I said, slowing my feet.

"No we shouldn't, Coyote," Salvador said, pulling me along, and he sounded kinda trembly, too.

"We should. We should tell that guy off." Pretty easy for me to say once I was already out the door, I know.

Salvador sighed. "No. Then he'll talk back and get even madder, and then your dad'll get madder and then there'll be a fight."

"So? Did you hear what that guy said? We *should* fight him!"

"It wouldn't be *we*, Coyote. It'd be your dad. You really want your dad to fight that guy?"

I looked back again.

The dude was a couple inches taller than my dad, and about fifty pounds heavier. And he was holding a bat. And Rodeo was, well, Rodeo. I'd seen the man get out of breath and sweaty just vacuuming the living room.

Rodeo was still talking, but now he was talking over his shoulder as he walked toward the door. The dude was just standing there with pouty duck lips and his bat in his hand.

"It's not right," I said, but my voice was small.

"No. It's not."

And then we were walking up the stairs onto Yager. Fig had concluded her business apparently, and Candace was sitting in the driver's seat and she took one look at me and Salvador and picked up on the vibe in a snap.

"What's going on?" she asked, but I looked and saw Wally sitting back on the couch and I kept walking right past her. I heard Salvador stop and talk to her in a low, hushed voice, so I knew he was getting her up to speed.

Fig had already hopped up onto Wally's lap, which I appreciated. A lot, maybe. He shouldn't have to be alone.

I sat down next to him.

I didn't know what to say.

But sometimes maybe the best thing to say is just the simplest thing.

"I'm so sorry," I said. "I'm so sorry that happened." I was surprised to find myself crying. I mean, nothing had happened to *me*. I sniffed and blinked hard to get that in check because there is nothing wrong with crying but I am not a big fan of someone making something all about them when it wasn't all about them.

Wally reached over and patted my knee. "I know," he said.

There was nothing else for me to say. But sometimes maybe the best thing to say is just nothing at all.

I sat there with Wally, saying nothing at all until Rodeo climbed aboard and said "Get rollin'" to Candace and then walked straight back and sat down on the floor crisscross-applesauce in front of Wally.

"Hey, brother," he said, fixing his magic eyes on Wally. "You okay?"

Wally nodded.

"Do you, uh, do you wanna talk about it?"

Wally took a breath in, and let the breath out. "There is nothing to talk about," he said in his deliberate way. He sounded very tired. "These things happen." He shook his head. "And I'm not even Chinese. My parents came from Thailand. Not that it should matter."

"This has happened before?" I asked.

"Of course," he said simply. "More and more, lately."

"That's . . . that's *awful*," I said. "Why?"

Wally shrugged. "These are scary times. Look at the world. People are scared."

Rodeo shook his head. "If the world is scary, that's all the more reason for folks to come together."

Wally smiled sadly. "That is a nice idea," he said. He didn't have to say the "but" for me and Rodeo to know it was there. The "but" was standing back there behind the counter with a baseball bat, in every sense and spelling of the word "but." "I think I'd like to just sit with Fig for a little while."

Rodeo nodded. "Gotcha. C'mon, Coyote."

Candace was driving, obviously, and Rodeo went to sit behind her and Salvador was sitting in one of the other seats and I plopped down next to him.

"Man," I said.

"Yeah. That was some BS right there."

"I wish there was something we could do," I said.

"Totally. I mean, that sucked. That really sucked. But there's nothing we can do to just, like, make everything better."

I sighed. And then something sparked in my mind. My head snapped up.

"Huh," I said, and chewed my bottom lip.

"Huh what?" Salvador asked.

"Give me your phone," I said. Mine was back in my room, and I didn't want to disturb Wally and Fig's private moment.

Salvador handed his over and I started clicking around.

"What are you doing?" he asked, but I kept at it.

Then I found what I was looking for.

"C'mere," I said, and jumped up and hopped over to where Candace and Rodeo were talking in understandably bummed-out tones.

"Hey," I said. "I got an idea." And then I pitched it. And they bought it. And I handed the phone over to Candace and she took a look and then flicked on the turn signal and then there we went.

Forty-five minutes later, we pulled into a parking lot. I hopped out with a few bills in my pocket and a few minutes later I was stepping back up onto Yager with a brown paper bag in my hand.

Wally was still sitting back on the couch. Salvador, Rodeo, and Candace were at the front of the bus.

"You wanna come with?" I asked them, low.

Rodeo shook his head. "Crowds are awkward, honeybird."

"It was your idea," Candace said. "Go on."

So I walked back to Wally. Fig danced around my feet as I went, trying her bestest to sniff the bag I was holding.

"Hey, Wally," I said.

He looked up at me. No magic smile. No sparkly eyes.

"Can I sit here?"

"Of course."

I sat beside him, and Fig jumped up beside me and I had to fight her off with an elbow.

"I got you something," I said. And I handed the bag over.

Wally gave me a little confused look as he took the bag, and then he unrolled the top and a smell wafted out. Big time. The smell that Fig had picked up on from the get-go. A salty, cheesy, meaty smell.

Wally sniffed. His eyebrows went up. He looked to me with wonder on his face. "Is this . . . ?"

I nodded at him.

He reached in and pulled out a greasy, white paper-wrapped square.

"You said," I said, "that everything is better with a Reuben sandwich."

Wally unfolded the white paper.

"It's corned beef, not pastrami," I said. "Like you said. I called and made sure."

Wally just stared at the sandwich, not saying anything.

I was getting nervous. And suddenly feeling a little ridiculous. This awesome, magic-smiled guy is the victim of a hate crime, basically, and I get him a *sandwich*?

"You don't have to eat it," I said, quick. "If you don't want. But it's supposedly . . . one of the best Reuben sandwiches in Indiana?" The internet had told me where the alleged *best* Reuben in Indiana was, but it was four hours away, so we'd had to settle for just a very highly rated Reuben, which at the time had still seemed better than nothing. "I guess I figured, you know . . . that the world can be craptastic sometimes. But at least there's sandwiches."

I've said plenty of dumb things in my life. But, boy, that was right up there.

Wally still didn't say anything.

But he brought half the sandwich up to his mouth. Took a bite. Closed his eyes and chewed.

And then his shoulders started shaking. His head tilted back, eyes still closed. The paper in his lap rustled.

"Are you okay?" I asked. "Oh my god, are you choking? Dad!"

I heard a thunder of footsteps as the rest of the crew rushed back.

But Wally shook his head and kinda nudged my arm and opened his mouth, and then I realized he wasn't choking. He was laughing.

"No, no," he said through laughter. He was talking with his mouth full of food which normally I'm categorically opposed to but in this case I was so relieved to just see him breathing that I didn't care. He chewed and swallowed as everyone else arrived.

"What's up?" Rodeo asked urgently. Him and Salvador and Candace gathered around, a half circle of worried faces.

"I'm fine, I'm fine," Wally said. "I was just . . . surprised."

"So the sandwich is okay?" I asked.

Wally put a hand on my arm and looked into my eyes. "The sandwich is wonderful." He held the one-bite-missing half sandwich toward me. "Try it. Please."

Now, I am not a huge fan of Reuben sandwiches. I think that putting sauerkraut on a sandwich is like putting barbecue sauce on an ice cream sundae. It falls squarely in the why-in-the-world-would-anyone-ever-do-that category for me. But it seemed rude to say no.

So I took a bite from the unbitten side of the sandwich half. And it tasted exactly like what a Reuben is, which is a perfectly good sandwich ruined by sauerkraut.

"Mmm," I lied. "Good."

Wally picked the other half up from the paper and held it out to Salvador. "Everyone try. It's marvelous."

Salvador looked at the sandwich and flickered a weak smile. I think he felt the same way I do about Reuben sandwiches. But, like me, he's polite. He took a tiny bite of the corner and then I was *sure* he felt the same way I do because I have seen that kid eat half a maple bar in one bite.

He nodded and smiled and I'm pretty sure fought back a gag and handed the sandwich to Candace, and on down the line it went.

"Oh, *man*," Rodeo said, shaking his head and rocking back on his heels. "That is *solid*."

We all chewed and looked around at each other for a second, and I know at least two of us were trying to ignore the taste of sauerkraut in our mouths.

"Why is no one else eating?" Wally asked.

"Oh," I said. "We just called and ordered yours."

"Aren't you hungry?"

We all kind of looked at each other and nodded.

"Well, then, get some food," Wally said. "And then we can put on some music. And maybe play some cards together." I'd taught Wally about Uno the day before, and he was a big fan.

"Like a . . . sandwich party?" I said.

"Exactly like a sandwich party. Because the world is scary," he said, looking at Rodeo. "Sometimes. And that is a very good reason for folks to come together."

"Well, all right," Rodeo said with a grin. "Sounds like a plan to me."

Us four started heading toward the front of the bus to go get our own sandwich party supplies, but Wally stopped me with a quiet, "Coyote."

"Yeah?" I asked, holding back.

"Thank you. For the sandwich." He wiped a few tears out of his eyes with the back of his free hand.

"Happy tears?" I asked.

"No," he said softly. "Real tears. But it was real laughter, too. And you were wrong, by the way," he said. "About sandwiches."

"I was?"

"Yes. Because the world *is* craptastic sometimes. You got that part right." He smiled at me, and it was a small smile, and it was mostly sad, maybe, but it also had at least a little bit of magic in it. "But it's not the sandwich that matters, Coyote. It's someone bringing you the sandwich."

# CHAPTER

## SIXTEEN

The sandwich party was a smashing success, and then we spent that night in the parking lot of a Walmart Supercenter. It's not as bad as it might sound. Way quieter than a truck stop, plus you can go inside to buy snacks and use the bathroom.

I heard my phone buzz a couple of times in the morning but I was far too asleep to care. Once I was finally *awake* awake, I shuffled inside the Walmart to brush my teeth and, I guess, *do my business*, and then I remembered the buzzing and walked straight back to my room to see what it was. Salvador was pretty soundly asleep in his sleeping bag, but on the off chance that he'd woken up and texted me and then gone back to sleep I wanted to be sure to keep my promise and text back.

It wasn't a text, though. It was a missed call notification and a voice mail.

I didn't recognize the number at first but then I realized that the area code was the same as the bookstore I'd been calling and calling in Maine and then my heart skipped four or five beats and I tapped through to the voice mail as fast as I could.

It's funny, how one phone call can change your life. I've had that happen a couple times, actually.

"Hey, there," the friendly guy leaving the voice mail said

into my ear. "This is Cal from One More Time Books up in Freeport. I got your messages about the lost book and I think I got some good news for you. Give me a call back whenever."

My heart went from skipping beats to cramming extra ones in.

Relief and joy flooded into me from all sides.

I bounced on my toes and spun in a quick circle.

I went to hit the "Call Back" button so frantically that I dropped my phone and swore and dropped to my knees to grab it and then hit the button just about hard enough to crack the screen and pressed the phone up to my ear.

The phone rang three times, though it felt like thirty, and I was just about to die but then the ringing stopped and the guy I now knew to be Cal said "Yello!" and I said "Hi there, my name is Coyote and I left you a few messages and then you called back and now I'm calling you back and it's about a book that I left there last summer?"

"Ah, Coyote!" Cal said. "Sorry I missed your calls for a while there. Had the shop closed up so's I could go down and visit my daughter in Key West."

"Okay," I said.

"Try to do that at least once a year. Gorgeous down there. Ever been?"

"Yes," I said, "but—"

"Bit of trouble getting back, of course, with all this Covid business, and—"

"The book!" I interrupted at a shout. "Sorry. But I need to know. You have my book, right?"

"Ah. *Black Bird*, by Mary Oliver, right?"

"Uh, no, it's *Red Bird*."

"Oh, oh, yeah, right. Always mixing up my birds. But, anyways. *Red Bird*. That's the good-news part for you."

My heart melted into a warm puddle of caramel and dribbled down to pool at my feet and a warm smile stretched like taffy across my face. It was a sweet moment, is what I'm saying.

"So you have it?"

"Nope!"

My mouth opened and closed like a goldfish.

"I . . . what?"

"We don't have your book here!" He said it all cheerful. "Never did! Checked our computers."

All the caramel at my feet curdled and turned to tar.

"Why . . . why is that good news?" I asked, barely.

"Didn't you say you were afraid you left it here on accident? Were gonna have to drive all the way over here to get it? Well, you didn't, so you don't! Saves you quite a drive. And, just for future reference, we could've mailed it to you, anyway."

"But . . . I need to find that book."

"Oh. Well, one less place to look, right?" Apparently him and Salvador had been comparing pep talk notes.

"Bye," I said, and hung up. It was rude, I knew; I should've thanked him for his help or wished him a good day or something. But I didn't have it in me.

I stood there, battling emotional nausea. I tried not to look over at my mom's ashes. Failed. There she was. Counting on me.

I'd started with four places to look. I was down to one. It *had* to be there.

"Pittsburgh," I whispered, then gulped. "It's gotta be Pittsburgh."

I was twitchy with anxiety on the whole drive to Pittsburgh. Which was, like, *hours*. So I was pretty twitched out by the time we got there. I didn't want to tell Salvador about the Maine thing yet because it was just too upsetting and obviously I couldn't tell anyone else so I just had to sit there on that devastating piece of information and act like everything was okay and try not to scream or burst into tears. So, not a great ride.

But it was gonna be okay. I'd walk into that thrift shop in Pittsburgh and find the book and read my mom's words and then off we'd go, setting her free and doing it right.

I was too on edge to come up with any wild stories or excuses, buffalo-based or otherwise, to get us to stop at the shop in Pittsburgh. So as we got closer to the city I took a break from my manic fingernail chewing and walked up to Rodeo and said, "Hey, there's a thrift shop I need to stop at in Pittsburgh. I'll give you directions." I was practically sweating through my shirt by that point.

"Coolio," Rodeo said, drumming his fingers on the steering wheel. But of course Candace, being Candace, had to jump in and try to cause problems for no reason, which was kind of her specialty.

"Again?" Candace asked, uninvited, from where she was sitting behind Rodeo. "What's with all these random stops?"

I bit my tongue. "Sometimes it's about the journey," I said, keeping my voice civil. Or, at least, trying to.

"The 'journey' of a thrift store?" she said, crinkling her eyebrows and shooting me a smile I was sure she meant for me to shoot back.

I did not.

"Yes, Candace," I said in a frigidly polite tone. "The journey of a thrift store."

"We've sure been hitting a lot of those," she answered, her own voice getting distinctly less friendly.

"Oh," I said. "Is *two* a big number for you?" I kept my voice light, but Rodeo glanced back with a little confused look on his face. The vibe was not hard to pick up on.

Candace's face was frozen in a little smile that was the exact *opposite* of Wally's.

"Is there something you're looking for?" she asked. And, boy. She asked it *weird*. She asked it exactly like a suspicious person would.

Which made me feel two things at once, and both of them big: *anxious* and *angry*. I'd never felt both extremely nervous and furious at the same time before. It's not a great mix.

I swallowed and clenched my fists and blinked a lot and breathed through my nostrils hard enough to make a sound. But I didn't stop smiling. Which felt creepy even to me.

"Yes. I am looking," I said, "for a flannel."

I'm not sure that in the history of human conversations there have ever been more boring words said with such seething drama.

"Oh!" Rodeo chirped from the driver's seat, I think trying

to cut the truly alarming amount of tension on the bus. "Like a shirt? Sweet!" No one said anything. "Love me a good flannel," he mumbled, losing traction.

Crickets.

Me and Candace stared each other down. Both smiling. Yeah. It was weird.

Candace blinked first. "Fine by me," she said with a shrug. Then she acted all fake casual and yawned and rubbed her neck. "But I'll tell you what. This trip is taking a toll. I'd kill for a real bed in a dark room that doesn't have traffic driving by. Don't know how you guys lived like this for all those years."

It was, possibly, a peace offering. A *let's-move-on* kind of comment. But I wasn't in the mood for hugs or handshakes. Especially if she was going to insult our whole way of life.

"Yeah," I said. "Fun trips aren't for everyone, I guess." I turned my back on her and plugged my phone into the stereo and started the directions to the thrift store, which I'd already punched in before the disastrous conversation.

"Twenty-eight minutes away," I said to whoever happened to be listening, and then marched back to pretend to read on the couch.

Twenty-eight minutes later, I got super excited.

Twenty-eight and a half minutes later, I got worried.

Twenty-nine minutes later, I started to get panicky.

Twenty-nine and a half minutes later, I was, once again, heartbroken.

Here's how it went.

First, we drove up a vaguely familiar street and I saw the thrift store, just like I kinda remembered it. Excitement.

Then, I noticed that there were no cars in the parking lot. Like, zero. Worried.

Next, after Rodeo parked and I started walking as fast and casually as I could up to the entrance, I saw a serious-looking sign on the door (plus I could see that the inside of the store was dark and lifeless). Panic.

Finally, I read the sign. Specifically, the words "closed indefinitely due to the pandemic." Heartbreak.

I cupped my hands around my eyes and pressed up to the window. Definitely dark. Definitely empty.

"*Crap crap crap crap crap*," I whispered.

Salvador came up behind me. "Shoot," he said.

I scanned the shadowy store. There, at the back: a wall of shelves, covered in books. Right freaking there. I could *see* them. And somewhere in them, I was sure, was the book I needed more than anything.

I stepped back and scanned the ground all around.

"What are you looking for?" Salvador asked, a little edge of worry to his voice.

"A brick," I said.

"Dude," he said. "Chill. Let's, like, talk this through."

"There's nothing to talk through," I said through clenched teeth. "The book is in there. I have to get it."

I eyed the bus. Rodeo, Wally, and Candace had gotten off but they had Fig on a leash and they were walking away, toward a little park so that Fig could once again get some work done on her business.

"Coyote," Salvador said. "Take a breath. We don't *know* it's in there. We still have one more place to look. So let's head to Maine. If the book's not there, we can grab a brick and come back."

Hot tears prickled in my eyes when he mentioned Maine and my stomach did a little somersault. There was nothing for me in Maine. This whole epic quest would be an epic failure if I couldn't get the book from those shelves at the back of that store right there in Pittsburgh. I didn't want Salvador or anyone else to know how badly I'd messed everything up, how much of everyone's time I'd wasted. I had to get in there and get that book and then everything would be fine. It would.

I swallowed the sharp lump in my throat and made myself talk less like a hot mess and more like a rational person.

"If we get to Maine and the book's not there and we have to turn around, my dad will figure it out. He'll know I lost the book."

"If you smash that window with a brick, he'll figure it out, too. Come on."

I growled. There's nothing worse than someone else making sense when you're not in the mood for it. I spun back around and pressed my face to the window again. Eyed those books. Then noticed something I hadn't before: a door, on the back wall. To an office, probably, or a storeroom. Half an idea sparked in my mind. It was barely a straw, but I grasped at it. I looked back at the rest of our crew, off in their own world at the park, not looking our way.

"Come on," I said, and took off at a jog.

"Where are we—" Salvador started to say, but then followed. Around the corner of the store. Past the side of the building. To the back. There was a dumpster and a little window high up on the wall and a little cement step that led to a back door. Maybe, just maybe maybe maybe, the owner was back working in the office.

I ran up to the door and knocked. Politely, with my knuckles, so if someone was in there they wouldn't think they were being robbed or something.

"Excuse me?" I called. Waited. No answer. I tried again. Nothing. I pounded harder, with the meaty part of my fist. "Hello?" I shouted. When there was still no answer, I grabbed the knob and tried it. Locked. I shook and yanked on the door, rattling the door on its hinges.

"Easy," Salvador said under his breath, and I saw him looking to the side, where there was a street and a sidewalk a little ways off. A couple was walking on the sidewalk, and they were definitely staring our way. I stepped back and waved and smiled. The guy waved back, a little uncertainly.

My stomach was in knots, my breathing fast.

"We gotta get in there," I said, pointlessly trying the knob one more time. I looked left, right, up and down, hoping for any idea or angle or ray of hope.

And I got one.

I bit my lip. Hard enough to hurt. It was a reckless idea, a far-fetched angle, a dim ray.

A scenario came together in my head. A plan, kind of.

I looked to Salvador. "We need to stay here tonight," I said.

He furrowed his brow. "Here at the thrift store?"

"No. But close. I've got an idea."

Salvador took a step back. "I don't like the look on your face right now, Coyote. The last time you looked like that, I got arrested."

I rolled my eyes. Yeah, sure, once upon a time I'd kinda stolen Yager and led the police on a high-speed bus chase after Rodeo got arrested for kidnapping, but it wasn't *that* big of a deal.

"Stop being so dramatic. You weren't officially arrested. I was. And Rodeo. But no one is getting arrested this time. I promise." I looked away. The kind-of plan was still kind of coagulating inside me. "You have a rideshare app on your phone, right? Like Uber or Lyft or something?"

Salvador swallowed. "Yeah," he said. It was his turn to look nauseous, apparently.

"Good. Come on."

"Coyote, I really don't . . ."

"Sshhh. Follow my lead."

We walked back around to the front, and everyone else was just walking our way.

"It's closed!" I called out, putting a lot of feeling into my cheerful *oh-well-who-cares?* tone.

"Aw, shoot!" Rodeo said.

"Let's hit the road!" I looked out of the corner of my eye at Candace. "Can't *wait* to get back on ol' comfy Yager." Sure enough, I saw her stick her tongue out.

"Ugh," she muttered.

Perfect. I didn't *need* her to play this part, but I thought she might, and it really helped.

"What?" I asked her, trying not to lean in too eagerly.

"Oh," she said, looking at me warily, I'm sure because of our previous conversation. "Nothing. I'm fine. It's just . . . we've spent a *lot* of time on that bus."

Fireworks in my heart. The good kind. Turns out Candace *could* be useful to have around, whether she liked it or not.

"Huh. You're right." I pretended to think it over. "You know, we deserve a little break. We've been driving all day every day and hitting thrift stores and dealing with racists and buying sandwiches and all sorts of stuff. What's the rush? It's getting late anyway. There was a motel a little ways back when we got off the highway. Let's spend the night, get a shower in. Hit the road in the morning."

Candace's whole face lit up. She looked to Rodeo hopefully.

"And," I said, snapping my fingers, "I'm like ninety percent sure that we passed a bowling alley, too."

One of the many weirdo things about Rodeo is that he *loves* bowling. Like, a lot. And, truly, he's terrible at it. I've been beating him since I was nine. I honestly think he just digs the shoes. But, whatever. I was trying to seal the deal. And I did.

A slow smile spread under Rodeo's beard. "Oh, man," he said, nodding. "I could go for knocking down some pins."

"Well, that settles it, then!"

Rodeo brought his hands up for a clap but then stopped. His eyes slid to Wally. "You okay with this idea, brother?"

Wally looked to me. "So, you mean it's like a . . . Pittsburgh party?" he said with a little smile. Wally had still been acting pretty bummed out since the whole gas station hate crime thing, which was super understandable. If a little bowling and good night's sleep could help cheer him up, that alone was worth it.

"*Exactly* like a Pittsburgh party," I said, beaming back.

"I am entirely okay with a Pittsburgh party," Wally said.

Everyone seemed pretty happy about the whole thing. Except for Salvador, who kept giving me worried glances and looking like he'd eaten some sketchy garbage-can food. Again.

And, boom. Phase One of my nuts-but-necessary plan was a go.

The Pittsburgh party itself was perfectly fine, but not at all the point of the whole thing, so I just spent the next few hours smiling and acting chill and trying not to vomit, checking the time too often, and sweating through my shirt. Again.

Wally got a room for himself, and Candace got a room for herself, while Salvador and Rodeo just decided to sleep in Yager to avoid any awkward sleeping arrangements. Candace did invite me to sleep in her room so we could have a little "girls' night," but I declined as quickly as I somewhat politely could. I would say that I appreciated the gesture, but like I said, I'm a terrible liar. We had burritos for dinner, and then Rodeo placed fifth out of five in the bowling (but probably first in the who-had-the-most-fun division, which is not nothing) and then, finally, it was time to turn in.

Then came Phase Two.

Darkness. Quiet. Lots of theatrical yawning from me. I was back in my bedroom, reading. Salvador was doing the same thing in his sleeping bag on the couch. Rodeo, same, in his blanket pile. Ivan and Fig were curled up together on the Throne, which was adorable but irrelevant.

"G'night," I called out as sleepily as I could, and clicked off my light.

A bit later, Salvador did the same thing.

Finally, Rodeo's little reading light clicked off.

Two *great* things about my dad, besides the fact that he loved bowling, which came in especially handy for my plan—he falls asleep fast, and he sleeps deep.

And, sure enough, in a shockingly short amount of time, the steady sounds of deep breathing and gentle snoring came from the front of the bus.

*Now,* I texted to Salvador. We'd both already put our phones on silent.

A couple seconds later Salvador slipped through the curtain into my room. We were both wearing shoes and nervous looks on our faces.

I slooooooowly unlatched and swung open the "Emergency Exit" door on the back wall of my room. Rodeo had long ago disconnected the alarm, so the only sound was a slight but grating creak of rarely used metal hinges.

I hopped down into the parking lot. Salvador landed beside me. I slooooooowly closed the door.

"This is a terrible idea," Salvador said.

"Some of the best ideas are," I said. "Let's go."

# SEVENTEEN

The rideshare car dropped us off on a dark street corner by the thrift shop.

"Geez. Can you believe that guy?" I asked as the car pulled away.

"What?" Salvador asked. "He seemed fine."

"He just *left* us here."

"Well, yeah. I mean, we told him to."

"Still! Seriously, who just drops off a couple of kids alone on a street corner in a big city in the middle of the night? I swear, some people just don't think about the consequences of their actions." I rubbed my hands together. "Ugh. Anyway. Let's go break into this store."

"Wait. Are we actually *breaking* in?"

"Are you really just piecing this together? What did you think we were doing?"

"I don't know. But you said we weren't gonna get arrested, Coyote."

"We're not. As long as we don't get caught. Follow me."

"How are we going to break in?"

Breaking in was Phase Three, but it was the first part that had occurred to me back behind the store earlier that day.

Even I had to admit that Salvador was fairly right in thinking that throwing a brick through the front window was a bad idea. And the back door was securely locked, and not an option. And the back window was useless, because the no-bricks-through-private-property rule applied to it, too, and it was too high up on the wall anyway.

Except for two things: The window wasn't closed. I was sure of it. It was slid open, just a couple inches. And, just as importantly: Yes, it was too high to jump to. But there was a big ol' dumpster pretty darn close to it, and that dumpster would make a heck of a stepping stool.

So, looking around to make sure no one was watching, I led us to the back of the building. And I pointed up at the window.

"See?" I whispered. "It's open!"

"You're not serious."

"I am. Watch."

With a jump and a shimmy, I slid myself up on top of the dumpster. I crawled along the black plastic lid to the back, where it met the brick wall of the building. Then I stood up and eyeballed the window. It was only about four feet above the dumpster, but it was a foot to the side. It was gonna be a stretch-and-jump situation.

"What am I supposed to do?" Salvador whisper-shouted from below.

"Just be the lookout!" I said over my shoulder. "I promised you wouldn't get arrested, remember? I'll go in, grab the book, slip back out, and off we go. Easy-cheesy."

I looked at the window. It was a rectangle, maybe a couple

feet tall and four feet wide. If I could slide the window the rest of the way open, it would be just *barely* big enough for me to fit through. But just barely big enough was all I needed.

"Can you grab me a stick or something to open the window with?"

"I thought I was just the lookout!" Salvador hissed.

"You just got promoted," I spat. "You're now lookout *and* stick-or-something-grabber. Congrats. Hurry up!"

A minute later Salvador handed me a scuffed-up, twisted piece of metal that looked like it used to be part of a bike. Or possibly a shopping cart.

"Perfect."

I leaned and poked and managed to push the window until it was all the way open. Then I stabbed and prodded at the screen until finally it snapped loose . . . and fell with a shockingly loud clatter inside.

Salvador and I both froze.

Then, somewhere in the darkness: the unmistakable high-pitched sound of a siren. My whole body flashed with electric panic. I said a word and spun around to jump down off the dumpster and flee the scene of the not-quite crime.

But then I froze again. Because on the road in the distance at the end of the alley, a car rolled by. A car that was *not* a police car, but a car which did have an incredibly loud and whiny engine that sounded *like* a siren which, apparently, is in fact an absolutely mistakable sound. The car kept cruising out of sight and the squeaky wail faded with it.

I gave my heart permission to begin beating again.

That car needed to get a new fan belt. And I needed to get a grip.

I started breathing again and turned to look back up at the window.

The opening looked small. And kind of far away, really.

"Coyote, I really don't think you . . ."

I knew that if I listened to Salvador I'd probably realize that he was making sense and then I'd lose my nerve and we wouldn't get that book and then . . . well, I couldn't really face that "and then."

*"This is for you, Mom,"* I mumbled under my breath. And then I leaped.

I caught the window frame with both hands.

And just hung there.

Sure, I'd done pull-ups before, in PE. But not very well. I wasn't, like, a real athletic star. The library was more my jam.

And, dangling against the brick wall, hanging a few feet (but what felt like miles and miles) above rock-hard concrete, it really showed. I groaned and gasped and kind of twitched a bit. But that was about it.

I was just about to drop when I felt something under my feet. Holding my weight. Taking the pressure off my hands.

It was Salvador. Chest pressed to the wall, arms up above his head, his hands under the soles of my shoes.

"You. Got. This. Coyote," he grunted between breaths. "I'll boost. You jump. On. Three."

Salvador had apparently promoted himself to burglar-booster as well. Which I was one hundred percent down with.

"Okay," I squeaked. I readied my muscles. My hands. My heart. My soul. I bent my knees as much as I could.

"One," I said.

"Two," Salvador gasped.

"Three!" we said together.

I felt Salvador surge beneath me, shoving up. I pushed off with my legs and gave it everything I had with my arms and I felt myself rocket up and my eyes came even with the bottom of the window frame then kept going right past it and I ducked my head and leaned into the opening and jerked myself forward and scrambled my feet in scraping kicks along the bricks and then my head was through and then part of my shoulders and I let go with one hand and thrust my arm through the window and kind of wedged myself there, mostly still dangling outside but now partly inside and I kept wiggling and struggling and kicking until I was balanced, my head and shoulders inside, bottom half outside, the window frame digging into my stomach.

It hurt. But I'd almost made it.

I squinted into the dark room I was on the verge of illegally entering. It was a little office. I could just make out some shelves, a few boxes, and right below me, a desk.

Something I'd never thought about before that moment but which quickly became painfully clear to me was that there is no good way to drop into an office headfirst. There was no way to turn around in the tight window, no way to swing my legs in ahead of my head. I was gonna have to dive. I didn't *think* I saw any knives or candlestick holders or anything particularly stabby on the desk.

"Are you stuck?" I heard Salvador dimly call from somewhere below my feet outside, and I realized that he was, basically, talking to my butt. This whole situation was already messy enough without adding that awkwardness.

"Here goes nothing," I said, and dove. Or, rather, crashed. "Dove" implies some sort of gracefulness. And there was definitely none of that.

A brief, exhilarating plunge through darkness. Then a definitely *un*exhilarating impact with a very hard surface: hands, then elbows, then face. My shoulders were just starting to hit when my momentum carried me forward off the desk and then it all happened again on the floor, this time with the added fun of my legs slamming into the desk. There was a clattery waterfall of little thuds and bangs as whatever junk had been on the desk came down to the floor with me. I've heard of people being *cat burglars* before. But I was definitely more of a *walrus burglar*.

I lay there for a second. And then just before I could start worrying about the noise my crash landing had made, the pain hit. It was kind of a general, all-over pain, but with some real highlights in my left arm and my face.

"Unngggh," I said, or something like that.

"Coyote!"

"Ungggh?" I asked, or something like that.

"Coyote, are you okay?"

I shook my head, trying to clear it.

"I'm calling your dad!"

That cleared my head. And quick.

"No!" I called, sitting up fast and ignoring the lightning bolt of pain behind my eye. "I'm fine! Great! Marvelous!" For the record, at least two of those three words did *not* apply to me.

I struggled to my feet, almost fainting when I made the mistake of trying to put some weight on my left arm. Definitely something off there. But that was a *later* problem.

"I'm gonna open the door!" I called through the window.

I stumbled toward where the door should be and then fumbled around with my good arm and found the knob and undid the lock and turned the knob and pulled and then, just when things were going kind of terribly, it all really went to heck.

The second that door opened, a blaring alarm started blasting. A high-pitched, ear-piercing, *wa-wo-wa-wo-wa-wo* kind of alarm.

I froze. Salvador, standing outside, gaped at me through the doorway.

I said some words.

"Come on!" he said. "We gotta go!"

*Wa-wo-wa-wo-wa-wo!*

In panic mode, I took one step toward him. And stopped. "No! I gotta get the book!"

"Are you nuts?"

"Possibly! But I have to get it!"

*Wa-wo-wa-wo-wa-wo!*

Salvador, who is a very good friend, stared at me for one second, then started pushing his way inside. "Okay, fine, let's look quick, but—"

"No! You stay out here. You can't get caught. Hide. I'll be out in a minute and we'll take off."

He looked around frantically. "Where can I hide?!"

"In the dumpster!"

"Are you serious?"

*"Or behind it or under it or wherever but I don't have time to talk right now I'm kind of in the middle of something I'll come back for you in a minute please just hide I don't want you to get in trouble there's no time!"* I said all that, kind of, and then slammed the door in his face.

And the race was on.

I shuffled blindly across the room to where I could just barely see a door, and I opened it and felt my way down a little hallway, and then I was walking out into the thrift store sales floor. I made my way toward the wall of books, and as I did, I fished in my pocket and pulled out my phone and turned on the flashlight.

I flashed the light over the wall of books and tried not to cry because, man, it sure seemed like a *lot* of books to try and skim with the cops probably on the way, and they weren't in any order or sections or anything.

But there was no time to cry. I jogged to the left side and started skimming.

*"Red Bird Red Bird Red Bird Red Bird Red Bird,"* I mumbled, my fingers racing along the spines as I hunted.

The wall of books had four big sections, and I tackled them one by one, top to bottom, left to right. I tried to ignore the throbbing in my arm and the dull ache in my face.

When I finished the first section, I stood up to start at the top of the next. The shock and adrenaline of my walrus fall was wearing off and the pain was getting worse with every breath. I rubbed at my eyes.

"Okay, okay, keep it together, Coyote," I mumbled. "I bet it takes ten minutes for the cops to get here. You got this."

I'm glad I hadn't actually bet. Because it was literally probably five seconds later that the store was lit up by *actually* unmistakable red and blue flashing lights through the front windows. Every cell in my body jolted.

I said some words. Swallowed back some terror nausea, which it turns out is even worse than emotional nausea.

I wanted to run. I wanted to burst into tears. I wanted to curl up in a ball on the floor.

But instead I shook my head. And I kept looking. It would all be worth it when I found the book.

Someone outside shouted something. I ignored it.

*"Red Bird Red Bird Red Bird Red Bird Red Bird."*

A bright flashlight beam swept the store. Froze on me. Some more shouting. Some more ignoring.

The front door rattled. But didn't open. Which was confusing for a second. But then I realized that, of course, the cops didn't have the keys to the place. I hoped they didn't get my brick idea.

I finished the second section and moved to the third.

More door rattling, more light flashing, more shouting. I stopped just long enough to turn toward the front and wave. Showed them my two basically empty hands, just to be safe. Winced when I waved my left arm, which was shifting rapidly from *super painful* to *excruciating*.

I couldn't see them through the glare of the flashlight, but the shouting and rattling did calm down a bit.

I was halfway through the third section when I heard the crunch of more tires from the parking lot and saw the flash of another set of headlights and then heard a car door slam and a conversation and then the jangling of keys in the doorway.

Great. Someone had shown up with the keys. Party pooper.

I got to the bottom of the third section and was just standing up when the door banged open and the flashlight framed me against the bookshelf and a voice called out, "Freeze. Police!"

I'm not gonna lie: It was scary. Scary enough that, for a second, I forgot about my arm and my face and, maybe, even the book I was desperately looking for.

I'd read books before where it said that someone was so scared they peed their pants and I always thought it was just exaggeration but, phew, it was a close call.

"It's just me!" I said, quick. "I'm alone! And unarmed! It's just me!"

"Don't move!"

"I'm not!"

"Keep your hands up!"

"I am!"

The voice and the light moved toward me and then the cop was standing there, a few feet away, taking me in. It was a female cop and she had a pretty solid frown on. When she'd gotten the break-in call, she probably hadn't been expecting to find a thirteen-year-old with tears streaming down her cheeks.

"What's going on?" she asked, and there was exactly zero kindness in her voice. Which was fair.

I swallowed and tried to manage my emotions, my terror, and my pain and still get some words out. "I'm just looking for something."

"What the hell are you looking for in my store in the middle of the night?!" asked a gruff voice, which I was guessing belonged to the store owner. Also fair.

"Sir, I'll handle this. Please stay back," the officer said. "What are you looking for?"

"A book."

There was a pause.

"A book?"

"Yes."

"Why in the hell are you—"

"Sir! *I* will handle this." She actually turned her head to bark that over her shoulder. She turned back toward me and blew out an exasperated sigh.

"Why did you break in and trespass to look for a book?"

I sucked a couple ragged breaths in. "I need it," I said, voice shaky. "I really, *really* need it. It was my mom's. And I lost it. And I need to get it back."

The cop shook her head. "Listen. I don't think your mom wants you out—"

"My mom's dead," I said, and the cop broke off quick. I wiped at my cheeks. "My mom died and this was her special book and I think I left it here on accident and the store was closed and I just . . ." I choked a bit and sniffed and then started again. "I just . . . *really* need it. Please. You can arrest me or whatever, but I just need to find it first. Please."

Another pause.

Then the cop said something into the walkie-talkie thing strapped to her chest, and then she backpedaled a few steps and there was a muffled conversation between her and the store owner, and then she walked back up to me.

"Go ahead," she said. "Make it quick. Then you're coming with me."

I was too happy to be scared about what would happen next. "Thank you thank you thank you," I said, and spun back to the shelves, to that fourth and final section where the book just had to be, it just *had* to.

Left to right. Book by book. Looking, desperately. Knowing that, at any second, I was gonna see those words that my eyes and my heart and my soul were looking for and then I'd have it, I'd have my mom's book with my mom's writing there in my hands and they could arrest me, they could throw me in jail, and it wouldn't matter because I'd have it and I'd be able to set her free, the right way. I'd be able to do that for her.

I finished a shelf. Dropped down to the next one. Finished that one.

The relief and gratitude I'd felt when that cop gave me the go-ahead was souring spine by spine into disbelief and devastation.

It hadn't been in Cheyenne and it hadn't been in Kansas and it wasn't waiting in Maine and I had nowhere else to look. It had to be here.

But, book by book and title by title and spine by spine, it wasn't.

And then I got to the very bottom shelf. And then I was halfway through it. And then I had to do an awful lot of blinking because everything was blurry. And then I was touching the title of the last book on the last shelf. And it wasn't *Red Bird*.

I took a shuddering breath. And I stood up. And I turned around to face the cop.

"It isn't here," I kind of managed to say.

The cop *tsk*ed her tongue. "You already checked all those?" she asked, flashing her light at the rest of the shelves. I nodded miserably. She sighed. "Sometimes it takes a fresh set of eyes. What's this book called?"

I gulped. "*Red Bird*. By Mary Oliver. It's black with red and white writing."

"Mmkay." She walked over to the end of the bookshelves and started scanning.

It's funny how kindness, which is the best thing in the world, can sometimes make you feel worse. And when that cop, who didn't know me, who had every right to growl at me and shout at me and arrest me, instead starting *helping* me? I kinda lost it. A sob broke free, and then another.

My crying before had been kind of a *light drizzle* or even *scattered showers* situation, but now I was in full-on *downpour*.

"Thank you," I choked out between gasps.

"Don't thank me. You live with your dad?" she asked, still skimming the books.

"Uh-huh."

"You got a phone?"

"Uh-huh."

"Call him. Give it to me when he picks up."

I sniffed. "Um. Could you . . . not tell him?"

"Excuse me?" She stopped searching to look at me.

"Please don't tell my dad about the book thing. You can tell him that I broke in and that I'm arrested or whatever but please please please don't tell him that I lost the book."

The officer frowned. She gave me a good long look. "Answer me honestly. Are you afraid that if he finds out, he'll hurt you?"

I blinked, and then realized what she meant. "Oh, no no no no," I said. "I'm just afraid he'll be, like . . . really sad. Like, *really* sad."

"Oh. Okay."

"So you won't tell him? About the book?"

The officer blew a breath out through her nose. "I will tell your father that you illegally broke into this store. And if he asks why, I will tell him that it's up to him to ask *you* why, because frankly that is none of my business and not a law enforcement issue."

"Thank you! Thank you!"

"Don't thank me. Call him."

So it was that a bit later I heard Rodeo's confused and sleepy voice in my ear.

"Coyote?"

"Hey," I said. My arm was really, really hurting and I was having a hard time concentrating. "I need you to talk to someone real quick." I'm pretty sure I heard him say "*What?*" but I was already handing the phone over.

I gave the shelves a fairly hopeless re-check as I listened to half of a very awkward and unfortunate conversation.

Eventually she hung up and handed the phone back and said, "He'll be here in a few minutes." She tightened her lips. "I'm sorry about the book. Doesn't look like it's here."

I nodded.

"Well." It was the gruff voice of the owner, sounding somewhat less gruff. "There is another box of books. In the back. Stuff I never sorted and shelved. Could be in there. I'll go grab it."

A funny little tingly feeling started spreading in my chest at those words. The feeling you get when you know that something awesome is about to happen. The feeling of a miracle just around the corner.

The guy walked into the back. A few seconds later his voice called out, all gruff again, "Hey! What happened to my desk?"

My stomach sank. "Oh," I hollered. "I did. Sorry."

He came back out grumbling and shooting me a scowl, but carrying a big cardboard box that did, kind of, look like a miracle. He flumped it down onto the floor.

"Knock yourself out."

I dropped to my knees and started digging with my good arm, hope burning like a flame in my chest.

And digging. And digging. Digging for that miracle.

Until there was a pile of books on the floor around me. And an empty box in front of me. And no *Red Bird* in my hand.

The thing about miracles is they don't happen all that often. If they did, we wouldn't call them miracles.

"This is impossible," I said, looking up at the cop and the store owner. My voice sounded broken. "I've read a million stories. This isn't how it's supposed to go. I was supposed to find it, just when I, like, thought all hope was lost." I shook my head. "What kind of story is this?"

"This ain't a story, kid," the owner said. "It's a thrift shop that you broke into. Pick up those books. I wanna go back to bed."

And then Rodeo was there. And the cop was filling him in.

Have you ever seen a man who never looks disappointed look *super* disappointed? I have.

At one point he looked around kind of confused and started to say, "Hey, where's . . . ," and I knew he was gonna ask about Salvador, and I made some serious eye contact with him and shook my head, and god bless him, he dropped it. I don't think at that moment he was interested in doing me any favors, but I know for a fact he wasn't interested in getting Salvador in any trouble.

Rodeo gave the owner fifty bucks for the busted screen, and he agreed not to press any charges. And then both the understand-ably grouchy owner and the surprisingly kind cop did me a solid and didn't say a word about the book that we didn't find. I shot them each my most serious silent *thank you so freaking much* eyes, and the cop kinda dipped her chin at me but the owner just scowled. Once again: fair.

And then it was me and Rodeo sitting in Yager. He sat there for a few breaths, eyes straight ahead, gripping the steering wheel. Didn't even start the engine.

"You really scared me," he said.

"I'm sorry."

"You can't do anything that . . . you can't . . ." He shook his head, looking for the words. "I can't lose you, little bird."

"You won't," I said.

"We'll talk about all this in the morning."

"Okay. But I think I need to go to the hospital."

His head snapped back toward me. "What? Why?"

I held up my left arm, which was pulsing with a pain that made my teeth clench. "I'm pretty sure I broke this."

"Serious or joking?" he asked, his voice going high.

"Serious."

My dad said some words. He started the engine and we started moving and then I said, "Wait! We need to pull back behind the store first!" Rodeo hit the brakes.

"Why?"

"Salvador's in the dumpster."

My dad blew out a long breath. He rubbed his nose between a thumb and finger. "Of course he is. All right."

# CHAPTER
## EIGHTEEN

*H*ospital emergency rooms in the middle of the night are well-lit but grim places. No one is there for any fun reason, and no one there is having the best day of their life. While we waited to see a doctor, I sat next to a guy who'd been stabbed. He was actually pretty nice.

Salvador (who, it turned out, had been hiding *behind* the dumpster, not in it) apologized profusely to Rodeo and I swore up and down that Salvador had tried to talk me out of the whole thing at every turn, so they were cool, which was good.

Cool with each other, anyway. They were both pretty unhappy with me.

There were doctors and nurses and X-rays and, eventually, a cast. A nurse did pull me aside at some point to really dig into how I ended up with a broken wrist and a black eye (which was news to me, but which made sense after landing on my face on a desk) and I realized she was making sure, just like the cop, that Rodeo wasn't the problem.

"The only way that man would ever hit me is if I was on fire and he was trying to put it out," I said. "Which actually kind of happened once." And then I told her the whole story of my little breaking-and-entering adventure, or at least the most relevant parts.

And at one point during all that waiting, Rodeo asked the question I'd been dreading.

"Why, darling? Why in the world did you go break into that place?"

I'd already settled on the only possible lie that had a chance of working. "I don't know," I said, looking sincerely glum. "I thought it'd be fun. You know. Sneak out, have a little adventure. I didn't think I'd get caught." That last part was the only true part and it was pretty darn flimsy as a story, but luckily at that point a nurse came in to poke me with a needle and Rodeo, who is a big baby when it comes to anything medical, had to leave before he passed out.

And then us three were driving home. Well, driving back to the motel parking lot. I had a bright pink cast on my arm and a real doozy of a black eye and we were all super sleepy and the sun was just starting to rise. Rodeo was driving silent without even any music on and Salvador was kind of sulking in the next seat over. It was super awkward.

"Okay," I tried. "So maybe that wasn't my best idea ever."

"Not in the mood, Coyote," Rodeo growled, and I even saw Salvador shake his head.

"Right," I said.

And then it started building inside me. I don't know if it was the pain, or the exhaustion, or the defeat. Most likely it was all of it put together, plus the fact that it was really starting to sink in that, amid all that midnight madness, I hadn't found the book.

And I had nowhere else to look. I had some vague plans about going through my notes and scouring my memory for other possible thrift stores or maybe calling one of the ones that "didn't think" they had it, but I was grasping at straws and I knew it.

What was building inside me wasn't just sadness and hopelessness, although there was plenty of that. What was building inside me was mostly *mad*. A big ol' steaming pile of mad.

Mad that my dad had kept that box of ashes secret from me for six years.

Mad that he'd kept my mom locked up for all that time.

Mad that he hadn't kept that book safe, that one priceless irreplaceable book that would tell us what my mom wanted.

Mad that I'd lost it. That I'd just picked it up and given it away and it had been right there in my clueless hands.

Mad that I'd looked and looked and looked and I didn't, couldn't, wouldn't find it and I'd never get to see what my mom had written down.

Mad that I didn't fit anywhere. Mad that kids at school made fun of me and didn't like me and all I'd wanted for years was to go to school and make friends and have friends and not be alone.

Mad even a little at Salvador, the best friend ever, because he was all Mr. Popular and kissing everybody and had a million friends and I didn't even have one besides him and he lived hundreds of miles away and how was that fair?

Mad that my dad had brought some sort of annoying *girlfriend* along on a journey that was supposed to be all about my mom.

Mad at my mom. For dying. For leaving me all this mess. I didn't feel good about that one. But it was there.

Mad at my sisters. For dying. And for making me do all this alone. Felt even worse about that one.

And somewhere in that silent bus ride that's all I became. When I should have been sleeping or apologizing or planning my next step, I just sat there hurting and seething until my anger was a white-hot ball inside me as we pulled into the motel.

None of this was fair.

And when a big ball of *mad* that white-hot builds up inside you and it's all mixed up with sadness and heartbreak and, yeah, maybe some embarrassment, sometimes all it needs is a target.

At that moment, Candace walked up the steps onto Yager.

Rodeo, apparently, had called her.

She looked from me to Salvador to Rodeo.

No one said anything.

"Well," she said at last. "Should we talk about this?"

Ooooh boy. It was that "we" that really lit my fuse. Like this, all of this, *any* of this, had anything to do with her.

I opened my mouth to say exactly that and a whole bunch more, but Rodeo beat me to it.

He actually kind of chuckled first. Which was very on-brand for Rodeo. But, let me tell you, when you're white-hot furious, there are few sounds more infuriating than a goddamn chuckle.

"Oh, it's one of those things. Just made a mistake. She must *really* want a flannel shirt."

He meant it as a joke, I think. He's a real let's-all-just-get-along type guy.

But then Candace kinda twisted her mouth and said the following words: "I don't think this is about a flannel shirt, babe."

*Babe? Babe?!*

She had the nerve to call my dad *that*, at that moment, with me right there? And she had the nerve to be *right* about something?

I stood up. I was shaking.

"What are you even doing here?" I asked. And, to be honest, my *ask* was pretty darn close to a shout.

Three faces turned toward me. Three open mouths.

"Seriously!" I pointed a vicious finger at Candace but turned my furious face to Rodeo. "Why did you bring her? How could you do that?"

"Coyote!" my dad started to say, but I was just getting going.

"Having *her* here, this woman I barely know, who apparently scratches your back and calls you *babe*, having *her* here along on this trip to put *my mom* to rest? This trip that is supposed to be about *her*?!" Tears were coming now, hot and angry. "That is a no-go, Dad. That is the biggest no-go in the history of no-gos. This is something we should be doing together. Me. And you. Me and you and no one else."

I paused to wipe my eyes and catch my breath and caught a glimpse of Salvador sitting there, looking awkward. "Well, and Salvador. He's basically family. Me and you and Salvador." Ivan, sitting on the dashboard, gave me an ears-back glare. I clicked my tongue impatiently. "And Ivan. But that is *it*. *She* should not be a part of this. I mean, who brings a *dog* onto a *bus*?" I chose in the heat of the moment to ignore the fact that in the last year I had brought both a cat and a goat onto the bus.

Rodeo looked stunned. Dismayed. Ambushed. But, also, maybe just a little mad. He looked quick to Candace and then back to me. He held his hands up and he got the little wrinkle he gets between his eyebrows when he's a little overwhelmed.

"Now hold up, darling. I am *not* loving this tone. I don't think you should—"

"No. Hush, Rodeo." My dad got interrupted. And not by me. By *Candace*, of all people. "She's right. I . . . I don't know what I was thinking. Coming along. This isn't my place." She stepped forward toward me and I saw that her eyes were all teary and I looked off to the side, breathing through my nose, holding tight to my anger. "I'm sorry," she said, technically to me even though I wasn't looking. "I'm sorry, Coyote. I shouldn't have come."

"Hey," I said, my voice shaking. "Look at you. Getting something right."

"Coyote," Rodeo said, his voice a warning.

"Sshhh," Candace said to him. "It's all right." Her voice was quivery, and I couldn't look her in the eye, which was fine because she stepped away from me and over to Rodeo. "It's time for me to go."

"But, Candace," Rodeo protested, and she said, "No, it's okay, really, I don't want to be where I'm not welcome," and I said, "And yet here you are." I pointed with my nonbroken arm. "There's the door."

Yeah. It was harsh. Even I knew it. I almost, for one little second, felt bad. Maybe I actually even did, a little.

But then I made the mistake of looking at my dad. My dad who was very far from perfect but who just wanted everyone to be happy. My dad who always tried to treat every soul he met with kindness and had taught me to do the same. My dad who had spent the last six years trying to not be sad. And failing, a lot. My dad who had just, finally maybe, actually started moving on. Who had, finally maybe, made a friend that wasn't his weirdo daughter. I looked at my dad.

And he didn't look mad at all. Even though he could have been. Maybe *should* have been. But, no.

He just looked . . . small. And defeated. Deflated. Hollowed out. His shoulders were slumped. And his eyes were all red and watery.

I opened my mouth. But nothing came out. And he wasn't looking at me, anyway. He was looking at the floor.

And then Candace was walking down the stairs and off the bus, and Rodeo was following behind, and they were talking low in the parking lot, and then they were hugging.

I was feeling like several different kinds of garbage. Physically and emotionally and mentally and spiritually, I was just wasted and burned and sour. I stomped back to my room and really wished I had a door to slam. Whisking a curtain closed just isn't as satisfying, no matter how hard you do it. I flopped down onto my bed way harder than you should with a black eye and a freshly broken arm and I winced and hissed but, what the heck, why not add a little more pain to the mix?

I was some version of asleep almost instantly. Somewhere along the line I heard the door opening and closing and voices and I heard Wally getting back on board and then we were driving and then we stopped and I sat up and peeked out my window and saw we were at the train station. Candace got off the bus with her big backpack and she had Fig in a little pet carrier. Her and Rodeo had some long goodbye. Which did include a significant hug. But no kiss. Which was good. I guess?

And then we were driving away and I secretly watched her walk into the train station and she looked really alone and kinda small and I saw Fig's big ridiculous ears through the mesh side of the pet carrier and even though Candace walking into that train station was technically me *winning*, I'll be honest, it didn't feel like it. Not by a long shot.

The thing about white-hot anger, maybe, is that holding it in feels awful, but letting it all out feels even worse.

And then we were rolling again.

I didn't know where we were going. I'd been calling the shots the whole time and we'd just hit our last dead end. But then I remembered: Rodeo didn't know that Maine was a dead end. He thought that was our destination, and Wally still needed a ride there.

So, off to Maine we were headed, I was sure. For no reason. Well, dropping off a friend is a pretty good reason. But what was I gonna do once we got there and Rodeo said, "Okay, darling, where do we set your mom free?" and I said, "Beats me" and then had to come clean about losing that book and making him drive all the way across the entire country for nothing? What then?

I didn't know what to do. I'd held the dark secret about

losing the book for so long that I wasn't ready to let it go just yet. I couldn't face the look in Rodeo's eyes. I couldn't break him more than I already had. Not yet.

And, man, I was tired.

So I laid back down. The problem wasn't going anywhere, unfortunately, even though we were.

I didn't dream about my mom while I was sleeping. But I think that, maybe, she was dreaming about me. Because when I woke up, hours later, with the bus rumbling down the road beneath me, I blinked and focused my eyes, and they focused all by themselves right on the memory box sitting on my bookshelf.

Once upon a time, I'd gone on quite a quest to save that old box. It was a whole thing.

It was a box that contained a bunch of worthless junk that meant the world to me. A memory box that I'd made with my mom and my sisters and that we'd buried in a park together, and then they'd died, all together, and left me and my dad, all alone.

Inside were pictures. And color pages. And locks of hair. And drawings. And notes. All those little things that families do and share and make before they disappear.

I'd loaded it on Yager first thing when we'd planned this trip.

Laying there, I still felt like garbage. Even more so, maybe. I think the super aspirin was wearing off.

But my eyes landed on that memory box.

Funny thing about that box. I looked through it, sometimes. And it always made me feel really, really sad. But it also always made me feel better, after.

At that moment, one thing I knew I could sure use was some feeling better.

So I crawled out of bed. Literally. My head was *pounding*.

And I sat down cross-legged on the floor in front of that shelf. And I pulled that memory box into my lap. And, like I did every time I looked inside, I took a deep, deep breath. And then I opened it up.

And I looked through it all. I looked at the pictures. At those smiling faces. Faces that I loved, so much. And missed, so much.

I looked at the sloppy, little-kid handwriting. The scrawled crayon and backward letters.

I remembered. I missed. I loved. And I felt really, really sad.

I don't know what I was looking for.

But I knew it when I found it.

It was down at the bottom.

My mom, apparently, had made us do this little family activity. We'd each done it, and we'd stapled our papers together. At the top of our page, each of us had drawn a crayon self-portrait. And written our name. And then, underneath the picture, the other two had written a sentence. Clearly, we'd been told to write what we loved about that sister.

On top was my older sister's. Her picture was the best, because she was the oldest. I looked at the picture. And I read the words. What I loved about her, apparently, was that she played babies with me. I remembered. And I missed. And I loved.

I skipped past mine, right to my little sister's. The picture was really something. Stick figure body, lumpy head, scribble hair, oversized smile. It was an adorable mess, because she was five when she drew it. And five was as old as she was ever gonna be. What I loved about her was that she was funny. I remembered. And I missed. And I loved.

Finally, I turned to my page. The little picture I drew of myself, with long hair and blue jeans and kind of frightening eyelashes. What my older sister loved about me was that I was fun to play with. I looked at what my little sister had written. She was just learning letters, and even with I'm sure a lot of help from Mom, her writing was a train wreck. But I could read it.

*I love Ella because she is always nice.*

Always nice.

Always nice?

The words were getting blurry. Dang it, Coyote. I thought I'd done enough crying lately. Apparently not.

That "always nice" was sticking in my head with the words "there's the door" and how alone Candace had looked when she walked into the train station and how Rodeo was gonna look when I told him I lost the book.

I carefully put all the treasures back inside the box, closed it, and put it on my shelf.

The memories, like always, made me feel really, really sad. But this time, they didn't also make me feel better. They made me feel worse.

I wanted to crawl back into bed and close my eyes and lay there for possibly ever.

My bladder had other ideas.

I stood up and grabbed the little bottle of aspirin and checked the time on my phone and swallowed one of the pills dry, and then I braced myself and opened the curtain to my room. I didn't want to face everybody, but I wanted to wet my pants even less.

Rodeo was driving, of course. Salvador was sitting up in one of the bus seats. Wally was reading on the couch. Ivan gave me a *hello* blink from Wally's lap. The bus seemed empty without Fig. And Candace, I guess.

I walked up and stood next to Wally. Rodeo saw me in the rearview mirror and we made eye contact and I said, "Bathroom break?" and he gave a thumbs-up but didn't say anything.

I looked down at Wally. He looked from my arm in a cast to my surely disheveled hair and then to my black eye.

"You should see the other guy," I said. Then shook my head. "Actually, the other guy is a desk. And he's fine."

Wally offered a small smile. "Rough night?" he asked.

I was guessing that Salvador or Rodeo had filled him in on all my nocturnal adventures, so I just nodded. And, dang it, started to tear up again. Honestly, I was gonna get dehydrated.

Wally reached up and took hold of my hand. Gently.

"Rough nights happen," he said. "But then there is the morning." And he gave my hand a little squeeze.

I looked out at the world flying by. It was almost sunset.

"But it's getting dark," I said.

Wally shrugged. "Of course. Always. But never forever." And he gave my hand another squeeze.

I was really glad I hadn't kicked Wally out, too. Not that I would have. *He's* not calling Rodeo "babe." But, still.

We stopped at a truck stop, and Rodeo gassed up Yager and I went to the bathroom and then bought a bag of Funyuns and the guy at the register had a black eye, too, and he looked at mine and cocked an eyebrow at me and I said "Fell out of a window" and he nodded and said "Dirt bike into a tree" and then we did a fist bump and out the door I went. It's funny, what you can bond with folks over.

I walked over to a little curbed-in area with some bushes and a spindly tree and a bunch of gravel. I wasn't quite ready to get back on the bus yet. Having one hand made everything tricky, and I held the Funyuns bag in my mouth and tore it open with my good hand.

I heard footsteps behind me and turned to see Salvador walking up.

"Hey," he said.

"Hey. Sorry again about almost getting you arrested."

"It's okay."

"I have something serious to ask you, Salvador, and it's really okay if the answer is no."

"I'm not breaking into anywhere else with you, Coyote." He pursed his lips. "Unless you *really* need to."

"No, that's not it." I blew out a breath. "I need you to button my pants."

"What?"

I waved my cast at him. "I couldn't get them buttoned. And it feels weird. I'll have to switch to my sweatpants. But, for now . . ."

Salvador was definitely blushing a little. "Oh. Okay."

And then he bent down and got it over with and it wasn't a big deal because it's just a button but when he straightened back up his blush faded and his face got all concerned. I was barely holding it together and apparently it was showing.

"How you doing, Coyote?"

"Not good."

"I can tell." He looked at Yager. Rodeo was climbing back aboard. Then he looked back to me.

"Maybe we should go up in the Attic."

I nodded. "Yeah. I think we should."

# NINETEEN

The Attic is just what we call the roof of Yager. It's one of my favorite places because it feels really alone but in a good way and kind of magical. And it's the place where Salvador and I really started becoming best friends, once upon a time.

There were rules about riding in the Attic, though. For obvious reasons. Falling onto a desk is probably nothing compared to falling from the top of a moving bus.

A cool thing about best friends is that sometimes they just *know* what you need, and besides knowing that I needed a ride in the Attic, Salvador also knew that I wasn't ready to face Rodeo yet.

So he's the one that went up to Rodeo and did the ask. There was a short little convo between them because I knew that technically we were in violation of one of the Attic rules, which is that I can only ride up there when it's dark. But I guess Rodeo knew what I needed, too, because then we were driving away, and not toward the highway. Taking turns that took us away from the houses and buildings and onto narrower roads with a lot more trees.

At some point I saw a sign that mentioned "Lord's Valley,"

which seemed both peaceful and scary at the same time. And then we were rumbling along a gravel road, and Rodeo brought Yager to a stop.

Salvador unhooked the rope ladder that was tied up to the ceiling by the hatch to the roof. He clambered up first and opened the hatch, and then I learned that climbing a rope ladder with an arm in a cast is almost as hard as buttoning jeans with an arm in a cast. Not impossible, though, and soon Salvador was helping pull me up and out and onto the roof.

We crawled forward, to the front of the bus, until we were by the little railing that Rodeo had installed. We lay there, on our stomachs, propped up on our elbows. The sun was somewhere behind the trees, sinking below the horizon. All around us, birds were calling.

Salvador looked at me. He kinda smiled. "You know, with that black eye you actually look kind of tough."

I wanted to smile back. But couldn't quite manage it. "I don't feel tough," I said.

Salvador nodded. "You wanna shout secrets?"

Shouting secrets is something me and Salvador did once, up in the Attic. It's cool because, if the engine's roaring, you can shout your secrets to the world and no one hears them but you.

"I don't feel like shouting," I said. "And I'm tired of secrets. Can we just talk?"

"Sure."

I thumped on the roof three times with my nonbroken fist. The engine started, and we started moving.

It's exciting every time, riding in the Attic. Not like heart-pounding-roller-coaster exciting, just being-up-high-flying-through-the-treetops-with-fresh-air-on-your-face exciting.

I looked to Salvador. And tried really hard to keep my throat and eyes under control because I thought it'd be nice to have *one* conversation without tearing up.

"I'm a mess," I said. "I'm a messy mess who makes messes." Salvador just blinked at me. "I lost the book and I completely failed at finding it and I was super mean to Candace and now she's alone with Fig and Rodeo's alone and I almost got you arrested again and I made you hide in a dumpster and button my pants and we're never gonna find that book and I'll never get to set my mom free the right way and I don't have any friends except for you and I'm surprised I even have you because all I do is ruin things and mess things up."

I'm glad we were just talking because that would have been a *lot* to shout. I probably woulda passed out.

Salvador took a second to process all that. "I think you've . . ." He frowned. "Kinda messed up a little here and there." He was being easy on me. Like, the easiest easy of all easinesses. I arched an eyebrow at him and opened my mouth to say something, but he jumped back in first. "Like everybody does, Coyote. Like *everybody* does."

I was not in the mood to be reassured. "No," I said. "Not like everybody. I'm not like *any*body." I huffed out a breath. "I don't *fit*, Salvador. I don't fit anywhere. And I'm afraid that . . . that . . . that I'll never find where I fit."

"Since when do you wanna fit in?" he said, trying to smile and make a joke of it.

I was also not in the mood for that.

"Since forever!" I said, and this time I actually *was* close to shouting. "You think that just because I, like, want to be my own person that I don't want that person to fit in or have friends or not be lonely? Can't I want both?"

He wiped his smile off quick. "Of course you can."

I wiggled up so I was kneeling, which was technically against the Attic rules, but I was all worked up and raw and hurting and it just wasn't a lying-down kind of moment.

"Well? Then? What's *wrong* with me?" I was definitely in full shout now.

Salvador's eyes widened and then narrowed, and he tightened his lips and got up on his own knees.

"There's *nothing* wrong with you!" he said, and now he was shouting, too. "I'm sorry that we can't find the book and I'm sorry you kinda messed things up with Candace and I'm sorry that you don't have any friends at school, but . . . but . . . you are Coyote *freaking* Sunrise!" He grabbed me by my shoulders. "You are the girl that gave me a violin concert. You're the girl that gave my *mom* a violin concert. You're the girl that drove a bus down the highway while being chased by the police and you're the girl who drove all the way across the country to find a book and you're the girl who—who—who . . . gave Wally a sandwich!"

He knelt there for a second, catching his breath. Then he leaned in a little closer and lowered his voice. "You are the weirdo who gave me a ride once. You say you're a mess and maybe you are but, man, I'm telling you, you're . . . you're an awesome freaking mess. You're my hero, Coyote Sunrise."

I blinked and blinked and blinked. Yager trembled under my knees. The world whirled around us.

"I don't feel like a hero," I said.

Salvador shrugged. "Who does?"

I swallowed and swallowed and swallowed. "I feel so . . . *lost*," I said. "I can, like, *see* the person that I want to be. Brave, and kind, and confident. But I just keep messing everything up and I just can't get there."

"Coyote, you *are* all of those things." I narrowed my eyes at him, and he tilted his head. "Or at least you're *trying* to be. And, like, maybe we can never really *become* the person we want to be, anyway, you know?"

"That's hopeful," I said.

"No, I mean . . . maybe we're just always *becoming* the person we want. We're, like, always, a . . . a . . ."

"Work in progress?"

"Yes!"

I thought about it. And I laughed, a bitter little laugh that wasn't fun or funny at all. I held up my broken arm.

"What kind of work is this? What kind of progress?"

"But you're still *trying*." He huffed out a breath and looked away from me, out at the world driving by, and then back to me. "I heard a story once, Coyote. About caterpillars. On a *Radiolab*."

"What's a *Radiolab*?"

"It's a radio show. Or a podcast, I guess. About science and stuff, kind of. We listened to it in science once."

"Okay."

"And this one was about caterpillars. And chrysalises."

"Okay."

"And it turns out that when a caterpillar goes into its chrysalis, it doesn't just grow wings and stuff on the body it has. It, like, completely *dissolves*. Into this gross kind of *snot* stuff. And then it comes back together in a whole new shape. A butterfly."

"That's . . . kinda bananas."

"I know! So, the caterpillar is just goo. But, also, if you cut into a caterpillar beforehand, you can actually find these super thin, tiny wings. They're already there. And then, in the goo part in the chrysalis, they're there, too. Before the butterfly. Before the goo. And that's . . . that's like you. Like you, figuring this out, and . . . and trying to, like, be who you want to be."

I frowned. "What are you saying, Salvador? That I'm, like, dissolved caterpillar snot?"

He rolled his eyes. "No, Coyote. I'm saying that life is a mess sometimes. That *you're* a mess sometimes. But . . . but that you had your wings all along." He gave my shoulders a squeeze. "You have to get through the mess to find 'em, maybe. But you had 'em all along, Coyote."

Gosh darn it. That boy. That coconutty, clueless, kiss-hiding boy.

He's all right, sometimes. Well, okay, he's a heckuva lot more than all right. And more than sometimes.

I leaned forward and grabbed that boy tight in a hug. I heard him kind of wheeze, I was squeezing him so tight. He just kinda knelt there, awkward in my arms, and I didn't care.

"Boy, you've got wings, too, Salvador," I said.

"Okay?" he mumbled back.

It felt good, hearing those words and hugging that friend up on top of a moving bus. But I wasn't kidding myself. Feeling good for a minute doesn't erase the hours of messing things up royally.

"I may or may not have wings," I said, pulling back. "But, man, I made a mess."

Salvador shrugged. "So? Clean it up." Once upon a time, that boy had said to me, *The book isn't gone, Coyote. It's just lost.* And he'd been right. And he was, I realized, right about this, too.

I thought about the mess I'd made. I thought about what I'd have to do to clean it up.

"I don't think I can do this alone," I said.

He gave me half a grin.

"Good thing you don't have to."

I gave him a full grin back. And blew out a holy-cow-this-has-been-a-lot sort of lip-fluttering breath.

"Well," I said. "I guess we should get started."

"Yeah," Salvador answered. Then he looked around at the world blowing by around us. "But . . . shouldn't we fly first? I mean, since we have wings, apparently?"

He shifted on his knees a little away from me and turned to face the front of the bus. He stuck his arms straight out like wings.

I laughed. Because he looked ridiculous.

"But one of my wings is broken," I said, waving my cast.

"Pffft. You've got a broken *arm*, dummy. Your wings are just fine. Come on."

So, what the heck. I spun toward the front, facing into the wind. Stuck out both arms, best as I could. Closed my eyes.

I'm not gonna lie. It felt more than a little ridiculous, kneeling there with pretend wings like a little kid. But I had the wind in my hair and my best friend beside me. So it also felt more than a little awesome.

Salvador whooped beside me.

I gave him a *yeehaw* back.

And, it turned out, maybe I *did* feel like shouting.

"I'm glad you're my friend, Salvador Vega!" I was shouting, but what I was shouting was no secret.

"I'm glad I'm your friend, too!" he shouted back.

I laughed, but not because Salvador was being ridiculous (although we both were). I laughed because, after all that, my heart just wanted to.

"I'm . . . super freaking fond of you!" I shouted, and I was gonna say "love" and we both would've known I didn't mean it like *that* but it still might've been weird, and he laughed and shouted back, "I'm super freaking fond of you, too," and then I shouted, "But I *hate* your new deodorant! You smell like a candy bar that just worked out!" and he shouted back, "Shut up!" but not in a mean way, and then we were both laughing and flying up there on that bus like a couple of weirdos.

Which, obviously, is exactly what we were.

# CHAPTER
# TWENTY

*A*fter flying like weirdos, it was time to get to work on the fixing part. Which I knew was not going to be easy, or possibly even possible.

"The first step," I said to Salvador in hushed tones back in my room once we'd gotten down from the roof, "is to call Candace. And the first step for *that* is to get her phone number. And the first step for *that* is to steal Rodeo's phone."

"That's a lot of first steps."

"Some plans are like that."

Stealing Rodeo's phone was easy because, I mean, it's Rodeo we're talking about here. During any given twenty-four hours his phone is "lost" for at least twelve of them. He's not a real keep-track-of-the-details kind of guy. So, in a matter of minutes, we were back in my room with Rodeo's phone and we had potentially *days* before he'd really notice and get concerned.

Then we had to figure out his passcode. First I tried my birthday. No-go. Which was a little hurtful, but whatever. I took a breath and tried my big sister's birthday (nope), then my little sister's (nope), then my mom's (nope).

"Careful," Salvador said. "One more wrong try and it'll lock."

I sat there, staring at the little number pad on the screen, thinking. His birthday? It made the most sense, but it didn't really feel like something my dad would do. Then an idea fizzed into my mind. I chewed on my lip.

Then I keyed it in. My parents' anniversary: 07/04/00. My dad had just said that he read Mom's book every year on their anniversary, so I knew he remembered.

The lock screen vanished, and we were in. Salvador pumped his fist silently and I had a little moment myself, also silent.

Maybe my dad was making new friends. Maybe, even, he was almost making a girlfriend. Maybe, a little, he was starting to move on. But moving on doesn't have to mean forgetting. His passcode was still the day he married my mom. Moving on, maybe, but holding on, too.

But then, of course, I had to do it. I had to talk to Candace. Which I wasn't super looking forward to, given all I'd said the last time we talked.

But I did it. Because digging out of a mess you made can be hard, sometimes really hard, but it's better than just sitting around, stewing in the mess. I mean, the only thing worse than changing a dirty diaper has gotta be sitting around in one, right?

So, basically, I knew that I'd really crapped my pants and I was ready to get out of 'em. Or something like that.

She answered right away, probably because I was using my dad's phone, so she thought it was Rodeo calling.

"Hey, babe," she said, which almost spun me right back into angry, which would have been super counterproductive.

"Hey, Candace. It's me."

"Coyote?" Her voice was just on the hostile side of surprised.

Or possibly the surprised side of hostile. But, to her credit, she then asked, "Is everything okay?" which was pretty thoughtful.

"Not really," I said. "But that's my fault." I took a deep breath. And then I changed the diaper. I started and ended with "I'm sorry," and even peppered a few more "I'm sorrys" in between, because that was really the main idea I was trying to get across.

And in the rest of that in between, I laid it all out. How I'd been feeling. How I was missing my mom. How Candace had pretty much been cool the whole time and my own distinct *un*coolness really had nothing to do with her. How I knew I'd messed it all up but I was hoping that, maybe, I could try to fix it. I even told her about my secret, about the lost book, which was super hard, but only fair for her to know that one reason I freaked out on her was that I'd been secretly freaking out on myself the entire trip. I didn't pause to give her a chance to talk or even hardly to take a breath because I didn't want to lose my nerve or my momentum.

Then I was done and we sat there, not talking for a second.

"Wow," Candace said.

"Yeah," I answered.

"You don't have to apologize, Coyote."

"Yes, I do."

"No, listen, I shouldn't have—"

"No," I interrupted. "I don't have to apologize for feeling weird about you and my dad. I don't have to apologize for being, like, kind of a mess about all this Mom stuff. But I do have to apologize for being mean. So I'm sorry. Really, truly sorry."

"Okay," Candace said after a beat. "Apology accepted. So . . . now what?"

I blew out a big sigh.

"Well. We got out of one dirty diaper. But now we gotta get a clean one."

"Excuse me?"

Then we got to talking. My first few first steps were taken care of. But of course I had a whole batch of second steps that needed to get handled.

Once I was off the phone with Candace, I jumped right into the first second step. "Hey, Wally," I said, sitting next to him on the couch.

"Hmm?" he said, looking up from his book.

"Look. I know you are an anxious driver and you made a conscious choice to be a passenger and only a passenger. But I really need your help. I need you to drive. I promise you won't have to change the oil or fix a flat tire. We need to get somewhere secretly without Rodeo driving, and Candace is gone and *I* don't want to have to drive this bus again myself."

Wally blinked at me. "You've . . . driven this bus before?"

"Yeah. It was kind of a whole thing."

"How did it go?"

"All things considered, pretty well. Nobody died. I kinda got arrested, though."

"Hmm."

"I'll sit by you the whole time. Please. I . . . I . . . I made someone feel craptastic. And now I'm trying to bring them a sandwich. Metaphorically speaking."

Wally nodded. "I thought so."

"So . . . will you? Will you break your own rule and drive this ridiculous bus through the dark so I can fix my big huge mistake or at least *one* of my big huge mistakes? And before you answer, I'd like to gently remind you that you told me that your new philosophy is to say 'yes' to things, so there's that. Will you?"

Wally closed his eyes, then opened them again. He shook his head, but he said, "Yes. Yes, Coyote, I will drive this bus for you."

Wally didn't quite seem like the hugging type, and consent is important, so I just gave him a hug with my eyes.

"Thank you thank you thank you," I said. Then we sat there looking at each other. I cleared my throat. Looked up at Rodeo in the driver's seat, who was yawning, which was perfect. Then back to Wally. Cleared my throat again.

His eyebrows went up. "Oh. Now?"

"Yeah. We're going seventy miles an hour in the wrong direction. So, um, *hustle*, if you could, thanks."

So Wally and I walked up and casually started chatting up Rodeo, who was yawning and rubbing his eyes (probably because he'd spent the night in the hospital with his hot mess train wreck of a daughter), and when I thought Rodeo was sufficiently warmed up I gave Wally a look and he said, "Excuse me, Rodeo. I have always wanted to drive a school bus. I was wondering if you would let me drive yours?"

It was a fairly off-the-wall request but Rodeo is a more-than-fairly-off-the-wall guy so he was super into it. Besides reading, really his only hobby is recreational school bus driving, and he was eager to share. He gave Wally a quick on-the-go tutorial, and then we pulled over to switch drivers and Wally got behind the wheel. After a couple clumsy lurches with the clutch, he got the hang of it, and pretty soon we were cruising down the road and Rodeo was giving Wally congratulatory pats on the back.

I waited a tick for another big yawn from Rodeo before saying, "You know, I can totally keep an eye on Wally if you wanna go lay down. I got a spot picked for us to spend the night about an hour down the road."

"Uhhh," Rodeo said, rubbing his cheek. "What do ya think, Wally? You good if I sneak in some shut-eye?"

"Of course," Wally said, all upbeat, but I was really hoping Rodeo didn't notice how nervously fake his smile was and how tightly he was gripping the wheel.

"Well, okay. You might need to stop for gas, though."

"I got it!" I said, maybe a little too quick. My dad's exhaustion was on my side, though, and he just mumbled, "Cool, cool," and stumbled back toward his blanket pile.

By the time we stopped for gas a few miles later, Rodeo was already snoring. So of course he didn't notice when we got back on the highway going the other way.

"How you feeling, Wally?" I asked when we were back up to highway speed.

"Terrified," he answered.

"That's normal," I assured him. "The terror totally died down for me. Until the police started chasing me. And that was even *after* the brakes went out and we all almost died. So you'll be fine."

Wally tightened his grip on the steering wheel. "I'm going to assume you're joking," he said.

"Okay."

"How far do we have to go?"

"Ummmm," I said, pulling out my phone and taking a look. "About six hours."

"Again, I'm going to assume you're joking."

"Okay." I reached past him and slipped a bottle into the cupholder. "I got us both some iced coffee at the gas station, just in case. Really appreciate this, Wally. Not joking."

Wally was an absolute freaking hero that night. Salvador stayed up as long as he could, but he was at least as tired as Rodeo (probably because he'd spent the night before hiding behind dumpsters and dashing off to hospitals with his hot mess trainwreck friend), so after a bit he got distinctly horizontal in his bus seat and then shortly thereafter he got distinctly quiet.

Neither of those was an option for me or Wally. Especially Wally. We both finished our coffees. I'd never had coffee before. It's really something. We told some stories. Played some Twenty Questions. Sang a bit. Got pretty loopy for a while in the middle when *everything* seemed funny and then again a little while later when *nothing* seemed funny. But on that man (who hated driving) drove. Absolute freaking hero.

Finally, we were pulling into the parking lot. It was still dark, but wouldn't be for long.

"What should I do?" Wally asked. He sounded numb.

"Park," I said. I felt numb. "Then go to bed."

"That's it?"

"That's it. We're . . ." I checked my phone. "Two hours early."

I looked to Salvador, mouth open, sleeping in the opposite seat; Rodeo's blanket pile rising and falling with his slumbering breath; Wally settling in on the couch; Ivan sleeping on the seat beside me. I knew I should probably go back to my bedroom. But that forty-foot walk was just more than I could handle.

I dropped my head back onto the seat. At least I assume that I did. Same with closing my eyes. I must've done that, too. 'Cause, man, I was *out* before I knew I was going out.

I was jerked awake by my phone going off in my pocket and it felt kinda like it was two seconds later but it also felt kinda like it was two days later but it turned out to be just two hours later, which made the most sense anyway.

It took a few seconds of blinking and looking around to remember where I was and why I was there and even, for a second, *who* I was. Yeah, I was sleeping pretty deep.

But then it came back to me and I looked at my phone and saw it was Candace calling, and I answered, ducking down and whispering and covering the phone with my hand.

A minute later, I was just hanging up and then Rodeo almost ruined it all by saying, "Who you talking to, sugarcake?" right in my darn ear, and I jumped and almost dropped my phone.

Rodeo was standing there next to me, rubbing his face and looking around all dazed-and-just-woke-up-y.

"What?" I said.

"Who are you talking to?"

"Um. You."

"No. I mean on the phone."

"Oh. It was . . . just a . . . salesperson. We're not interested in saving thousands of dollars by transferring our credit card debt to a new Sapphire Club card with a very low introductory interest rate, are we?"

Rodeo sniffed. "I ain't even sure what that means," he said.

"Yeah, I figured."

"Where are we?"

I didn't want to tell him the whole truth just yet so I met the truth halfway and said, "Eh, some parking lot somewhere."

"Yeah," Rodeo said. He eyed a convenience store that was across the road, which was good, because it meant he wasn't looking toward the train station. "I'ma go hit the bathroom and see if they got any coffee," he said, and stumbled his sleepy way out the door, which was more perfect than I could have planned.

So it was that my surprise reunion—and my first attempt at cleaning up one of my messes—actually kinda worked.

Rodeo came tromping back up the bus stairs a few minutes later, Styrofoam cup of coffee in his hand. Salvador and Wally were sitting up at the front, looking discreetly out the windows. I was standing in the middle of the bus, waiting for him.

"Hey," he said, looking all confused. "The fella in there said we're in Ohio."

"Dad," I said, but maybe not quite loud and firm enough.

"But that don't seem right," my dad went on. "I mean, we were heading east when I went to sleep, right?"

"Dad," I said again.

"Ohio is *west* of Pennsylvania, ain't it?"

"Dad," I said for a third time, but firmer. "Shut up." I said it gentle, though, in a sort of nice this-is-for-your-own-good kind of way.

Rodeo looked at me.

"Come here," I said, and backed toward my room. I stopped right by the curtain that was my door.

Rodeo shuffled my way and stopped in front of me. "What's going on, Coyote?"

For a moment, I looked for my words. I'd done something wrong. And now I wanted to do something right. I blew out a shaky breath.

"Do you remember our first Christmas on the road?" I asked. "I mean, after the, uh . . . the accident? Our first Christmas when it was just you and me?"

Rodeo got that wounded look in his eyes that he used to always get when we talked about my mom or my sisters or what happened to them, the look that used to mean he was going away inside himself and leaving me for a while. But, this time, he stayed.

He shrugged, and nodded a "yes."

"We didn't talk about it," I said. "About Christmas coming up. Even though I know we both saw it coming. And even though we didn't talk about it one bit, I was still kinda hoping. Hoping that when I woke up, there'd be . . . a tree or something. Some presents. You know?" My voice broke, but I cleared my throat and kept going. "*Christmas.* But I came out of my room, this room right here behind me, and it was just you. Sitting there, looking out the window. No tree. No presents.

Just you, looking sad as . . . sad as . . ." I didn't know how to finish that metaphor. Because what could be as sad as the saddest person in the world?

Rodeo heaved out a ragged sigh. "I remember, darling," he said, scratchy and so quiet I could barely hear it even though I was standing close enough to him to smell his coffee.

"And that whole day, we didn't say a word about it. You didn't even say Merry Christmas to me." I stopped to breathe, because I was having a hard time getting the words out. "We just laid together in your bed all day and listened to the rain on the roof and didn't say anything and that was it. The whole day."

Rodeo closed his eyes and lowered his head. "I know, honeycakes. I'm sorry. I was sad."

"I know you were. I was, too. But that day, I was even sadder."

"I know, darling."

"No, you don't," I said, but I said it soft, not mad. Because I wasn't mad. "I'd already lost so much. My mom. My sisters. My friends, my house. I'd already lost *so* much. But that day I realized that . . . that the losing wasn't over. I'd lost Christmas, too. Not just that year, but probably every year. Just when I thought I couldn't lose any more, I kept losing. And that was hard. *Really* hard." I wiped tears off my cheek that I hadn't even entirely known I was crying. "It wasn't right, making me lose Christmas, on top of everything else. Losing all that future happiness. You shoulda said it, Rodeo. You shoulda said Merry Christmas. Even if it was hard. Even if you didn't really mean it."

Rodeo shook his head, eyes still down. "I know, darling, and I—"

"Geez," I said, "for freak's sake, could you just let me finish? I ain't lecturing you here, old man. I'm apologizing."

Rodeo looked up at me kind of sideways. "Really?"

"Yeah. I know maybe I've got kind of a funny way of apologizing, but you got kind of a funny way of doing just about everything, so just zip your lip for a minute and let me finish. Agreed?" It sounds mean but I said it quiet, and with a little smile, and with my voice still cracking, so overall it had more of a *let's-get-through-this-thing-together* vibe.

Rodeo gave me a hint of a smile back. "Agreed," he murmured.

"Good. What I'm saying is, that was wrong, what you did. But I know why you did it. And now . . . now I'm doing it, too. Or, I have been. You lost Mom. Your best friend. And with what I've been doing and how I've been acting, I've been trying to make sure you lose any new friends, too. Any new happiness. And that ain't right. It's not right, Dad."

"What are you saying?" my dad asked.

I blew out a big breath. "I'm saying that maybe we've lost enough. Maybe we should be done with losing for a while. Maybe it's time to do some finding."

Rodeo was looking at me, pretty confused, which was fair.

"I'm saying I'm sorry." I reached behind me and grabbed the edge of the curtain. "And I guess what I'm saying is . . . Merry Christmas. Merry Christmas, Dad."

And then I swooped the curtain to the side.

And there was Candace, standing there. Holding Fig in her arms.

Rodeo's mouth dropped open.

"Hey," Candace said.

There was a moment of us all just staring at each other.

"Well," I said to Rodeo, who was standing there with a little grin growing on his face. "Give her a *howdy*, old man. Geez."

Rodeo took a big step toward her and wrapped his arms around her and held her tight enough that I was worried about Fig's safety, who was pinned somewhere between them.

"Or a hug," I mumbled, looking away. "Sure."

After what seemed like an unreasonably long time, Rodeo let her go. They both turned to me, all shining eyes and sheepish smiles.

"I'm sorry for . . . everything," I said. "I think it's"—I sighed and shook my head and forged ahead—"*cool* that you're friends, or whatever."

"I think you're pretty cool, too, Coyote," Candace said.

"Obviously," I said, through my own smile. I was feeling pretty good about how me and Wally and Salvador had managed to pull this off. Pretty good about cleaning up some of my messes and maybe finding my wings a little.

But then Rodeo said, "Now, let's fire up this bus and finish this quest. Where we headed, Coyote?"

My smile faded almost as fast as my good feelings. I swallowed.

"Uh, yeah," I said. "About that."

# CHAPTER

## TWENTY-ONE

And then, yeah, I told him. I mean, I had to. There was no more hiding it, and that horrible secret was one of the messes I knew I needed to clean up. And with nowhere else to go, it was time to actually face the music.

Unlike the apology I'd just made, I opted for the direct, rip-off-the-Band-Aid approach. I did it fast and I did it in one breath and I did it looking at the floor, mostly.

*"So here's the thing about that, Daddio, I actually lost Mom's special book sometime last summer, well I mean I dropped it off somewhere because I didn't know it was Mom's special book at the time, and I was too afraid to tell you, so this whole time I've actually been trying to find it, which is why I broke into that store, but now I've already looked everywhere and I think it's gone like gone gone and I'm so so so sorry, and I know you'll never forgive me and I'm not asking you to and I'm so sorry."* I gulped in a breath. "And so, yeah, I guess that's about it."

Somewhere, a car honked. A truck drove by on the street, playing jaunty horn music out its windows.

"Wait," Rodeo said to me at last. "So . . . where's the book?"

I did a little huff. It wasn't a great time for my dad's flaky cluelessness. Ripping a Band-Aid off once is more than enough.

Although, to be fair, I had been talking awfully fast and it probably had been mostly a mumble.

"I don't *know.*" My voice was starting to shake. "It's gone, Dad. I'm sorry."

"I'll, uh, let you two talk about this," Candace said quietly, and walked up to join Salvador and Wally.

My hands were shaky by then, too. Eyes a little blurry and burny. I couldn't look my dad in the eyes.

I heard him, though. Blow out a long breath. "You mean, you haven't had the book . . . this *whole* time?"

"No. I mean, *yes,* I haven't had it. You know what I mean."

"So . . . this whole trip, you've been . . ."

"Yeah. Lying. And looking. I've been retracing our route from last summer, hitting the places we stopped at. I'm actually kind of shocked you haven't noticed. I mean, didn't you think it was weird that we kept hitting all the same little stores we went to last year?"

Rodeo frowned. "Huh. Yeah. Now that you mention it." He shrugged. "I guess I was just kinda enjoying the ride." My dad closed his eyes in a grimace, but not before I saw them start to fill up. His lips were tight. He rubbed his face with his hands. "Whew," my dad said, letting out another breath. Then, "whew," another one.

There'd been a part of me that had hoped that he wouldn't care; that he'd just laugh and give me a hug and say something like, "Heck, honeybird, who cares? It's just a book! Let's get tacos!" I mean, it really was within the realm of possibility.

That wasn't what happened, though. Losing that book hit him hard. Which was fair.

He kinda wilted backward and sat on the couch. He put his head in his hands.

I sat down next to him. "I'm so sorry," I said. "I can't believe that I—"

"Sshhh," he said, shaking his head.

I *sshhh*ed. My dad never *sshhh*ed me. My stomach somersaulted. I knew then that my dad was mad. *Really* mad.

I was wrong.

Because he looked up at me and his eyes were red-rimmed but there was exactly zero *mad* in them. "This ain't your fault, Coyote," he said. "Not one little bit. It's mine."

I opened my mouth to argue but he went on before I could, his voice low and hoarse.

"It is. I hid those ashes all those years. I never told you about them. Or the book. Or how she wrote in it. How were you to know, little bird? That book is lost because *I* didn't take care of it."

Again, I started to talk, and this time he held up a hand to stop my words.

"It's okay. It is. It was one hundred percent my fault. But it was an accident." He took in a shaky breath. Looked down at the floor. "I've been thinking a lot about your mom on this trip. A lot. And I know . . ." He shook his head. "I know she wouldn't care about this. About us losing that book."

"You don't think," I said, my voice small and trembly, "you don't think she'd be . . . mad at me?"

I know it was a little kiddie thing to say. But that's all right. Because when it came to my mom, I *was* a little kid. And I always would be. I'd never had the chance to grow up with her.

"Mad at you? Aw, *heck* no," my dad said. "Not a speck. Not about that silly book. Or any of this." He frowned. "Well. She might've been mad about the Pittsburgh burglary. That was *nuts*, Coyote. But none of the rest of it. If she was sitting here, watching us be all mopey and stuff, I know she'd laugh. And roll her eyes. Especially at me. She rolled her eyes at me *a lot*." He kinda smiled. I kinda smiled, too. "And she'd tell us to get over it. To not worry about stuff that doesn't matter. And she'd say something like, all we gotta do to do this thing right is just to . . . do it *together*, you know?" He put an arm around me. "So let's do it. Let's do it together, Ella. Yeah?"

I sniffed. And I leaned into him. And I nodded. And that nod was not a lie at all. That nod was the truth.

"Yeah," I said.

And we sat like that for a while. Me and my dad.

And it felt good. Good to finally have all those lies and secrets and fears gone. Felt good to just sit there in the truth together.

After a while, my dad did a little breathy chuckle through his nose. "Man, honeycakes. I can't believe what you been doing. This whole secret mission. I mean, how did you even know what you were looking for, exactly?"

"Well, I knew the title." I slid my phone out of my pants pocket and clicked through to the picture of *Red Bird* that Rawley had found. "And we had this picture. So we just kept looking, scanning the—"

"When did you take that picture?" Rodeo asked, leaning in.

"What? Oh, I didn't. It's just from the internet."

Rodeo squinted. "How did it get on the internet?"

I rolled my eyes. I was not in the mood to give my dad a lesson on the basic concept of the internet. Again.

"It's just a picture someone took of a copy of the book. In some bookstore somewhere. It doesn't matter. We were just using this so we—"

"But that's the book," Rodeo said.

I bit my lip in frustration. "I know, Dad," I said, keeping my voice as patient as I could. "We did an image search. On the internet. You can just type in what—"

"No. I mean, that's *it*. That's your mom's book!"

"For the love of god, old man, I *know* it is!" All the patience was definitely out of my voice by then. "*I did an image search and I—*"

"Ella!" my dad shouted, shocking me into silence. "Listen to me! I know what an image search is! I'm telling you, that's *the* book! Like, the exact actual copy! Do the pinchy-pinch!"

"The what now?"

"The . . . the . . . backward pinchy-pinch thing!" he said, snapping his fingers like a crab in my face.

"Oh. Like, zoom in?"

I did the pinchy-pinch, zooming in on the book in the picture. My dad dragged his finger across the screen, moving it so we were looking at the edges of the pages.

"See?" Rodeo said, pointing. "Those are the pages we taped!"

I blinked, heart racing.

I could see it. A little piece of tape, holding two of the pages together. And the same thing, later in the book, holding two more pages together. The pages where my mom and my dad, had written down their secret final resting place.

"This is *the* book, Coyote!"

My mouth went dry.

I jerked my hand away from my screen, suddenly terrified that I was gonna click something wrong and make the website disappear and then not be able to find it again.

I was better at technology than Rodeo, sure, but that's kinda like saying you're better at Ping-Pong than a koala bear. It's a low bar.

"Salvador!" I straight-up screamed.

His wide-eyed face popped up from behind one of the bus seats at the front. Based on my shriek, he probably assumed I'd burst into flames.

"What?!" he asked, jumping up.

"Where is this book?" I demanded, holding up my phone. He hopped up and jogged back to me, but his face went all confused when I held up my phone to him.

"We don't know, Coyote. That's why we did this whole—"

"No!" I shouted, suddenly understanding Rodeo's frustration from a moment before. "Where is this actual copy of this actual book? This *exact* one. Where is it?"

Salvador blinked. Then, I think, he got it all without me having to explain. His eyebrows shot up. "Are you serious?" he mumbled, taking the phone from me. He did some tapping and then read from the screen: "It's a used bookstore. Called Beach Reads."

"Where is it?"

"Um. Griffin Bay, Ohio?"

"Griffin Bay, Griffin Bay," I mumbled, tapping my fingertips on my lips. Then my mouth dropped open. I slapped myself on the forehead. "Griffin Bay! I totally forgot!" I pointed a finger at Rodeo. "You!"

He held up his hands. "What did I do?"

"Last summer! After Indiana, but before Pittsburgh. You had a D.E.A.D. Dream. You were craving, like, a fish sandwich or something."

Rodeo thought for a second, then his eyebrows went up. "Not just any fish sandwich," he said. "A fresh *perch* sandwich, with—"

"Whatever! So we drove all the way up to, what, Lake Erie, so you could get one."

Rodeo smiled the special kind of smile he does only when he's remembering a great sandwich. "Yeah we did," he said, nodding. "Man, that perch was hot and crispy and *perfectly* fr—"

"Not the important part here, Father," I said, snapping my fingers. "We stopped for that sandwich *and* we stopped at a used bookstore. I remember! *In Griffin Bay, Ohio!* Salvador, quick, what's their phone number?"

Salvador did some tapping and squinting. Possibly a pinchy-pinch or two. "Shoot," he said, looking up. "No number listed."

"Are you kidding?" I asked, slumping back against the couch. But then I sat right back up. "Wait a minute. We're *in* Ohio. Right now. How far is Griffin Bay from here, Salvador?"

More tapping and squinting. "Uh. Geez. A little more than an hour, is all."

I jumped to my feet. Pointed at Rodeo, then up at the front of the bus. "Bus. Drive. Now."

Then I marched right up to the front, to the big ol' silver bell we had bolted to the ceiling up by the front door. We called it the Holy Hell Bell, and we called it that because, holy hell, it was *loud*. And only to be used on very special occasions.

I grabbed the ringer thing and rang the bejeezus out of it. And that clattering brass lived up to its name. If my other arm wouldn't have been in a cast, I would've plugged my ear for sure.

Ivan and Fig both ran for the back of the bus, which was fair.

"Grab a seat, everyone!" I hollered over the racket of the bell. "This quest is back on!"

# CHAPTER
# TWENTY-TWO

An hour is sixty minutes long no matter how you cut it, but *whoo-boy*, how long those sixty minutes *feel* can really vary depending on how desperate you are to be done with 'em.

I'm sure that Rodeo drove as fast as he safely could, but it didn't feel like it. A possibly cool thing about being on a bus, though, is that if you're heading somewhere and you're all uptight about it, you can pace around as you go. As long as you're not the one driving, I guess.

So I paced for a few dozen miles of highway, up and down that bus. I was, maybe, about to get my mama's book back. Or I was, maybe, about to find out that the bookstore had sold it in the last nine months, and that I'd hit another (and probably the final) dead end. Not a lot of room for in-between there. So the stakes were sky-high, and my heart knew it. So did my stomach. And my armpits.

And then we were pulling up. It was a cute little lakeside town that I remembered, more or less. A two-block downtown with shops and cafés that most folks would call *charming*. Me included. I remembered the bookstore, off the main drag on a little side street. As Rodeo was pulling Yager over to park on the side of the street, I was already standing by the bus door. That's normally very much not allowed but, you know, extraordinary circumstances.

The first bus-sized parking spot Rodeo found was half a block away and I covered that half block at a dead run.

I pulled up panting at the glass door and took one breath to settle myself and fan the little flame of hope in my heart and then I turned the knob to go in.

Well, I *tried* to turn the knob. Which, of course, was locked. I rattled it and twisted it both ways and tried pulling and then pushing the door, but it was a no-go. Pittsburgh all over again.

"*No,*" I whispered, "*no no no no.*"

Salvador jogged up as I was stepping back, sizing up the display windows full of books on either side of the door.

"No bricks," he said, proving he was a pretty accurate judge of my decision-making process.

I growled and took two steps down the sidewalk toward the corner.

"No breaking in the back door, either," he said. "You're almost out of arms."

Fig and Rodeo and Candace and Wally came walking up. One of them was on a leash.

"What's up?" Rodeo asked.

"It's locked!" I said, voice starting to break.

Candace stepped to the window and held her hands up to peer through.

"Okay," Rodeo said. "Take it easy. We'll ask around, find the owner . . ."

"Found him," Candace said, face still pressed to the window. She looked back at us. "He's in there."

I leaped forward to squint through the window, and sure enough I could see an old guy standing at the back behind a counter. He was looking our way, too, which was no surprise since there was a whole crowd standing outside his store and I'd just been rattling his front door like it was a Holy Hell Bell.

I rapped my knuckles on the glass and gave a wave that I hoped was more *friendly* than *maniacally desperate*.

The man offered a wave back that was more *cautious* than *welcoming*. Which was fair.

I beckoned him with my hand. "Excuse me?" I called through the glass. "Could you help us, sir?"

He hesitated for a second before flooding my heart with gratitude by walking around the counter and toward the door.

I stepped back as he opened it, but just a crack.

He was big and tall, with white hair combed flat to his head and large metal-framed glasses and an untucked button-down shirt that hung out over his belly and a general vibe of careful kindness. Which I get. Because *kindness* is great but *careful* is smart, especially when you've got a maniacally desperate girl with a black eye and broken arm banging on your locked door.

"I'm sorry," he said. "But we're closed. On account of the coronavirus."

"Sure," I answered fast, before he could shut the door again. I yanked a mask out of my back pocket and slipped it on. "Sorry to bother you. But I just need to grab a book real quick."

His eyes gave a quick scan of our crew. Between my fresh-from-the-emergency-room look and Rodeo's usual bearded funkiness and Candace's shaved and dyed head and the mismatched pair of Salvador and Wally—not to mention whatever the heck Fig was—I wasn't at all surprised that he was skeptical of letting us in.

He smiled but shook his head. "I'm afraid I can't let—"

"It's just one book," I interrupted. "I know exactly which one. And I know you have it. Or, *had* it, at least. And I *really* need it."

The man's carefully kind smile faltered a bit and he opened his mouth and I could tell he was gonna give me another "I'm sorry" so I beat him to it.

"You see that bus down there?" I asked, pointing up the street toward Yager. He looked up the street and frowned, but he nodded. "In that bus is a box. And in that box are my mom's ashes. She . . . she died." I probably didn't need to say that last part. I think pretty much someone is *required* to die before they get turned into ashes and put in a box. Or at least they would die during the process.

But I forged on. "In a car accident. With." I took a steadying breath. "With my sisters. But before she died she wrote down, in the pages of a special book, where she wanted us to scatter her ashes. And then I lost that book. I left it here. On accident. Please. You don't even need to sell it to me. I just need to see what she wrote. That's all. *Please.*"

The man's mouth had slowly opened as I'd talked. He blinked at me. And he took a couple seconds before he spoke. "Well," he said, "I'm real sorry about what happened to your family." He paused. "Truly." He said it right into my eyes, his *careful* turned all the way into *kindness* now. "My wife has a health condition and we can't risk her getting exposed to this virus, so I'm gonna have you stay out here. But if you tell me the name of the book, I'll go in and look for it."

"*Thank you thank you thank you,*" I said, and yanked my phone out of my pocket and tapped around until I had the picture of that book up on the screen and I held it up to him. "It's *Red Bird* by Mary Oliver. Poetry. This copy right here that you posted. Thank you times a million."

But the man didn't turn around and go look for the book. He just stood there, eyebrows high on his forehead. "Oh, my," he said, and looked back to my eyes. "I remember that book." Man, I did *not* like that word "remember" there in that sentence. I think he saw my heart start to break because he held up a hand. "It's okay. It's not here. But I know where it is."

I almost collapsed. The happy kind of collapse, if there is such a thing. I was all tingly.

"You do?"

"I do. I gave that book as a gift. Just last week. To one of my best customers."

"Where are they? What's their address?" I asked.

"Hold on," he said. "I can't just send you to her house without her permission. She's . . . had a hard time, lately. But I think she'll understand. Wait here. I'll give her a call."

So I did some more pacing, but this time on a sidewalk instead of a bus. I tried not to do too much staring through the window at him standing back there at the counter talking on the phone, but it was hard. After approximately thirteen and a half years, the bookstore door swung open again.

I wanted to ask "Well?" or "What did she say?" or "*For the love of god is she going to let me have the book?!*" but I didn't have the breath for it so I just looked at him with what I was sure were maniacally desperate eyes.

"If you keep going up this street, you'll come to a four-way stop," he said, pointing. "Take a left. Go down three blocks, and you'll be at Griffin Beach Park. There's a gazebo. She'll meet you there with the book in a little while. Her name is Doreen."

I wanted to say a million thank-yous but I only had the heart for one real, deep, true one. So I gave it to him.

"Thank you."

He smiled. "Good luck," he said.

# CHAPTER
# TWENTY-THREE

I was doing even *more* pacing—this time around a gazebo—when I saw Doreen walking up.

I knew it was her. It wasn't, like, *magic* or anything. I mean, she was the only person in the park beside me. And she was carrying a little black book. But, still, my breath caught in my throat when I saw her coming.

She was old. Like, really old. Thin and kind of bent over a little. Moving kinda slow, but still moving pretty well. A puff of white hair on her head.

I was standing alone in the gazebo. I hadn't asked everyone else to stay in the bus, but I guess they'd just kind of known that this was something I wanted to do alone.

She walked up to me. She was wearing a cloth mask made out of fabric that had pictures of cats on it, which I thought was a good sign. I was wearing my mask, too.

"You must be the girl," she said, "who needs the book." She had an English accent, and a gentle voice, and warm eyes. I loved her right away, whether she was giving me the book or not.

"Yes, ma'am," I said.

She nodded. "Let's sit. But let's keep our distance."

There were a few picnic tables in the gazebo, looking out over the green grass of the park and the blue water of the lake. We sat on a bench together, one of us on either end, four feet of bench between us.

"I understand this was your mother's book? And she passed away?"

I nodded. I kept looking back and forth between Doreen's eyes and the book she held in her pale hands.

"I'm terribly sorry," she said, and I nodded again.

"Me, too."

"And a sister, as well?"

I swallowed. "Two sisters, actually."

Doreen clicked her tongue. "Oh, dear," she murmured, and then she reached toward my hand with one of hers. But she couldn't reach. She sighed. And she reached into her purse and pulled out a little bottle of hand sanitizer and gave herself a squirt and rubbed it in and then handed the bottle to me and I did the same and then she stood up and shuffled a couple of feet over and sat down beside me and then she patted my hand.

All that, just for that.

It was beautiful.

"Did Jeffrey tell you why he gave me this book?" she asked.

"No," I said, guessing that Jeffrey was the bookstore owner.

"He gave it to me because he is kind, and because I was sad. I was sad because . . ." She stopped talking for a breath, and I heard her swallow. Her eyes got thick and glossy with tears, and she looked out at the dancing water of the lake. "I was sad because my sister died."

"I'm sorry," I said, which is kind of the only thing to say, as silly as it is. I meant it, though. Losing a sister is hard.

"Thank you, dear." She exhaled and pursed her lips. "It was very hard for me. Very hard. I wanted to take care of her. But I couldn't. She had Covid, so she was in the special ward they had. And she couldn't have visitors. And so she was alone. Even at the end." She stopped. Shook her head. Pulled a little white handkerchief out of her pocket and dabbed at her eyes. "Sisters are meant to take care of each other," she said, her voice shaky. "It was very hard."

Now it was my turn to reach out. My turn to pat *her* hand.

"So I was very sad. *Am* very sad, really. And so he gave me your mother's book. Because he knew that my sister loved poetry. Mary Oliver especially. And because he is a good friend."

"Did the book help?" I asked.

"No. But Jeffrey giving me the book helped. A little."

I nodded, remembering what Wally had said about sandwiches. I got it.

Doreen cleared her throat. "The lovely thing about having a sister is that it's like being born with a best friend. We had been together my whole life. Even when we were apart. It's always been me and her. And now it's just me. Me, and her ashes."

"You have her ashes?"

"I do. And I understand you have your mother's?"

I nodded. "What are you going to do with them? Your sister's ashes, I mean?"

"Oh, I don't know, dear. I don't know. What are you going to do with your mother's?"

"I'm supposed to scatter them. In some place that she wrote down in that book."

She must have heard something in my voice. Because she asked me a question. "Do you want to?"

I breathed in. Breathed out.

And then I shrugged. Just like nodding your head can sometimes really be a lie, shrugging can sometimes really be the truth. And the truth of that shrug was a truth I hadn't really shared with anyone yet: not my dad, not my best friend, not even really myself. But it was the truth. *Did* I want to scatter my mom's ashes, say goodbye to her forever?

I thought of my mom, who made me heart-shaped pancakes and hummed my nightmares away and read books to me in the bathtub and scratched my back until I fell asleep and, no, *no no no no no*, I did not want to let her go.

But, at the same time, I kinda did. She wanted to be set free. My dad wanted to set her free. It had been a long time. And all that tight holding on I was doing? It didn't actually feel all that good, really.

I rubbed at my eyes and sniffed and shrugged again.

"I don't know," I said. "I'm supposed to. And my dad wants to. But I don't know what to do."

Doreen gave my hand a little squeeze. "That's all right," she

said. "You don't have to know, dear. Be gentle with yourself."
She patted the book on her lap. "Your mother chose a poem in
this book? And she wrote something for you there?"

"Yeah," I whispered.

"Well, then maybe that is where you should start," she said.
And she pressed the book into my hands.

# CHAPTER

# TWENTY-FOUR

I held that book and while I held that book I held my breath, too. I felt the smoothness of the cover on my fingertips. That book, that I'd searched for and hunted and chased. That book, that my mom had held in her hands. That book, that I had lost. Now, found.

The moment felt electric. But electric in a quiet way. Like stepping barefoot into an ice-cold creek in the woods. If it had been a scene in a movie, there wouldn't have been soaring violin strings. There wouldn't have been any music at all. There would have been silence. Or, maybe, the beating of my heart.

"I think," I said. Cleared my throat. "I think I'm gonna," I added. Then I kinda pointed with the book at a bench, sitting by itself a little ways away from the gazebo.

"Of course, dear," Doreen said.

And I got up and walked over to the bench and sat down. It was probably a nice bench, in a nice park, with a nice view of the lake. But I didn't notice any of that, or care.

I looked at the cover of the book. It was a little ragged, with some creases and a ripped corner. Which is pretty much standard for anything that's under Rodeo's care for a few years. I turned it so I could see the edges of the pages. And the tape. Two pieces.

One, I knew, was my dad's. And one was my mom's. He'd said that hers was toward the back of the book; his, the front. So I paged back to the second piece of tape. Which was actually kind of tricky, since one of my hands was pretty useless in its cast.

But I got there. And I slipped my finger under the tape. And I took a breath. And then I slid my finger up, pulling the tape free and opening to the poem that my mom had picked as her favorite.

It was called "Mornings at Blackwater." It was short. Less than twenty lines.

That poem had been taped closed for years. Lost. Now, found. I would be the first person to read it since my mom had, years before. Hers were the last eyes that had seen those words. Hers were the last fingers that had touched that page.

Using my good hand, I pressed the book open on my lap.

And I saw it. My mom's handwriting. Neat. Small. Black ink. She'd written her words sideways, in the gutter of the book where the two pages came together. My heart skipped and, quick, I covered her words with my hand. I wasn't ready to read them, just yet. So I read the poem instead.

This is what it said:

> For years, every morning, I drank
> from Blackwater Pond.
> It was flavored with oak leaves and also,
>     no doubt,
> the feet of ducks.

And always it assuaged me
from the dry bowl of the very far past.

What I want to say is
that the past is the past,
and the present is what your life is,
and you are capable
of choosing what that will be,
darling citizen.

So come to the pond,
or the river of your imagination,
or the harbor of your longing,

and put your lips to the world.
And live
your life.

It was all blurry by the end. Very. Lost in tears, really.

It was funny. I'd been sad and scared because I thought I'd forgotten what my mom's voice sounded like. Like I was losing that. But when I read that poem, it wasn't my own voice saying the words in my head and my heart. It was hers, again. Found.

I felt her. I felt *her*. I heard her voice. Talking just to me.

*Darling citizen.*

I know it's silly, maybe. Because those weren't even her words. They were the poet's, Mary Oliver's. And my mom didn't even choose that poem for *me*, but just because it was her favorite. I mean, she didn't even *mark* it for me. That was for Rodeo.

So I had no right or reason, maybe, to think I could hear her voice, through all the years and all the distance and all the heartbreak and joy and everything, saying those words, and saying them just to me.

But, here's the deal. I think that the universe is funny, sometimes. And by *funny*, I mean *beautiful*. And by *think*, I mean *know*. The universe is beautiful, sometimes. And, sometimes, you don't need right or reason to know something is true. And, I tell you, I heard it. For the first time in way too long, I heard my mama's voice. Talking to me. Just to me.

I don't know how long I sat there, with her voice and those words. Long enough for my eyes to clear and my cheeks to dry.

I sucked in a big, lung-filling breath. Let it flow back out. Turned the book sideways. And then I spread my fingers, so I could see, at last, where this journey would end. So I could see, finally, where my mom had chosen for her final resting place. So I could see the words that my mom had written.

Her handwriting, even after all the years, was familiar. I remembered it, the flowing loops and neat letters.

I read those words.

And my heart filled up. And my eyes filled up, once again.

But my heart also sank, just a little. And I frowned, just a little.

# CHAPTER
# TWENTY-FIVE

*A* few minutes later, my dad sat down beside me on the bench.

"Hey, little bean," he said, careful.

"Hey."

"How you doing?"

"Okay."

"Did you, uh . . . did you find it?"

"Yeah."

He put an arm around me. Pressed his lips to the top of my head. "So. Where we headed?"

"I don't know," I said. And I handed him the book, held open to the right page.

Funny: My dad did the same thing I did. I saw him cover Mom's words with a finger while he read the poem. His breathing got rough and he sniffled and rubbed at his eyes while he read the poem Mom had chosen. And, just like me, he took in and let out a big breath before reading what she'd written.

His shoulders got all shaky again. I leaned into him. Let him have his moment.

When his breathing and sniffling had calmed down enough, I asked him, "Why do you think she wrote that? What did she mean?"

My dad swallowed. "I think she meant that...that she doesn't care what we do with her ashes. I think she wrote that because, if she were gone, that's all that matters. It's the only thing that she really wanted us to know."

I nodded.

Here's what my mom wrote on the page in that little book next to that beautiful poem that she had chosen just for us:

*I love you. I love you. I love you. I love you.*

That's it. *I love you.* Written four times. Nothing else.

I rubbed at my eyes with the heel of my hand. "Why do you think she wrote it four times?"

My dad pointed with one finger at the first *I love you.* "For me," he said. His finger slid to the second. "For your little sister." Then to the third. "For your big sister." His finger moved again, and stopped on that last *I love you.* My skin went all tingly. "For you," he said softly. "That one's just for you, Ella."

I'm gonna skip over the next few minutes. It was a hard moment. But a special one. A moment just for me, and my dad. And my sisters. And my mom.

A moment just for our family.

# CHAPTER
# TWENTY-SIX

Eventually my dad gave me a squeeze and then got up and walked over to join Candace, who was walking Fig on a little path down by the lake. I looked back and saw that Wally was sitting next to Doreen at the picnic table, and Salvador was standing a ways off, leaning against the gazebo. I gave him a little wave and he walked my way.

"Okay if I sit here?" Salvador asked all careful and gentle because Salvador is, in fact, a high-quality and thoughtful human being.

"Yeah," I said.

So he slid down next to me and we sat there for a while, *Red Bird* closed on my lap.

"Well," I said, after a while. "It's kind of a dead end."

"Really? She . . . didn't write anything?"

"She did. But all she wrote was 'I love you.'"

"Oh," Salvador said. "That's, uh . . . that's actually kinda cool."

"Yeah," I said. "It is."

Another few moments of silence.

"You wanna see the poem, though?" I asked. "It's a good one."

"Sure."

I sat there while Salvador read "Mornings at Blackwater."

"Wow," he said. "Your mom seems like she was pretty amazing, Coyote."

"Yeah. She was."

I looked out at the water, and the trees, and the grass, thinking about it all. I was feeling mostly at peace about the whole thing. I'd done everything I could. And a lot that I shouldn't have, honestly. And I found the book. And if my mom didn't want to write down a place, well, who was I to complain?

She'd written down something better. Something more important. I would've liked to do it *right*, but maybe that was her point, kind of. I could do it right in my own way. The rightest thing was just to know that she loved me. I felt okay about that. Mostly.

But then Salvador said something. And the something he said was, "Huh."

"What?" I said, still looking out at the world and feeling mostly okay.

"Why do you think she underlined this part?"

It was my turn to say "Huh?" but I said it with a question mark.

I looked down to where Salvador was pointing on the page. To those five words in that poem, underlined lightly in pen. So light you could barely see it. Especially if your eyes were all tear-filled and you were having a big hearing-your-mom's-or-wife's-voice-for-the-first-time-in-six-years moment.

I snatched the book from his hand. Blinked and blinked, to make sure. Bit my lip, thinking. Confused, for just a second. And then it came to me.

"Oh my god," I said. I looked to Salvador. "Salvador. You're a genius."

"I just . . ."

But I wasn't listening. I stood up and then jumped right up onto the bench.

"Rodeo!" I hollered. "Rodeo!" I jumped up and down on the bench. My dad turned toward me. "I know how to do it right!" I shouted, waving the book in the air above my head. "I know where to go!"

# CHAPTER
# TWENTY-SEVEN

The words that my mom had underlined were these ones: *So come to the pond*.

No biggie, right? Except that it was.

Because there was a place that we used to go. A drive, up a mountain. And then a hike, through the woods. Uphill, sure, but short. Not too hard for little legs. Not too far to bring a blanket, and a backpack of food.

We would go there, together. From time to time. Our family. With snacks and water bottles and books and, sometimes, a lunch.

It was, technically, a lake. That's what the maps and the trail signs said. But it was a very small lake. Even a six-year-old could throw a rock across it. If they were lucky. Way too small for boats, or fishing. But just the right size for splashing, and picnics.

It was one of our special places. In the spring, with the melting snow and greening plants and rowdy birds. In the summer, with the blue skies and the smell of hot pine needles. In the fall, with the crisp air and brightness of the changing larches.

We called it *our pond*.

Of course.

# CHAPTER
# TWENTY-EIGHT

We all gathered around the picnic table. Even Doreen. Rodeo and Candace had come hustling up after my shouting, and I showed Rodeo the underlined words that Salvador had found and I told him the idea that I had and then I asked, "What do you think?" and his eyes got all misty and he smiled and said, "Well, heck yeah, of course you're right, of course that's what she meant."

He threw up his hands. "So what are we waiting for?"

I gulped, remembering my shrug to Doreen. I was glad that we'd found that *right way* to lay my mom to rest that we'd been looking for. But I still wasn't sure that I was ready to let go. But I was relatively sure that maybe I was ready to try. So I put on my bravest smile.

"Let's roll," I said. Then I remembered something and turned toward Wally. "But . . . we're supposed to take you to Maine. The pond is all the way back in Washington State."

Wally just raised his eyebrows. "Ask, Coyote," he said.

I grinned. "Hey, Wally. Do you wanna drive in the wrong direction all the way across the entire freaking country with us to maybe scatter my mom's ashes?"

Wally smiled his warm, magic smile. "Yes," he said.

And I smiled back.

Then I looked over and saw Doreen. Sitting by herself.

I stepped over to her. And I talked quiet, so she wasn't on the spot.

"You said you were all alone," I said. "With your sister being gone."

She nodded.

"Do you have a job?"

She laughed. "Goodness, no, dear."

"Do you have any pets?"

"No."

We both knew where I was going with this. Doreen smiled at me, but it was an uncertain, I-don't-know-about-this kind of smile. I got it.

"Well," I said. "Do you . . . do you wanna go on a trip? A trip that is also kind of a saying-goodbye-to-someone-you-love trip? A trip to maybe scatter ashes?" I leaned in closer and said right into her eyes, *"It's okay if you don't. Really."*

Doreen's mouth puckered. "Oh, my. I don't know, dear. At my age. Do you even have room for me?"

I realized that Doreen, maybe, hadn't seen us pull into the parking lot. "You see that big ol' bus over there? That's our ride. It seats fifty-six, and we've only got five in our crew. Seven if you count cats and rat dogs. So, yeah, room is not an issue."

"Is it . . . *safe*?" she asked. "With everything going on?"

"I don't know," I answered, wanting to be truthful. "We've been washing our hands lots. And masking up everywhere. And none of us has a fever or cold or anything. But it's up to you, of course."

I moved in even closer, to be double-sure that our words were just between us. *"No pressure. But you wouldn't have to be alone, for a while. And we could remember our sisters, together. If you want to."*

Doreen looked away. Out at the water.

"Oh, dear," she said to herself. Then she sighed. And looked back to me. And I could see a little smile in her eyes. "I think perhaps I would, dear. Yes."

I stepped back and felt a grin spread across my face. "Good answer. Now, I have three more questions for you."

Her answers, by the way, were the Bible, her great-grandfather's farm in Wales, and egg salad.

An hour later, give or take, we were parked outside Doreen's apartment. She'd packed a bag and let her neighbors (and Jeffrey, the bookstore owner) know that she was going, and we were all back aboard Yager. She was sitting right up front, next to Wally.

"This is quite a to-do," she said.

I shrugged. "All we have to do is drive this old bus twenty-five hundred miles across the country. Easy-peasy."

"Easy for you to say," Rodeo grouched, stretching his back in the driver's seat. "That's a long way, chickadee."

"Well," I said, "we've got two drivers. Three if you count Wally."

"Please don't count me," Wally said.

"Fair. Three if you count *Doreen.*"

"I haven't driven a car in thirty years," Doreen said.

"Okay. Three if you count *me.*"

Rodeo shook his head. "Absolutely not."

"Ugh. Fine. Two drivers. But that's plenty. Twelve hundred miles apiece. No biggie."

Candace, sitting in one of the other bus seats, crinkled her brow. "Um. But where's everyone gonna sleep?"

"Huh," I said. It was a fair question, and something I hadn't considered. "Wally's been sleeping on the couch. I guess Salvador could fit in my room?"

"Nope," Rodeo said, quick.

I lowered my eyelids at him. "Ugh. He has a *girlfriend*, Dad."

Rodeo frowned and shot a look Salvador's way. "Then definitely nope."

Salvador blushed an adorably dark shade of mortified and found something super interesting to look at out the window.

"We'll just . . . get another bed," Rodeo said.

"Two beds," Candace said.

I snapped my fingers. "A bunk bed!"

"But we need it, like, *now*," Rodeo said. "Or at least before bedtime. Where can we find a bed that quick?"

Candace blinked at him. "Uh, Craigslist or Facebook Marketplace."

"Okay," Rodeo said, starting up the engine. "How do I get there?"

"Oh, honey," Candace said, and pulled out her phone.

And that is how, a few hours and a couple hundred miles later, we ended up with a very used but perfectly serviceable bunk bed smack dab in the middle of Yager, flying down the road toward the sunset.

# CHAPTER
# TWENTY-NINE

*O*ur trip from the lake in Ohio to the pond in Washington was, mostly, uneventful. A lot of driving. A fair amount of talking, and card-playing. Some disappointing burgers and some truly sensational nacho fries. But *mostly* uneventful is not the same thing as *totally* uneventful, and a couple of eventful events did happen. One in particular.

The first of the eventful events started very uneventfully.

It doesn't matter where we were. But we were in North Dakota. Candace was driving.

I was sitting up on the top bunk. Well, I was laying on the top bunk. Buses, apparently, aren't built to hold bunk beds. Or bunk beds aren't built to be on buses. Either way, there was only enough room between the top mattress and the ceiling to kind of slither in and lay down. Lying on my stomach and propped up on my elbows, I could touch the ceiling with my head. It was kind of cozy, though, and felt kind of private, which was good, because I'd given Doreen my room.

I had the box of ashes open. I don't know why, exactly. I think maybe I was trying to get used to the idea of saying good-bye to my mom. I was paging through the copy of *Red Bird*, reading some of the other poems. Which were pretty great. I was imagining her, flipping through those same poems, looking at that same ink on those same pages.

"How's it going, darling?"

My dad's voice popped me out of my thoughts. He put his arms up on the bed and rested his chin on them.

"Pretty good," I said.

"How you feeling about all this? About, you know, what we're going to do?"

I looked at the ashes. "I don't know. But it's what she wanted. So I guess we should do it?"

"Mmm," my dad said. "I guess we should." I was kinda glad that he wasn't all gung-ho about it, either.

I looked at the book. There was still one piece of tape. My dad's pages.

"Hey. Can I look at what *you* wrote? In the book, I mean?"

"Sure, I guess. I kinda forget what I wrote."

I gently tugged the tape loose and opened to the pages. I saw his words right away, on the page of a poem called "Boundaries." He'd scrawled it in his usual all-capitals script.

"Bake me into a loaf of bread," I read aloud. I blinked. I looked up at him.

Rodeo frowned, then broke into a big grin. "Oh, yeah!" he said, laughing. "I remember now!"

"*Bake me into a loaf of bread?!*" I hissed.

"It was a joke."

"A . . . *joke*?!" I sputtered. "That's a heckuva thing to joke about, dirtbag!"

"Maybe," he said stubbornly.

"Maybe? There's no maybe about it! She gave you an honest answer to a serious question, and you gave her some ridiculous *joke*?"

He shrugged. "Well. I figured, if I died, she'd be sad. And I didn't want her to be sad. So I thought maybe that'd make her laugh." He sighed and looked away and then looked back into my eyes. "I didn't care what she did with my ashes, butterfly. I just wanted her to be happy. I'd rather she was laughing than crying, you know?"

Darn it. Darn that unshaven, unhinged weirdo. I hated how he could make so much sense and seem so darn *good* when I knew for certain that he was in fact an unshaven, unhinged weirdo.

But then a thought hit me. "What if she woulda done it, though?"

"What?"

"What if you woulda died and she looked to this page and wasn't sure you were joking and then actually baked your ashes into a loaf of bread?"

Rodeo scratched his chin, brow furrowed, considering. "Well," he mused, "that woulda been gross, I guess." He arched an eyebrow. "But, I am gluten-free, at least."

I opened my mouth. Closed it. Slugged him on the shoulder with a clumsy backhand. "Something's wrong with you," I said.

"Yeah," he said, rubbing his shoulder. "A heckuva lot, probably."

I blew out a cleansing breath. Let the poetry book fall closed.

"Ugh. Let's lighten the mood," I said. Then I looked around the silent bus. At Salvador, reading on the couch. Ivan, asleep on the back of the couch behind Salvador's head, Fig curled up beside him. Wally and Doreen, chatting in one of the seats up front. Candace up in the driver's seat. The world, blue-skied and sunny out the windows. "You know what I'm thinking? I'm thinking it's time for a Blowout."

Rodeo grinned. "Abso-freaking-lutely," he said.

"You handle the tunes," I said, and then I wormed my way down from the bunk. "Salvador!" I called. "Help me out! Open the windows!" I was already on the other side of the bus, sliding the windows down one by one.

"Which ones?" he asked.

"All of them!"

Me and him moved from the back of the bus to the front, opening every window as we went. By the time we got to the front, wind was gusting all around us and Rodeo had his phone plugged into the stereo. He winked at me and then gave the Holy Hell Bell a healthy ringing.

"It's time for a Blowout, folks! Hit the gas, hold on to your hats, dance if you want to!"

And then he pressed play. And one of our favorite Blowout songs ("The Way We Move") by one of our favorite souls (Langhorne Slim) blasted out the speakers. It was all drums and piano and guitars and shout-along choruses.

And that's all a Blowout is, really. Windows open as far as they go. Music blaring as loud as you can stand. Yager moving as fast as it can, within (or maybe just a little bit past) the limits of the law. It's swirling air and rocking music and it's pure freedom and it's something we'd invented years before, anytime we needed to wake up or perk up or cheer up.

Wally and Doreen were smiling uncertainly. Candace started bopping and boogying in her seat, in a way that was hopelessly nerdy but also undeniably endearing.

I danced my way toward the back of the bus, spinning and hopping. My hair blew wild.

I'd found the book. Against all the odds. And I'd cleaned up my messes. I'd, maybe, grown my wings a little. I didn't know how it was gonna go when we got to where we were going, but I didn't have to know that yet.

I was on a bus with my best friend and my dad and three new friends and the world's best cat and a perfectly fine dog. And my mom, kinda. It was gonna be okay. It was, maybe, even gonna be awesome.

And even if it wasn't, that moment right there with those folks and that music? *That* was awesome. You gotta take your awesomeness when you can. Because you never know how long it's gonna last.

Case in point.

I shimmied my way around the bunk bed a couple times. Rodeo and Salvador had danced their way back toward me. To call what either one of them was doing "dancing" was pretty generous, but I was feeling generous, so there you go. Doreen and Wally were still sitting down, but they were looking back at us with big smiles, hair swirling around their heads. It was adorable.

"You guys are bananas!" Salvador laugh-shouted over the music to me and Rodeo.

"Of course," I hollered back. "It's our superpower!"

And to prove it, I reached for a cape. Well, what I reached for was a blanket. From the top bunk, which happened to be right at my eye level. I grabbed the edge of the blanket and gave it a wild, reckless, caught-up-in-the-moment yank.

Now, in almost any given situation, reaching for a cape is a great idea. With very little downside.

However, this particular given situation was a bit different.

Because on top of that blanket was a box. And in that box were ashes. And somebody had left that box of ashes on top of that blanket, and they'd left it there unlatched and open. That someone was named *me*. And, of course, there was seventy-mile-an-hour wind whipping around the bus like a tornado.

So, yeah.

The box flew up into the air. Lid open. Spinning and tumbling through the swirling wind.

The world went gray. And dusty.

We all froze. At least, I did. I'm assuming Rodeo and Salvador did, too. I couldn't see them, though. Because I had Mom in my eyes.

Candace, apparently, glanced in the rearview mirror. Because she pretty freaking abruptly hit the brakes. Which is not a great thing to do when three people are standing up on a bus and not holding on to anything.

I don't blame her, though. I'm not sure what the exact *right* thing to do is when you're driving a bus and then three dancing people suddenly fling somebody's cremated remains through the air, but hitting the brakes *does* seem like a fair response.

Either way, Rodeo and Salvador and me lurched, stumbling to the floor, ashes still whirling around us. We tumbled to a heap on our hands and knees and butts while Candace pulled Yager to a skidding stop on the shoulder of the road.

Everything stood still. No one said anything. Candace must've gotten ahold of Rodeo's phone, though, because the music cut off.

I heard footsteps coming our way. And then Candace's voice. "Oh. My. God."

I rubbed my eyes clear. Scooted back and up onto my knees. Looked around.

Mom was everywhere.

The floor. The bed. In the air. On me and Rodeo (laying on his back) and Salvador (sitting with his back against the couch, shaking his head).

The box lay open and mostly empty on the floor beside me.

My dad slowly pulled himself up to his knees, facing me. Gray ash was covering his face and his mangy long hair and his straggly beard. He looked like a ghost. Which makes sense, I guess, because after all a ghost is a dead person, and he was at that moment covered in dead person.

Candace was looking down at us from a safe distance, eyes wide, one hand over her mouth. Wally and Doreen appeared beside her.

"Oh, dear," Doreen said.

Rodeo looked at me, blinking. "What do we do?" he asked.

I looked around at the disaster surrounding us.

Ash everywhere. Ash, that was all that was left of my mom. Ash, that I'd just found, after all these years. Ash that we'd gone on a whole journey to put to rest.

I swallowed.

I really only had two choices.

"Well," I said. "I think she'd rather we were laughing than crying, Dad."

And then I snorted. I'm not gonna lie. It was a fake laugh. A whole big part of me wanted to burst into tears. But in life, sometimes, if we're lucky, we get to choose. And I chose to laugh. A fake laugh to get me started, sure. Along with a mostly fake smile. But an almost-real laugh followed. And then a partly real snicker. And by then my smile was mostly sincere. And then I sat back on my feet and started laughing for real.

Because, I mean, the whole thing was definitely pretty horrifying. But also, unquestionably, kinda horribly hilarious, too, right?

A funny thing about laughing at inappropriate times is that it's oddly contagious.

Salvador broke first. I could hear him trying to hold it in, but it was no use.

Then Candace. Wally added to the mix with a robust belly laugh. I heard Doreen laughing through a few "oh my goodnesses."

Finally, even Rodeo joined in. Laughing. Real laughter, too.

So we all stood or sat or knelt there, covered in my mom's

mortal remains, laughing our fool heads off. I mean, what else could we do, really?

Eventually, we did our best to gather her up. Carefully, we shook her from our hair and clothes. Swept her into little piles. Scooped her back into the box. Everyone pitched in. We only got a little more than half of her back, but it was better than nothing.

At one point, as we all quietly cleaned, I looked over and saw my dad. Kneeling, by himself. Mostly turned away from me. He was looking at his hands. Kind of turning them over, rubbing his fingers together. Looking at that ash. That ash that was my mom.

And I remembered: He'd never looked in the box. Not before, not with me, not on this trip. This was the first time he was seeing Mom again.

"Hey, baby," I heard him say, quiet and ragged. So quiet only I could hear. So ragged I had to blink and look away.

I walked over to him on my knees. Close. Put my hands on his elbows.

"Hey," I said. He just swallowed. His eyes were full. "You better not cry," I said. "Or you'll get all muddy." He smiled, a little. But the tears started anyway. "She woulda laughed," I said, fighting my own tears.

Rodeo breathed in, breathed out. "Yeah," he said. "I know. That's why I'm crying. She was really . . ." His voice broke off. I leaned in and squeezed him in a tight hug. Both our faces were getting a little muddy, I think. Tears tracing trails through ash.

"Yeah," I said. "She was."

We knelt there for a while, my dad and me, in each other's arms, in a bus full of friends, covered in the ashes of the woman we loved and missed. All three of us, together.

"You know," he said after a while, "this actually helps." He gestured around us at the absolutely bonkers thing that had just happened. "I've been having a hard time, all this way. Hard time getting my head around letting go. Scattering the ashes. Saying goodbye."

I nodded. I, after all, had been feeling exactly the same way. Still was, actually.

"But, now . . ." He smiled and kind of chuckled. "Now, seeing 'em . . . I'm totally ready. I'm ready, Coyote. Because you know what? This here?" He held up an ash-covered hand. "This isn't your mom."

My stomach dropped. "Oh god," I said. "Who is it?"

"No," he said, quick. "These are your mom's ashes. But they're not your mom. She's here," he said, patting his chest with his palm. "And here," he said, tapping mine. "And here," he said, pointing back and forth between us. "That's the important part. This here is just dust. Ash. I can say goodbye to this ash. 'Cause I know I'll be holding on to the important stuff. Right?"

I wiped at my eyes and gave him a grin.

"Right," I said, and hoped that I meant it. I think I did.

After a bit, we'd gotten just about all of my mom picked up that we could.

At the next town, we stopped at one of those self-service car washes and sprayed each other down. It was almost certainly the first time anyone had visited that particular car wash to spray a dead body off themselves. At least I hope it was. While Rodeo, Salvador, and myself hosed off, Doreen and Wally and Candace wiped down the inside of the bus with some wet rags.

And an hour later, we were back on the road, munching potato chips and singing along to Neil Diamond like nothing had happened.

Yeah. I've lived a pretty weird life. But that was one of the weirdest days for sure.

# CHAPTER
## THIRTY

I got a little more anxious with every mile. The whole ash disaster hadn't given me quite the coming-to-peace-with-this-whole-letting-go thing that it had given Rodeo. Even after cleaning Mom out of my ears, I still wasn't one hundred percent on board with letting her go.

My emotional nausea jumped into higher gear when we crossed the state line into Washington. The state we used to live in. The state we'd really only ever come back to once. The state where our pond was.

When we crossed that state line, that letting-go moment jumped straight from a someday-maybe kind of thing to an in-a-few-hours-like-probably-before-dinner kind of thing. Which is really an entirely different kind of thing.

I paced restlessly for a while—I'd really been doing more than my fair share of pacing lately—and then finally settled in on the couch.

After a few minutes, Doreen walked up to me, taking her time. After the whole ash blowup, she'd stopped wearing her mask on the bus. I guess that kind of thing just brings folks together. She was definitely a full pod member for sure.

"Okay if I sit?" she asked, and I scooted over to make room, eager for something to think and talk about other than, you know, scattering a parent's ashes. She sat down with a little grimace and groan, and then mumbled something to herself.

"What?" I asked.

"Oh, nothing," Doreen said with a little laugh, "just something I say when something hurts."

"What do you say?"

Doreen smiled. "I say, 'How lucky am I?'"

I gave her a look. "You say that when something hurts?"

"I do. Or when I forget something. Or when my eyes can't read something that's printed too small. Any of those lovely things that start to happen to you when you get old."

"Okay, I'll bite. Why do you say that?"

"Because it's true! The lucky bit, I mean." She reached over and patted my leg. "You're young. I once was, too, believe it or not. I used to be a competitive swimmer—can you imagine? And when I first started getting old, I hated it. My hair went gray. I got all wrinkly. My knees hurt. My vision went. There were plenty of reasons to be crabby and grouchy. And I was, sometimes." She gave my knee a squeeze. "But then, I realized something. I realized how very, very lucky I was. I mean, for goodness' sake, I outlived my knees! I outlived my hair, and my eyes, and my skin!" She laughed and threw her hands in the air. She looked delighted.

"And that's a . . . good thing?"

"Good?" Doreen said with a little shrug. "It's a *lucky* thing, at least. Because there are plenty who don't, dear." Her voice got quiet. "Too many. People I've known and loved, wonderful people, who didn't get to outlive very much. Didn't outlive their parents. Didn't outlive their childhood, even. People I've known and loved and lost too soon, who never got to see and feel all that I've got to see and feel." She shook her head. "How much would they give to have more time? To outlive their knees?"

She pulled in a good, deep breath. Slow. Let it out. Her voice had gone a little shaky at the end, but when she started talking again, it was back to its strong warmth.

"So when good things happen—sunsets, delicious meals, beautiful music, new friends—I think: *How lucky am I?* But, also, when those unpleasant, being-an-old-person things happen— achy knees, a sore back, and false teeth—I think: *How lucky am I?*" She smiled, and her smile was just as magic as Wally's. "My goodness, how lucky am I?"

She looked at me.

"Oh, dear. I've made you sad."

"No," I said, smiling and shaking my head. And, yeah, maybe wiping at my eyes a little. Which I'd also been doing more than my fair share of lately. "Not at all. Just the opposite. I think that's . . . I think that's amazing."

Doreen chuckled. "I don't know about amazing. But it's *true*. And it gets me through the day. Simple gratitude, dear, is woefully underrated."

We sat for a few moments, the bus humming beneath us, the world flying by out the windows. I looked and saw Wally sitting in a seat near the front of the bus.

"Speaking of new friends," I said, giving Doreen a playful nudge, "you and Wally have sure been hanging out a lot together."

"He's lovely," Doreen said, not taking the bait.

"Yeah. So . . . is there any chance you two are becoming, you know, more than friends?"

Doreen threw her head back and laughed. "Oh, dear." She patted me on the hand. "It may be hard to believe when you're young, but there is no such thing as *more* than friends. If you have a friend, a true friend, you have all that you really need."

Man. Doreen was dropping wisdom on me left and right.

And, in that moment, it all added up to something for me. Sometimes you knew something all along but you didn't know you knew it until something makes you know you knew it, you know? So it can feel like a surprise, even though you had it the whole time. Yeah. What Doreen was saying about gratitude and friendship was making me see all sorts of things in all sorts of new ways that maybe weren't all that new.

"Thanks for the talk." I gave Doreen a shoulder hug. "I've got a phone call to make."

And then I slipped back into my room and closed the curtain behind me and pulled my phone out of my pocket and called the only person I had in my "Contacts" besides Rodeo and Salvador.

Audrey picked up on the third ring.

And why did I call Audrey, a.k.a. the Ostrich, a.k.a. the only other lobster in my middle school crab pot, right there at that moment? I don't know *exactly* exactly why, but I do know it had something to do with all the stuff that Doreen had said.

It had to do with Salvador calling me a butterfly. And the way Ivan curled up in my lap when I sat down. Or how Wally smiled and shared his favorite sandwich with me.

Because back at school, I was a lobster. But so was Audrey. And as far as I knew, she didn't have a Salvador. Or a Wally. Or a Doreen. Or an Ivan. I don't think she even had a Fig. And I didn't love that. So, I figured, at least she could have a Coyote.

And also, there was this: I'd been awfully focused on all the friends I didn't have at school. But the fact of the matter was that every day when I went and sat down alone in the library, someone came and sat down next to me. And she made me laugh. And she'd brought me a cupcake on my birthday. And she'd even drawn a special dragon, just for me, for Christmas. How lucky was I?

"Hey," she said.

"Hey," I answered. Really great start.

"So have you done the whole burial thing yet?"

"How did you know that's what I'm doing?"

I could almost *hear* her blink and shrug through the phone. "It seemed pretty obvious that's what you were going to do."

"Oh. But, no, I haven't. Yet."

"So you still have your mom?"

"Yeah." I thought of the Blowout incident. "Well, I've got like sixty percent of her."

"Oh. Well, that should do it."

"I think so." I hadn't really had a plan for how the conversation would go, but if I would've, I don't think it would have been following it. I cleared my throat. "How are you doing?"

"Fine. Pretty bored without school. I made a pretty neat dragon out of clay, though."

"That's cool," I said, and actually kind of meant it. "Hey. Why do you like dragons so much, Audrey?"

"Because they're cool," she answered without skipping a beat.

"Right. But why do you think they're cool?"

This time, Audrey did skip a beat. She skipped a lot of beats, actually. And when she started answering, her voice sounded different.

"Because they can breathe fire," she said. "If someone is being mean to them." Another skipped beat. "And because they have thick armor," she said. "So thick you can't get through it to hurt them." For some reason, even though I couldn't see her, I knew that her eyes were blinking wetly behind her glasses. "And because they can fly away."

We both sat there for a few breaths. Well, I was standing, technically, but still.

"Dragons *are* cool," I said at last. "Do you know why I like you, Audrey?"

"No," she answered, and she said it honestly.

"Because you're cool, too. I've met a lot of people. And a lot of people are the same. Which is fine. But you're different. And you're cool, Audrey. Even cooler than a dragon."

"Nothing is cooler than a dragon," she said, like *I* was the one missing the point.

I pursed my lips. "Okay. You're just as cool as a dragon, then."

There was another pause. A few more skipped beats.

"Thank you," she said. Then she said, kinda quick, "You're cool, too, Coyote."

I sighed. I thought about messes, and mistakes. And I thought about caterpillar snot and wings.

"I'm working on it," I said. I blew out a big breath. "I'm glad you're my friend, Audrey."

Another skipped beat. Shorter this time.

"I didn't know we were friends."

"Neither did I," I said, honestly. "But I think we are. And I'm really glad we are."

"Oh. Good. Then I'm glad you're my friend, too, Coyote."

"I don't know when I'm getting back," I said. "But when I do, do you wanna have a sleepover? We could sleep in my bus, which is pretty cool. And you could finally meet Ivan." I'd shown her about a thousand pictures of him, so that introduction was probably overdue.

"Okay," Audrey said. "But I'll have to bring my own pillow. I've got a tricky septum."

"Um," I said. "Okey dokey."

Then we hung up.

I stepped out of my bedroom. And I saw my dad, bobbing his head to the music up in the driver's seat. And Salvador, sitting and talking to Candace, saying something that made her laugh. And I saw Fig, and Ivan, and Wally, and Doreen. All of us, rambling on this bus on this crazy quest. A quest that, sure, maybe had some of the achy-knees-and-sore-back type stuff in it. But a quest that also definitely had a lot of the delicious-meals-and-new-friends type stuff in it, too.

How lucky was I?

An hour before, I'd been feeling nauseous and unsure. I still was. But now I was also feeling pretty darn lucky, too.

Doreen was right.

Gratitude: woefully underrated.

# CHAPTER

# THIRTY-ONE

*A*nd then we were there.

Yager rolled to a stop in a gravel parking lot. Rodeo killed the engine.

It was a little trailhead parking lot, surrounded by trees. There was a breeze. It wasn't sunset yet, but it was getting there. The sky was darkening in the east, and starting to go pink and yellow behind the pines to the west.

There were no other cars in the parking lot. It was just us, on that bus, in those trees, under that sky.

No one moved. They were waiting for me, I knew. They were giving me that moment to decide. No one was looking at me. But I knew they were all watching me.

I was sitting next to Wally. "*I don't know if I can do this,*" I whispered to him.

He put a hand on my knee. "*You don't have to,*" he murmured back.

"*But I want to,*" I said. "*I think.*" I swallowed. "*Like . . . I want to set her free. But I don't want to let her go.*"

Wally nodded. And then he took a few moments to think. Which is something that more people should do more often, honestly.

And then he said, "*I remember, when I was a child, playing on the playground. Climbing all over everything. Swinging and dangling on the monkey bars. You, too?*"

I nodded. And instantly a memory flashed into my mind of hanging from the monkey bars with my mom's hands on my hips, her voice behind me saying, *Don't worry, honey, I won't let you fall*. A memory that didn't help at all with my current trying-to-let-go-of-her problem, by the way.

Wally continued, in his gentle whisper. "*I remember, sometimes, when I was trying to hang on, how my hands would hurt. And I would almost fall. So I would have to let go, with one hand, and shake it out. And then hold on again.*" He had been looking away, out the window, but now he turned to look into my eyes. "*Do you understand? To keep holding on, I had to let go. But I wasn't really letting go. I was just . . . changing my grip. So I could hold on* better."

I got all tingly. And I nodded. 'Cause I got it. And I liked it. Changing my grip.

"*Thank you,*" I said.

"*Good luck,*" he answered.

And then I stood up.

And I walked back to the shelf where the box was. Which was one hundred percent closed and one hundred percent latched, of course. I'd started being very careful about that. For obvious reasons.

I picked it up and held it against my side with my good arm.

Candace and Salvador were sitting together on the couch.

"You coming?" I asked.

Salvador shook his head. "I think I'll stay here," he said. "But if you want me to come, I will." Because, you know, he's the best.

"It's okay," I said.

"You got this, Coyote," Candace said.

I gave her a thank-you nod.

I walked toward the front door. And I stopped next to where Doreen was sitting. I noticed she had something in her lap. It was a big, metal, vase-type thing. An *urn*. I knew what was inside without asking. She was holding it like something very, very precious. Which it was.

"Would it be all right if I came with you?" she asked.

"It would be lovely," I said, borrowing one of her words.

"It isn't far?"

"No," I said. "And we'll help you."

Rodeo was waiting in the driver's seat. He looked like I felt: Sad. Unsure. A little overwhelmed. But also, maybe, ready.

He looked into my eyes and tightened his lips, but didn't say anything. Neither did I.

The three of us walked off the bus and closed the door behind us and started up the trail through the woods. Rodeo held Doreen's arm, since I had one arm in a cast and one already holding a box.

It was a beautiful day. Or the end of a beautiful day. Birds, wild with spring energy, flew from limb to limb and sang their hearts out around us. We walked up a slope, and around a corner, and through a little meadow. And then up over a rise.

And then there it was.

I didn't plan on stopping when I saw it. But my body stopped all on its own. Because my heart told it to. Doreen and my dad stopped with me.

It was a quiet scene, all around me. But it wasn't a quiet scene inside me. Because seeing that pond brought back a roar of memories and feelings and echoes and voices. A beautiful roar, maybe. I could, for a moment, see and hear it all: family picnics and inside jokes and giggling laughter and silly hugs and hide-and-seek and warm held hands. Family.

I knew why my mom had chosen that pond. She'd known. It was perfect. A quiet place that sang with memories.

The pond was even smaller than I remembered. Which makes sense. Because I was so much bigger. The last time I'd been there, I'd been a six-year-old with two sisters and a mom. Now I was a thirteen-year-old with a box of ashes.

Sometimes it isn't the world that changes. It's us.

I took a breath. A breath of air flavored with pine needles and spring moss.

And then together we walked down the little slope. To the bank of the pond.

Doreen let go of my dad and stepped back. She was giving us the moment.

I looked out at the pond. It was pink, now, reflecting back the light from the sun, which had disappeared over the horizon. I'd see it again, though. And, in the meantime, it had given me this beautiful moment, in this beautiful place, with this water painted by light. Gratitude.

I looked up at my dad. His eyes were pink, too. As were mine, I bet. I nodded at him, and my nod was kind of a question mark. He nodded back, and his was a "yes."

I handed him the box. With my arm in a cast, I couldn't hold it and open it at the same time. He cradled it in his arms. I reached with my good hand and undid the latches. And then, carefully, swung open the lid.

And there she was. There, in that place she'd chosen and written down.

But it wasn't her, of course. It was just ashes.

And this wasn't a letting go. It was just changing our grip.

But, still.

I did some blinking and sniffling and wiping of my eyes.

I'd already done more crying during the course of this adventure than any person should probably do in a lifetime, except that's not true at all, because there's nothing wrong with crying, not even a little bit. I mean if you're feeling something true and deep and powerful and so you show that you're feeling something true and deep and powerful, what on earth is the problem with that?

And I was. I was feeling something true and deep and powerful.

I loved my mom. I loved her, I loved her, I loved her. And I was really sad that she was gone. But it was time to let some of that sadness go, a little bit. So I could hold on to her, even better.

I thought of the words of the poem my mom had chosen.

*The past is the past and the present is what your life is, and you are capable of choosing what that will be, darling citizen.*

I reached into the box. And I filled my hand with ash.

I held it for a second. Felt it there against my skin.

And then I tossed it. Out and away, letting it fly through my fingers.

It dimpled the pink water of the pond. Wisped and swirled a bit in the breeze, wrapping around me and my dad. Like a hug.

My dad did the same. A handful held. And a handful set free.

We took turns. Until the box was empty. Until the ash was gone.

*She* wasn't gone, though. Not at all.

I thought of the words that she'd written in that book, beside that poem.

"*I love you, too, Mom,*" I whispered.

My dad closed the box. Clicked the latches.

"Give me a sec, okay?" he mumbled.

"'Course," I said. I bumped his shoulder with my head, then walked back toward Doreen.

She was standing a little ways away, the urn in her hands.

She unscrewed the lid, and looked inside.

I heard her breath catch. And I thought that maybe she, like my dad, hadn't looked at the ashes. That maybe she was seeing them for the first time.

"*Oh, my darling,*" she said to the ashes, her voice choked.

And, boy. My throat got all tight at the way she said that. Hearing her call her sister *darling* like that. It was something.

Rodeo called me *darling* all the time. But it was a whole different thing, the way Doreen called her sister *darling*. There was *so much* love in that word, when she said it. There was love in it when Rodeo said it, too, but when Doreen said it, there was *decades* of love in it. A *lifetime* of love. And a lot of loss, too. It was *I love you* and *I miss you* and *I've always loved you* and *I'll always love you* and *I'll always miss you* and a whole lot more, all wrapped up in two little syllables.

Doreen closed her eyes. Took a few breaths. And then she screwed the lid back on.

I moved in next to her, so our shoulders were touching. "Not yet?" I asked, soft. I got it.

Doreen shook her head. Her eyes were full of tears, and sunset. "This is the perfect place for you and your mother. But I don't think it is for me and my sister."

I put my good arm around her and gave her a squeeze. "Well, if you ever figure out the perfect place, let me know," I said. "We can give you a ride."

Doreen smiled. "Thank you," she said. "That would be lovely."

Rodeo turned and made his way back toward us. He gave me a little smile. It wasn't a happy smile. But it was a peaceful smile.

"Should we go back to our friends?" I asked, which is a wonderful thing to be able to say.

My dad nodded.

"Yes, my dear," Doreen said, and linked an arm through mine. "Let's do."

# THIRTY-TWO

Doreen and my dad and me climbed back up onto the bus together, with one empty box and one full urn.

Three people and one cat and one Fig looked at us. The humans had questions in their eyes. I gave them each a smile and a nod.

I'd done a fair amount of thinking on the walk back from the pond, and a whole lot of feeling. Thinking and feeling about my mom, and my sisters, and this quest, and my old friend, and my new friends, and my life up 'til now, and my life from here on out, and letting go, and holding on, and *once upon a time*s, and *happily ever after*s.

I'd even thought about all the crabs in the crab pot back home. A lot of them were definitely caterpillar snot. Or they'd been caterpillar snot to me, at least. But who knows. Maybe they just hadn't found their wings yet, either.

And I thought that, just maybe, there was a world in which I would've been a crab, too. If the universe hadn't gotten broken, and I hadn't spent five years living in a bus with a wild man, but just lived a normal crab life. I might have laughed at me, too, and my weird name, and my habit of saying things which are, apparently, incorrect things to say.

So, in some weird way, I felt *grateful*. Grateful, sort of, for everything that had happened to me. Even the bad stuff. 'Cause, yeah, there'd been plenty of sadness and heartache and emotional nausea along the way. But there'd been an awful lot of great stuff, too.

And, in the end, it all added up to make me the kind of person that wasn't mean to lobsters. And I liked being that kind of person. The kind of person my little sister thought I was.

At first, I thought this was a story about going on a journey to scatter some ashes. Then I thought it was a story about going on a journey to track down a book. And for a little while there I thought it was a story about cleaning up messes. And a story, maybe, about growing wings. But maybe a story, like a person, can be more than one thing.

And maybe, way down in the middle, it was really about *finding*. Finding ashes and finding books and finding friends and finding where you belong and finding clues and finding wings and finding a way and then, at the end, finding peace. Because we lose a lot, all of us, on our journeys. There's no way around that. But we find a lot, too, if we're lucky. And I was.

So I stood there on that bus in a world that was turning to night and I looked at those faces looking back at me and I felt grateful. Grateful that I'd found them. And grateful that they'd found me.

"Well," my dad said. "What should we do, little bird?"

And I reached up and gave the Holy Hell Bell a helluva good clanging.

"Listen up, darling citizens!" I said. "We're going to get pizza. A lot of pizza." There was a murmur of approval, but I wasn't done. I reached down and plugged in the Christmas lights, and the bus went from dusky shadows to cheerful brightness. I grinned. "But first, we're going to dance. Put on some music, old man. Good music. And put it on loud. We need to have a party."

"Why?" Salvador asked, laughing.

"Because," I said. "Because I feel . . . emotionally triumphant. And because my mom was awesome. And my sisters were awesome. And Doreen's sister was awesome. And you're awesome," I said, looking at Salvador. "And you're awesome," I said to Wally, "and you're awesome," I said to Candace, "and you're awesome," I said to Doreen, "and you're awesome, Dad. Even awesomer than a dragon."

"Aw, thanks, sweetie," my dad said without even asking for an explanation, which was a very *my dad* thing to do.

"You're awesome, too, Coyote," Candace said.

"Obviously," I answered.

I reached down into the little *special occasion* bin we kept under the front seat and pulled out a couple of maracas and two tambourines and started handing them around.

"This bus is like *life*," I said. "Or, maybe, life is like this bus." Crap. I was really starting to sound like Rodeo. And I could tell, because he was smiling and nodding along, but everyone else just looked a little confused. But I didn't care. "And here we are on it together. We weren't always on it together. And we won't always be on it together. But we are right now. And that's pretty freaking awesome." I gave a tambourine a good, jangling shake, and then I looked at Doreen. "I mean, how lucky are we?"

She gave me a smile. A great smile. A *lovely* smile.

Rodeo belted out a *yeehaw*, and the rest of the crowd cheered.

And the speakers came to life, blaring out some song that Rodeo picked and it didn't matter what song he picked because it was perfect no matter what.

And I danced. We all did. And we laughed. And we sang. And we hugged. Me more than anyone.

Because once upon a time I had a mom and two sisters. And then I didn't. And I wish, in that time in between, we'd done a little more laughing and dancing and singing and hugging. But that time in between, that's not just *then*. It's also *now*.

And because, once upon another time, there was a bunch of weirdos dancing in a lit-up bus in a dark parking lot at the foot of a mountain. And I don't know about the happily-ever-after. No one does. And no one is really actually happy ever after, forever. It's all ashes eventually.

But for a while, and from time to time, we can fly. So we ought to. Because I was gonna have to say goodbye to each one of those folks someday, somewhere, in some way. That's a fact. But we weren't saying goodbye yet. There's a whole lot of meantime in there, if we're lucky. And until we do say goodbye, there's plenty of time to fly.

I looked around at that bus. And I looked around at those folks. And I looked at my beautiful-crazy, great-hearted dad. And I looked out at the world around us outside the windows.

And I danced. And even though I felt a whole heckuva lot, I only thought one thing. I thought it for the world, and I thought it for my mom and my sisters, and I thought it for my friends, and I thought it for my dad, and I thought it for everyone and everything around me. And I thought it for myself.

*I love you. I love you. I love you. I love you.*

# ACKNOWLEDGMENTS

As Doreen says, simple gratitude is woefully underrated. And I am profoundly grateful to enough folks to just about fill up Yager.

To my editor, Brian, for being such a stellar travel companion on this journey. Your insight and perspective made this book immeasurably better. And to the whole team at Macmillan/Henry Holt: Carina, Kelsey, Tatiana, Katie, Naheid, Abby, Aurora, and everyone else who played such an important part in making this book happen.

To Celia, for once again hitting an absolute home run with the beautiful art. Coyote is so lucky to have you to bring her (and Fig!) to life.

To the Mary Oliver estate for allowing her remarkable poem to play such an essential role in this story. She is my favorite for a reason.

To all you readers and parents and teachers and librarians who've taken Coyote into your hearts. I'm so glad and so grateful that so many of you have loved her as much as I do. She'd absolutely let you on the bus (and so would I), no matter what your favorite sandwich is.

And lastly (and mostly) to my family. Just for being awesome, and for being my first readers. Thank you for giving me so very much to be grateful for every day, Karen and Eva and Ella and Claire. *I love you. I love you. I love you. I love you.*